EX APPEAL

OTHER TITLES BY CATHY YARDLEY

Ponto Beach Reunion

Love, Comment, Subscribe
Gouda Friends

Smartypants Romance

Prose Before Bros, Green Valley Librarian book 3

Fandom Hearts

Level Up
Hooked
One True Pairing
Game of Hearts
What Happens at Con
Ms. Behave
Playing Doctor
Ship of Fools

Stand-Alone Novels

The Surfer Solution
Guilty Pleasures
Jack & Jilted
Baby, It's Cold Outside

EX APPEAL

CATHY YARDLEY

 Montlake

Published by Montlake, Seattle

www.apub.com

Amazon, the Amazon logo, and Montlake are trademarks of Amazon.com, Inc., or its affiliates.

ISBN-13: 9781662503962
ISBN-10: 1662503962

Cover design and illustration by Philip Pascuzzo

Printed in the United States of America

*To my fellow nerds, geeks, and recovering honors
students . . . welcome to the Herd.*

PROLOGUE

One Year Ago

"Emily, wait!"

Emily MacDonald power walked blindly down the outdoor paths of Ponto Beach High School, so angry she was surprised her hair didn't catch fire.

She had just wanted to go to her ten-year reunion and blow off some steam with her friends. It had been a miserable month on the heels of a crappy year and, if she was honest, a fairly shitty decade. All the bright-eyed dreams she'd had when they'd all graduated, when she'd been a computer hacker with the world laid out like a red carpet, had died shortly after graduation. She had figured she'd have a drink at the cash bar and catch up with her "Nerd Herd." Just . . . forget.

What she had *not* been expecting, and the last thing she had needed, was seeing Vinh. The cherry on the shit sundae that was this night.

She could hear his footsteps behind her, and she picked up the pace, darting past the English building and heading toward the portable history classrooms. "I don't want to talk to you, Vinh."

He was jogging to catch up. "I can understand why," he said, barely sounding out of breath. She refused to look over at him. "But I was hoping you'd at least hear me out."

"Why should I hear you out?" Emily kept on storming, but it was harder because she'd actually decided to wear heels and a dress tonight. Considering her normal work uniform was a beat-up pair of Converse, jeans, and a T-shirt, she wasn't going to be beating any speed records tonight. She wanted to get away from Vinh, but she didn't want to break an ankle doing it.

"Because it's been almost *ten years*," Vinh growled. "And I want to say I'm sorry."

Now *that* stopped her. She was about to respond when she heard some other people, a little ways off near the chem building, laughing and talking. She grabbed Vinh by the lapel of his expensive (no doubt custom-tailored) suit and yanked him into a darkened corridor. "You waited ten years to say you're sorry? And you're wondering why I'm not more thrilled to see you? *Are you shitting me?*"

Even in the dim light of the corridor, Emily could see Vinh's pained look. She also couldn't help but notice that he looked sinfully, ridiculously handsome. He had been pretty damned cute when they had been in school, in a quiet way, and she'd always been attracted to him. Now, dressed in a suit (and she didn't even know suit kink was a *thing*, but she totally understood it now) he looked good enough to eat . . . and her body was reminding her it had been a while since she'd had a decent bite.

Nope. Kitchen's closed, you horny bitch. Vinh is off the menu.

She glowered at him.

"I had reasons for breaking up with you," he said, and just like that, she remembered all the reasons why no matter how hot he looked, there was no way she was going back to *that*.

"I don't care if dumping me saved the planet from an asteroid," she said between gritted teeth. "You *hurt* me, Vinh."

He let out a deep sigh. "I know. I didn't want to, but . . . I don't know. It seemed like the best choice at the time."

Now the jaw she'd been clenching dropped open. *"The best choice at the time?"*

She saw him wince. "If I could just—"

"My father had died a few months before," she said. "I had to drop out of school because Mom was essentially having a nervous breakdown. And you thought, 'You know what? This is the *perfect time to dump my girlfriend*'?"

He rubbed his face with his hands. "There were a lot of other things going on . . ."

"Oh, I know," she said. "You were *busy*. You needed to *succeed*. You had to focus on your schoolwork so you could get your fancy internship, so you could launch your now obviously stratospheric career. Am I wrong?"

Now he glared at her. "This would be easier if you'd just listen to me."

"Why the *fuck* would I want to make it easier on *you*?"

He let out a huff, walking in a tight circle, as if to somehow burn off frustrated energy. "Because it's been ten years?"

It could've been ten millennia, and she'd still be pissed as hell. Perhaps that made her spiteful, or petty, or vengeful.

She really didn't care.

"How can I put this bluntly?" she said.

"You mean you haven't started?" he interrupted, with that dry humor that she used to *love*, God damn it.

"I don't want to see you," she said. "Ever. You want to apologize, fine—whatever blows your hair back. Doesn't mean I have to forgive you. But we're not talking about it, or anything else, ever again. If you were on life support, I would unplug it to charge my phone. Are we clear?"

He was quiet for a long moment. "I . . . see. I figured you would still be angry, and rightfully so. But I think I underestimated how much you hated me."

"This isn't hate," she lied. "Believe me, hate would take way too much time and energy. But that doesn't mean I have to put up with your bullshit self-recriminations and pretend we're friends either. Go sell it to someone who's buying, Vinh. Considering what you do for a living, I can't imagine I'm the only stop on a redemption tour."

Another pause. "Been keeping track of me, huh? And my stratospheric career, as you said?"

She cursed herself inwardly. That had been sloppy. "Just what I hear from the Herd."

"I wanted to see the Herd," he said. "It's been a while."

"Nobody's fault but yours," she muttered. "It's not like they've gone anywhere. Well, not the townies, anyway."

"But if I'm being honest, the one person I wanted to see was you."

"Well, you have." She crossed her arms. The night wasn't cold, but she felt like shivering. And possibly crying. But she'd rip her own hair out at the roots before shedding one tear in front of this man. "Time to get going. Unless you want to hang out with the Herd."

He looked pensive. "Not sure I fit in there anymore."

"That's on you. Not my problem." She straightened her back. "I'm leaving. You do what you want."

He looked like he was going to reach for her for a moment, his hand sneaking out. Then he dropped it, sighing.

"Take care of yourself, Emily."

Without another word, he turned and walked away.

She watched him, her breathing going shallow and rapid, her hands balling into fists. How dare he? How *dare* he show up and ruin her night?

She blinked away tears, then looked around. She was standing in front of one of their old classrooms—AP Computer Science—the place where she'd developed her love, and skill, for hacking.

It was also where they had sneaked off to and made out during lunch, before Vinh had gotten his car.

A tear tumbled down, and she knuckled it away.

Fucking reunions. She was definitely skipping the next one.

CHAPTER 1

It was Thanksgiving, and Vinh Doan spent it the same way he had for years: in his windowed office at Aimsley & Company, working his ass off. He wasn't even in business casual, much less jeans—he wore one of his usual bespoke suits, this time in a deep navy with a slight pinstripe, over a royal-blue custom shirt. Other companies might allow for khakis and polos. Hell, other companies probably discouraged people coming in on Thanksgiving.

Aimsley expected their people to show up looking not only like they were ready to work but like they *owned* the world and their work reflected that. Even when he'd started out as an intern, he'd done what he could, skipping meals to afford better clothes so he could look the part. He *was* Aimsley, from his silk tie to his Italian-leather shoes. Which meant he wore them no matter what day it was.

For the highest echelon, there were no Thanksgivings, no Christmases, no birthdays. There was only the job. If you weren't onboard with that, you were in the wrong company . . . something they very quickly rectified. Only the best of the best survived long term at Aimsley.

At the risk of sounding immodest, he believed he was even better than that.

His only nod to the holiday was not wearing a tie, although he had one at the ready in case one of the senior partners came in. He was all right with the high-priced, high-fashion uniform of a custom-tailored suit. It was something his mentor had taught him was actually a strategic tool, a way to visually make an impression and gain the upper hand. Still, he had to admit: he hated ties.

Lots of people who worked for Aimsley were off with family, judging by the reduced staff buzzing around the office, but fewer than most "normal" people would imagine. They were a global consultancy, with clients who were dealing with problems in any number of countries that didn't celebrate Thanksgiving. Hell, for that matter, they had domestic clients for whom problems didn't stop when office hours did. Aimsley's team of consultants were fixers, the superheroes of the corporate elite, the ones who came in and cleaned up messes with discretion and creativity. They strategized. They maneuvered.

They made things go away.

They also got paid an exorbitant amount for this service . . . and the better you were at it, the better you got compensated. He was one of the best, and he was well aware of it—and made sure that his superiors were well aware of it too.

He'd closed his doors, and he fortunately had a modicum of privacy, so he took a moment to rub his eyes with the heels of his palms, trying to ease some of the strain. He had thought he'd be more excited about his recent promotion to vice president of internal operations. He'd gone up the ranks relatively quickly, thanks to his gift for getting clients out of jams, from the intensely personal (getting rid of blackmail material) to the larger scale (rebranding and covering up a coup attempt by plutocrats in a foreign country). It had meant a lot of travel. He'd been all over the world, even though he couldn't describe landmarks in any of the places he'd been. He was quite familiar with airports, conference rooms, and hotel rooms, though.

But his subsequent promotion had been less about changing how the company operated and more about dealing with sticky situations the company found itself in now. His reward for his competency was to clean up a mess closer to home.

He grimaced as he looked over the accounts. Aimsley had been a front-runner in investing in cryptocurrency, and he'd seen why immediately. The team members liked to show off their technological savvy, being front-runners of the flashy tech and wearing their early-adopter badges proudly. But he had known, even then, that there was a very specific reason why they'd chosen crypto. It was the same reason any criminal organization used crypto: the blockchain was sacrosanct, in theory . . . and very, very hard to track.

If you wanted to hide something, you did it over crypto. Simple as that.

Unfortunately, after the collapse of the Silk Road and a few missteps that had been made public, Aimsley needed to address their own branding for the first time in their seventy-five-year history. Rather than being seen as the consultant geniuses they'd built their reputations on, they were now facing a word they hadn't dealt with before.

Accountability.

He sighed. The thing was, like with any other client, the challenge wasn't getting them on the straight and narrow. They didn't want to be on the straight and narrow, per se. They wanted to do what they'd always done, and so did their clients. They just didn't want to look bad doing it. They wanted the rebrand, the polish, the accolades. They wanted the mess cleaned up and the problem neatly vanished.

That was, in a nutshell, his job. And he was damned good at his job.

He supposed he ought to feel worse about it, but he didn't. On the other hand, he didn't necessarily feel good about it either. He felt neither pride nor shame.

He frowned. He really didn't feel anything, if he thought about it, which he rarely did. Except maybe tired.

That's . . . weird. And a little unsettling.

He twisted, trying to crack the tension out of his neck and back. He had until Monday to clean up a toxic trail of cryptocurrency. He didn't have time for an existential crisis, dammit.

His phone buzzed with a text, and he grabbed at the distraction from his sister like a life preserver. He didn't laugh, but he did smile when he opened the attachment to see what Tam had labeled "Cthurkey," an unholy combination of turkey, googly eyes, and octopus tentacles coming out of its "mouth" (i.e., the neck hole of the turkey).

VINH: That is cursed. That's worse than the potato-salad-in-a-jug photo you sent me on the fourth of July.

TAM: LOL yup! It's going to be hard to top this one. What are you doing?

VINH: Working.

He could almost hear his sister's sigh, even though she was three thousand miles away.

TAM: Because of course you are. Are you doing anything else? With anyone?

The numb feeling intensified. If numbness could intensify, anyway. He shrugged, then realized she couldn't see it. His fingers flew across the small keyboard.

VINH: Eh. I don't even like turkey. And will like it even less now, thanks to your Eldritch god of fowl.

There was a long pause.

Ex Appeal

> TAM: Given any thought to coming out for Herdsgiving? It's at our house this year, and you could crash here.

Vinh let out a low exhalation. After some communication issues and emotional processing, Tam and her boyfriend, Josh, had finally gotten their act together last Valentine's, had gotten engaged in September, and were now settled down in domestic bliss, living together in Ponto Beach, the Southern Cal beach community where they'd grown up. He'd known Josh for as long as Tam had, making Josh one of his oldest friends. He was happy that the two of them were together . . . glad that she finally seemed content and that she had finally found work that she not only excelled at but also enjoyed. He'd hated seeing her deal with shitty boyfriends and even shittier jobs.

Still, that didn't mean he wanted to witness his oldest friend and his twin sister in connubial bliss, and it sure as hell didn't mean he wanted to be next door to them sleeping together. Nope. No. Brain bleach.

> VINH: First, you know I'd get a hotel room if I went back to Ponto. Next, I can't go to Ponto. I'm swamped with work.
>
> TAM: Fun sponge. When are you NOT swamped with work??
>
> VINH: That's why I get paid the big bucks.
>
> TAM: Bleh. A bunch of the Herd's gonna be here on Saturday if you change your mind.

He grimaced. That, honestly, was one of the main reasons why he didn't want to go. He could easily get a hotel room, holiday or not, and he didn't care that much about seeing Tam and Josh all snuggly or whatever. But the rest of their group of friends from high school, the self-titled Nerd Herd, were a little more of a problem.

11

Specifically, one particular member of their crew.

For a second, his mind flashed with a picture: bronze-blonde hair, flashing hazel eyes, the quirk of a Cupid's bow smile.

He closed his eyes, willing himself back to blankness.

VINH: Tickets would be expensive this late.

TAM: Boo, hiss! You just said you get paid the big bucks. Isn't there some private jet just laying around? C'mon. It'll be fun.

He pressed his mouth together in a thin line. Tam was one of the few people he let push at him. Anyone else, he'd have shut down by now—forcefully, coldly, if necessary. But Tam was the closest person to him on earth, which admittedly wasn't saying much. He recognized he probably ought to keep in better contact with his twin, but he knew that she was aware that if she ever really needed him, he'd be there. He had absolutely no intention of going, but at the same time, he wasn't going to be a dick about it.

TAM: This isn't about Emily, is it?

Just like that, his chest felt like someone had hit him with a sledgehammer.

Emily.

He closed his eyes, trying to force down the scramble of emotions that emerged. He deliberately hadn't thought about Emily since his misguided attempt to see her the previous year, at their ten-year reunion. She'd made it clear she wanted nothing to do with him. He'd taken the L, cursing himself for letting his judgment lapse. He'd known better.

VINH: Gotta go. This work isn't going to do itself.

TAM: Fine, fine. But you keep bottling this stuff up, you're going to have a stroke before you're 40

TAM: Love you

Vinh still felt the acid burn of his thoughts of Emily, and a quiet, desperate pang that he hadn't felt in longer than he could remember.

Stop it. It doesn't matter. You've got success. That's what matters. That's what's always mattered . . . even to Emily, even if she wouldn't admit it.

He sighed. Then he quickly typed back.

VINH: Love you. We'll catch up at Xmas.

Then he shut his phone off, slowly, deliberately, and put it in his desk drawer. With a few more meditative breaths, he felt the comforting cold envelop him. Work. That was what mattered.

By eight o'clock that night, he was the only staff left in the office as far as he could see when he went to get coffee from the machine in the break room.

"Late night?" Carlos, head of the cleaning crew, asked with his usual expansive cheer. "And on Thanksgiving?"

Vinh shrugged. "I don't like turkey," he said, just as he had to Tam. It was a canned response, but it generally worked. He would probably go home, have a spicy ramen pack, and say, *The hell with it.* Maybe wash it down with a beer. Maybe a few beers, honestly.

"Shoulda said something. You could've had food with my familia," Carlos said with a smile, and Vinh forced himself to smile back. He wasn't known to be friendly, especially among the other staff—mostly because there was a corporate culture where you couldn't really trust anybody, especially when the org chart shifted like a shaken Etch A Sketch. But if Vinh had learned anything from all the jobs he'd done in college—waiting tables, cleaning classrooms, working at the library—he knew that the last thing he was going to do was make someone in the same kind of job feel like shit. He got gifts for his assistant and for the IT department. He gave tips to the cleaning crew. And he'd gotten closer to Carlos, who always handled his floor and kept his office pristine—and who usually bumped into him when he was in the office working late.

"I don't really celebrate Thanksgiving at this point," Vinh responded politely, "but thanks."

"You work too hard," Carlos said, with a little shake of his head.

"You know, I'm hearing that a lot lately," Vinh said. "But you're working on Thanksgiving too."

Carlos shrugged. "Tanya is going off to college next year. I gotta make it up where I can."

Now that, Vinh could relate to. He reached for his wallet, then pulled out a few hundred-dollar bills. "For her fund, then. Happy Thanksgiving."

"Whoa, now, that wasn't . . . I didn't mean . . ." Carlos looked at the money, pride warring with temptation.

"I'm a miserable bastard who makes too much money," Vinh added. "Just let me do this."

Carlos looked at him, then nodded, taking the money. "You have a good one," Carlos said. "Maybe take a little time to yourself."

Vinh nodded, even though he had no intention of taking a break.

By ten o'clock, he was probably the only person in the building besides security. His clothes were rumpled, and his temples throbbed a little. While what he was doing might not be considered entirely ethical, it was legal and passed his own moral sniff test. At least he was getting them out of the mess they'd gotten themselves into. At least from now on, they would have their money in legit, trackable accounts, and it'd be accounting's headache.

Who are you kidding? The next time they needed a "creative" solution, he'd be tapped. It was the job.

He'd shifted things, rearranged things, rewritten history. He still didn't feel anything, other than a bit of punchiness.

Finally, he got to the last big account, the one he'd been putting off. It was a client based in Eastern Europe—or rather, a domestic client *working* in Eastern Europe. They'd created a huge infrastructure there for factories, transportation, the whole smash. In order to get things done as quickly as they'd wanted, it meant "incentivizing" certain elements, known more bluntly as bribes . . . and it was no small amount. They'd needed a discretionary fund that they could use at a moment's notice, and they'd needed it to be just that: discreet.

Read: they needed a secret slush fund, and they'd put aside $10 million.

He sighed. Massaging $10 million wasn't like shifting budget items. This was going to be a huge pain in the ass.

Or at least he thought so, until he opened up the account, and froze.

Account balance: $0.00.

He stared at it, uncomprehending. Ten million dollars had just vanished. From an account only he had access to.

And he'd had nothing to do with it.

Oh shit.

CHAPTER 2

"How the hell do you *lose* ten million dollars?" Roger Holmes, one of the senior partners Vinh had never gotten along with, was red faced and yelling.

By nine o'clock the next morning, Vinh was sitting in a conference room, across the table from the five senior partners of Aimsley & Company, all of whom were none too pleased to show up to work on the day after Thanksgiving. That said, they were even more incensed at the reason *why* they were there. They sat on the opposite side like a jury, glaring at him.

Vinh took a deep breath. He had been up all night, hadn't even gone home, so he was rumpled and frazzled. He *loathed* being anything less than perfectly attired, which spoke to how dire this situation was. He'd tried everything he could to find out what had happened. Had it been a bank, cleaning out an account of that magnitude would've tripped some flags, and he would've been contacted. The problem was, they'd specifically chosen crypto so they could move assets fluidly, without question and with utter anonymity. So the fact that someone had cleaned out the account hadn't triggered any sort of warning, which was how Vinh was in this position in the first place.

"I somehow got hacked," Vinh said. "At least, that's what it's looking like. I'll know more when I contact the crypto company again. As far as they can tell at the moment, it's a legitimate transaction. They can't tell me where the money's been moved to, and I can't get my hands on it. Yet," he quickly added.

His mentor, Winston St. John, regarded him seriously. He was wearing a bespoke suit, no doubt from the same personal tailor he'd recommended to Vinh all those years ago, and he looked sharp as a razor. Vinh's chest felt like it was being squeezed in a vise. Of all the people he could disappoint, Winston was the worst. He'd been the one who had tapped Vinh to get his first job here, despite his lack of legacy or connections. He'd recognized Vinh's talent and cultivated it. Letting him down hurt more than anything Vinh could remember in years. Even his own family's withering judgment didn't sting like this, and they'd raised him to feel each failure like it was an incurable personal defect.

"This is bad, Vinh." Winston's voice was agitated.

I fucking know *it's bad!*

But rather than letting that ill-advised comment fly, he simply nodded, feeling the cringing acceptance of a screwup on a monumental scale.

"I still don't know how this could've happened!" Roger shouted, slamming his palm on the table. "How you could have *let* this happen!" The other senior partners nodded in agreement, their faces the picture of frowning concern.

"That's enough, Roger. We don't have all the information yet, so let's not rush to judgment," Winston tried to temporize, but Roger was on too much of a roll.

"How do we know you didn't just steal the money?" Roger demanded.

Vinh, who was already running on a sleep deficit and was pissed at himself, turned to Roger, his stare contemptuous. "Because if I were planning to steal, I would have and could have stolen more than that. Also, *I wouldn't have told you.*"

The five of them stared at him. Vinh cursed himself silently.

Winston nodded. "You're right, of course. If you'd wanted to rob the company, you would have been more than capable of taking more, and doing more damage, come to that."

Vinh wasn't sure if that was meant to be a vote of confidence or an indictment. Roger didn't look appeased, but at least he shut up.

"That still leaves us with a not-insignificant amount of money missing, though," Winston said, taking point in the proceedings. Fortunately, only Roger seemed to be unhappy with this shift in meeting leadership, but Winston had been with the company the longest and had the most seniority. Also, politically speaking, he was the one with the most support and probably the last person in the company you wanted to fuck with. Vinh didn't let his "summers in Martha's Vineyard" blue blood charm fool him. As much as Vinh admired his mentor, he recognized the truth: he was ruthless and brilliant and had no qualms about gutting you if he saw you as a threat.

Vinh needed to make sure Winston didn't see him as a threat.

"Well, obviously, he needs to recover or replace the missing money, however he can, because we're certainly not eating that big a loss," Roger continued doggedly, picking up momentum. "If he can't, we should look at criminal proceedings. And there's no way he's still employed here!"

Vinh grimaced. *How am I supposed to replace the money if I'm fired?* But Roger was pure vibes, no logic at this point. It would be throwing gas on a fire. "I need to figure out how this happened. I can't do that from the outside."

"Ha!" Roger rolled his eyes. "Do you really think we're letting you keep your job? Do you think we're letting you *stay in the building?* Do we look that naive?"

Vinh clenched his jaw. "If you don't let me get to the bottom of this, how do you know it won't happen again?"

"So you want more access to our computers?" Sarra Friedman, another board member, second in seniority only to Winston, finally chimed in. She was dressed more casually in a sweater set and a pair of wool slacks, her ashy-blonde hair cut in short waves. Vinh would guess that no one had told her what today's meeting was going to be about. She seemed already irritated that her vacation had been cut short, and he knew from previous interactions with her that as the only woman on the senior partner board, she hated appearing too casual, since it might be perceived as being unready. Now, she looked downright perturbed. "Absolutely not. You said you could rob us if you'd wanted to, but what if this is a ploy to get more access? So you could clean us out and run?"

Jeremy and Tyler, the final two senior partners, made rumblings of agreement. Roger looked like she'd suggested Vinh was going to rob the joint at gunpoint. Vinh grimaced.

"We only have your word that you didn't steal the money," Roger said. "Even if you could have stolen more money . . . why should we trust you? Why should we believe you? Why shouldn't I pick up the phone right now and get someone over here to slap cuffs on you and perp walk you out of the building in front of all of Manhattan?"

Perp walk? Seriously?

Vinh looked at Roger, leveling the ice-cold glare that he was infamous for. Seniority or not, Roger shut up, at least.

"Because," Vinh said, "to claim that I stole money would mean that you'd have to account for where it was and what it was. Technically, that money wasn't supposed to be there at all, much less attached to Aimsley or its client."

Roger's eyes widened.

"If you wanted me arrested," Vinh explained, his voice as mild as a weather reporter's, "I suppose that it would fall on me to explain what the account was used for. Maybe share some files with authorities. That sort of thing."

The five went silent. Even Winston seemed shocked. Which, to Vinh, was surprising.

He was using tactics straight out of their playbook, after all.

"Are you threatening us?" Roger finally said.

Vinh couldn't help it. He rubbed his hands over his face. "I've been up for over twenty-four hours. I'm not threatening you. I've devoted my adult life, since I graduated, to working here. I've been loyal. And right now, I'm telling you: something's wrong. I don't know how this could've happened, and the fact that someone could get to *me*—any of you who know me ought to know that this is a huge, dangerous problem. Either you've got a hacker out there that can crack our company's security—in which case, you ought to be looking at the rest of our accounts—or you've got someone rogue on the inside who is capable of theft."

Someone who's trying to set me up.

Winston sighed heavily. "You're right. This is a serious breach in security," he said slowly, despite Roger's strangled yelp of disagreement. "However, Sarra has a point. Whether you're being set up or not, the bottom line is, you can't be involved with this, Vinh. We can't have a suspect participate in his own investigation."

Vinh winced. He'd anticipated this, much as he hated it. "Am I fired, then?" he asked, impressed that his voice sounded calm. If anything, he sounded weary.

"You should be," Roger muttered. "We should put it to a vote."

Winston's stern glance was quelling, and Roger quieted. "We should vote," Winston said with his usual tone of command, looking at the five of them. "Before we do, however, I'd like to remind everyone here that Vinh has been an invaluable member of the Aimsley family. He has gone above and beyond in some of our most challenging situations. How he handled the Aquarius problem was downright masterful."

"He did pull off that miracle in Buenos Aires as well," Tyler agreed with audible hesitation. "And Bolivia. I still don't know how you managed to pull off that thing with the drug lords, getting those workers out of there."

"There is also the fact that Vinh has been, ah, very involved in some of the more . . . delicate aspects of our current brand rehabilitation," Winston added.

Read: Vinh was in the process of cleaning up some of the more problematic elements of their past so they were squeaky clean on paper and, quite frankly, he knew where a lot of the bodies were buried. Vinh could almost see when the truth of that matter sank in with the rest of the board.

"So what? Are we supposed to give him a golden parachute before cutting him loose?" Roger asked, crossing his arms like a mulish toddler.

"*Now* we put it to a vote," Winston said. "I propose a one-month suspension while we conduct an in-house investigation to see what happened to the money. Vinh's good, but we have other equally good consultants who can get to the bottom of this, I'm sure. In the meantime, all your security access is going to be suspended. You're barred from the building. Does everyone agree to this?" he asked, almost as an afterthought.

Of course, Jeremy and Tyler agreed, as did Sarra. Roger cleared his throat, then finally did, dragging his feet.

"I brought in this client," Roger said, which explained why he was so pissed. At least in part. "I'll set up the team, with my own consultants, and we'll find the proof we need."

Vinh didn't like the sound of that. Roger was already biased, and his instructions would probably be something like "Find me what I need to nail Vinh to the wall."

"Fine," Winston said, and Vinh's stomach fell like a frozen cannonball. "All right. We'll reconvene as soon as we have more evidence and a better sense of what's going on. In the meantime, I would suggest all of you talk to the other partners, vice presidents, and consultants. They don't need to know the details of what happened, but we'll want to control what information is leaked out. The last thing we need is other clients getting wind that their money isn't safe. And I want you to make sure that all security measures are stringent. Vinh's right. If it happened to him, I hate to think of what could happen to any of our other consultants. He's always been one of our best."

Roger huffed, then got up and strode out. Jeremy and Tyler whispered back and forth to each other, shooting suspicious looks at Vinh, while Sarra didn't even try to hide her open disdain as she walked past him out the door. That left Winston and Vinh in the conference room, alone.

"I'm going to have to have security escort you out," he said, and to his credit, he sounded apologetic. "And you're not going to be allowed in the building. You're also not allowed to talk to anyone else from the company. You have to realize that."

"I need to clear my name, Winston," he said. "You know I didn't do this."

Winston sighed. "Of course I do."

His belief buoyed Vinh, until his next sentence.

"But it's not what I believe. It's what you can prove. And like I said, this looks bad. You have to know that."

He nodded.

"So you'd better hope that Roger's people can figure out what's going on."

That's not encouraging.

"We'll contact you when we know what's going on," Winston said, with clear dismissal.

He wasn't going to let that happen. His face burned with humiliation as he was escorted by Chance, the security guard, to gather his few belongings out of the office. He could be grateful that there were still a lot of consultants out for the holiday, but there were enough of them there to try and curry favor at how hard they worked and how many billable hours they put in that there were plenty of witnesses. Word would spread as soon as he left the building. He went to the car HR had summoned and headed back to his building. He was exhausted, but his mind was speeding like a bullet train.

Obviously, whoever had set him up wanted him to take the fall. It felt almost personal, somehow, although at this point he was so punch drunk it was impossible to make that determination clearly. The problem was, he now needed to figure out what, exactly, had happened, how it had happened, who was responsible. And he needed to get the money back. He was too damned careful for this to have happened.

So how had it?

Hacking. No matter what else, he felt like it was computer related. So . . . he needed a hacker to catch a hacker. But he couldn't just go on the dark web and hire some black hat to break into the company. For God's sake, he was trying to improve his situation, not make it worse. He needed the ultimate oxymoron: a hacker he could trust with the most important thing in his life—his career.

He got out of the town car, then gathered his cardboard box of belongings. His brain tumbled through possible options as he walked through his lobby and headed for his elevator, despite being on the verge of too exhausted to function. And as he shut and locked the door of his condo behind him, he finally realized there was, in fact, a hacker he knew that he could trust.

Too bad she hated him.

CHAPTER 3

"Okay, Mom! I'm going to Tam and Josh's house!" Emily MacDonald called out as she carefully wrapped the pie she'd baked in foil. "I'll be back late!"

Her mother emerged from down the long hallway, looking aggrieved. "You're going out?"

Emily nodded, tugging on her coat. "It's Herdsgiving, remember?"

And not a moment too soon. Emily worked as phone tech support for a local company, one that outsourced to a number of different businesses and had shifts going twenty-four seven, and this week had been particularly stressful. She tried to remind herself that people got frustrated by technology, and with the holidays, there were a lot of additional pressures as people tried to clear their desks before Thanksgiving. That didn't stop it from stinging when people hurled curses at her for things not working. It really didn't help that often people heard a woman on the phone and either assumed she didn't know anything or tried hitting on her. She'd spent Thanksgiving with her mother and brother, exhausted, but had gone back in to work on Friday because she needed the hours and other people wanted her to cover their shifts. The company got paid by how many calls they handled, and they kept adding more clients on. She supposed it was better than working two jobs, like she had when she'd worked at a call center for a mobile phone company and then cleaned houses or done holiday retail work. But every now and then, she'd think about what she actually loved. She'd grit her teeth when she heard people doing everything they could to leave their computers vulnerable, security-wise, because they were irritated by tech or because they couldn't be bothered to "remember a hard password" so they left it as "password1!" or whatever.

To a recovering hacker, that stuff was downright insulting.

After a rough week, it was Saturday night, and she was ready to blow off some steam with her best friends.

Her mother shook her head. "You and the Herd. I remember when they all hung out here. Remember? The pool parties? And the graduation party you had? Greg was just out of college . . ."

Emily gritted her teeth. She loved her mother, but when she headed down memory lane, it could last a while—and, unfortunately, could go in uncomfortable directions, depending. Her mother's rosy memory was right: the parties had been awesome, so cool that people had actually crashed them. Yes, a nerd party, crashed. Her mother had always made tons of food, her brother had come home from college and exuded cool, and her father had been a big, boisterous, charming figure, telling jokes that he punctuated with his joyous laugh.

Now, the pool filter was on the fritz and barely worked—the pool had a greenish tinge. One more item on the long list of things that needed to be addressed in the house.

Emily cleared her throat. "Well, I'm going to get going . . ."

"Speaking of Greg," her mother interjected, and Emily suppressed a groan. "He called. He got a new job."

This was not a big surprise. Before their father had died, Greg had been what could charitably be described as a *free spirit*. He'd gotten into mischievous trouble, pulling pranks with his high school friends, dropping out of college. Since their father's death, Greg had leapfrogged from one job to another, every now and then taking a few classes at community college before leaving it behind. She didn't judge him for that—it was hard to figure out your place, and Greg had been close to their father.

Still, she was leery of what he decided was a "job" after a bad incident shortly after their father's death—one that involved a scam with a few friends that had narrowly avoided landing him in jail. "What is he doing now?" she asked, her tone careful.

"He's a mechanic."

Emily nodded, feeling awash with relief. "That makes sense, actually. He's always tinkering with his car, and he's been able to bring mine back from the dead more times than I can count." Which was good, because money was a little tight for repairs. "Anyway, I need to . . ."

"Ask me where he's working!" Her mother's blue eyes sparkled with amusement.

Emily sighed. "Where's he working?"

"Antarctica!"

Emily gaped. "He's *where*?"

"He'd been interested, and he went to some job fair," her mother bubbled. "And there was an opening! Except he had to leave immediately."

"Are you kidding me?" Emily blurted out, her tone more harsh than usual. She took a steadying breath, then asked more calmly, "So quickly he couldn't talk to me? The day after Thanksgiving? Why?"

"He said that the flights to McMurdo Station don't happen that often, and there are weather issues. It's not like you can just hop on a commercial flight! So when somebody dropped out, they needed him on the plane immediately, or they'd take somebody else, and he wouldn't have a chance for months," her mother said, appearing entertained. "Doesn't that sound exciting? What an adventure!"

Emily ground her teeth.

Her mother was oblivious to her dismay. "Anyway, Greg said he'd FaceTime us later, after he lands and settles in and whatnot, and then he'll explain everything!" She paused, biting her lip. "Oh! That reminds me. He asked if you'd take care of his pets?"

Now Emily didn't even bother to stop the groan. "Are you *kidding*? Take care of his pets?" She shuddered. "Why the hell didn't he text me before he left? He took the time to talk to *you*. Why didn't he take five minutes to talk to me?"

"He only called me to ask what I thought he should pack," her mother said, with a note of chastisement. "This is a big opportunity for him, and he sounded so excited. But he couldn't expect them to let him transport all those animals, could he? So I said of course you'd help."

Emily closed her eyes for a second. She counted to ten. Then she opened her eyes.

"I'll figure something out," she said. Maybe she could trade favors with Hayden or something. She knew the Herd would help her out if she needed it—it's what they did. They were loyal and supportive, and she loved them like they were her own blood family.

That said, she hated being the one who always *needed* help. It was lowering.

"Fine. I'm going to head over to . . ."

"One other thing." Now her mother looked nervous. Emily braced herself. "The property tax bill . . ."

"Yes, I know that's due," Emily reassured her. "We've got it, don't worry." It was, after all, the reason Emily had given up her apartment and moved back to her childhood home. Her mother had been having trouble keeping on top of everything—the bills, the repairs.

"It, um, went up." Her mother's eyes were round with worry and confusion. "By a lot."

Now Emily felt her chest clench. *Jesus.* Because of course it had.

"We'll figure it out," she said, then gave her mother a hug. "Okay?"

"I know it's unfair," her mother said quietly. "But your father loved this house so much . . ."

It was like a punch in the gut. He'd been dead for nearly a decade now, but her father still haunted the house, in the most bittersweet way. Emily had loved him, and she still missed him.

And at times, she resented the hell out of him.

"Don't worry. I promise, we'll figure it out," Emily repeated. "Now, I've gotta go, or I'm going to be late. You going to be all right?"

Her mother nodded, her eyes bright, sparkling with unshed tears. "Don't worry. I've got that new show I wanted to watch. And I'll eat some of that second pie you made."

"That's the spirit." Emily gave her mother another hug, then tugged on a sweatshirt, grabbed the pie, and headed out to her car. It was an ancient Mazda Miata, in a faded red. Her father had given it to her as a sweet-sixteen present, and she'd been thrilled. Now, it let out sounds of displeasure as she turned the key.

"Come on, Ruby. Don't be that way," she coaxed it, trying the key again. The engine turned over, thankfully.

With Greg in Antarctica, how was she going to get her car fixed? She frowned.

One more thing.

She squared her shoulders and pulled out of the driveway, negotiating her way through the neighborhood. Her father had been so proud to get the house in this development. Other people might have called them McMansions, but he'd been thrilled. He saw it as a step in the right direction, until they could get a real mansion, or at least a house with an ocean view. With the obliviousness of childhood, she'd never thought about it. It was just home. She hadn't compared it to her friends' families' houses, figuring they were largely the same—except for Josh, who lived in a tiny house that had seen better days and was obviously in a worse area of town. She hadn't really clocked the differences in economic status, had never thought it was a big deal.

She knew better now. Fortunately, her friends had never called her on the blindness to her own privilege, especially once she'd fallen on the other side of that scale.

She made her way to Tam and Josh's house, her car creaking angrily as she tried to keep up to speed on the freeway. Fortunately, she didn't have too far to drive. Josh had bought the house as his business had taken off, and he now owned his own nice home with an ocean view. Considering how hard he'd worked for it, she was thrilled for him. And even more thrilled that he and Tam had gotten over their issues and were now engaged. If Tam were any happier, she'd have to split, osmosis-style, into two people to contain her joy.

There were going to be other people there too. Happy couples. Her good friends Tobin and Lily, famous YouTubers, would probably be there. Her friend Asad and his boyfriend, Freddie, who had been easily accepted in the Herd, despite lacking the high school history the lot of them shared. She grimaced, gripping her steering wheel a little tighter. She hoped that other people showed up as well. She loved her friends, but since so many of them were now coupled up, it was hard not to feel a little . . . not jealous, exactly, but out of place as someone so solidly single. She hadn't been in a relationship in years at this point, and honestly, she was okay with that. The last thing she needed was another set of expectations, another person to accommodate, another list of things to handle.

Still . . . seeing them all loved up and happy made her wish there was someone in her life whom she could snuggle up to and watch a movie with. And sex would be nice. She frowned. Well, sex with someone who knew what he was doing would be nice.

See: not needing another person to accommodate.

The last guy she'd slept with had basically blamed her for not getting off, insisting that he knew what he was doing and asking what *her* problem was.

Yeah. There were worse things than being single.

She finally pulled into the driveway, and the car shuddered to a grateful stop. She grabbed the pie from the passenger seat. It was almost seven—hopefully she wasn't too late. At least she hoped she had beat Hayden, who was notorious for not having any sense of (or attachment to) time. She hurried up the walk, already feeling a sense of calm warmth start to radiate through her.

This was the Nerd Herd. Her best friends for decades, her foundation, her core. She rang the doorbell, a smile curving her lips.

These people? They were her home.

The door opened, and she stared. It wasn't Tam, or Josh, or any of the regular Herd. The man answering the door was taller than her, with jet-black hair in a short, stylish cut and obsidian eyes framed by mile-long sooty eyelashes. Cheekbones you could probably chisel marble with. His broad shoulders filled the hell out of—she swallowed hard—a gray Henley long-sleeved shirt, with the sleeves pushed up to reveal some really hot forearms. He was wearing a pair of worn jeans that completed the look. She could feel her mouth go dry. *Holy hotness, this man is . . .*

Wait.

She shook her head, then blinked. "*Vinh?*" she croaked.

He nodded, staring at her intensely. Just like she remembered. "Hello, Em," he said, and his voice did that rumbly low baritone that had melted her for years.

Her first love.

Her first heartbreak.

And the one man she had *not* been expecting to see here today.

She dropped the pie. Then she turned and, without one ounce of shame, *ran*.

CHAPTER 4

The last time Vinh had seen Emily, she'd told him to fuck off. Literally. Specifically, to "fuck *all the way off.*" She'd said, point blank, that she did not want to see him. She'd been defiant and angry. And kind of glorious.

Whatever he'd been expecting, he hadn't been prepared for her simply running away.

In fact, the last thing he needed was for her to disappear, since the whole reason he was at Herdsgiving was because he needed to talk to her.

Despite being in socks, he bolted after her, avoiding the pie she'd unceremoniously dumped on the ground. She had actually made it to her car and was yanking the door open when he said, "Whoa! Wait, wait, wait. Let me explain."

She paused, looking at him in total fight-or-flight panic. Then she closed her eyes, taking a deep breath. When she opened them, they were shards of hazel ice. "What are you even doing here? Did Tam know you were coming and not tell me?" She glared at the house, obviously feeling betrayed.

"No. It was a last-minute thing," he said quickly. "Something came up, and . . . well. I needed to see you."

Her eyes went wide. "*Me?* You needed to see me?"

He nodded, shifting his weight, taking her in. She was wearing a zippered sage-green sweat jacket that made her eyes greener, a pair of black jeans with a hole in the knee—one from actual wear, not a fashion statement—and battered old sneakers. Her blonde hair was darker, the color of caramel, and cut in a severe bob that accentuated her jawline. She looked half-pixie, half-punk.

She looked fucking edible. And he wanted to devour her.

Calm it down, you idiot. This was *not* the time. He had enough problems without trying to pursue something physical with the one woman who could get him out of his current mess. And the one woman who hated him with the fire of a thousand suns.

Focus.

He cleared his throat. "I need your help."

Now she goggled. "Dear diary," she muttered. "Today, a bitch really tried it."

"I'm not asking for a favor," he said. "Well, I am asking for a favor. But I don't expect you to just help me out of the kindness of your heart or anything. I know . . . well, how we left things. And I know it was all my fault."

"That is for damned sure," she concurred. "What kind of favor?"

Here was where it got tricky. "The kind that involves you and computers."

Her eyes narrowed, and she crossed her arms. "Let me guess: you're not asking me to build you a website."

He took a deep, calming breath. "No. But it is work related."

Which was true. Sort of.

Winston had sent him a message saying that the board had set a deadline. If they didn't have concrete proof that someone else had done it, and/or the money back by January, Vinh would be on the chopping block. He'd lose his job, that much was evident. But as much as he'd threatened them, he knew that any chance of getting a job elsewhere—at one of their competitors, maybe—was severely curtailed. At that level, it was often about who you knew, and they'd poison the well wherever he wanted to move. He needed to get this resolved in-house, and then he could think about moving somewhere else.

At this point, he was running on borrowed time. But without access to his computer accounts, and without someone who knew the ins and outs of hacking, he was at a loss. What he was asking someone to do was crack into the Aimsley computers, a company known for working with some of the most prestigious companies in the US. He needed someone who could research what had happened and help him get the money back. He also needed someone who wouldn't then be tempted to simply pocket $10 million for themselves and leave Vinh in an even worse position than he was.

He needed a hacker he could trust. And that left only one person.

The fact that, after all these years, his attraction to her struck him like a bolt of lightning was horribly inconvenient, but there they were.

"I know your company, Vinh," Emily said, dragging him back to the present. "They're the ones that were all golden with tons of accolades, but now it's coming out that they have some questionable business practices, right? Odds are good that whatever you want me to do, I don't want to do. Hell, I may not even want to *know* about it."

"Rumors of Aimsley's . . . *problems*," he said as delicately as he could, "are greatly exaggerated."

She quirked her mouth in a sarcastic smile. "What hat would I be wearing, Vinh?"

He huffed out a short breath. He knew what she was asking. Hackers could be classified into "hats"—white hats for security testers, black hats for trolls who broke in illegally, installing malware, stealing, or just melting down systems for laughs.

"Gray," he admitted. "Bending the laws for a good cause, though."

Her eyebrows jumped up. "Vigilante, then?"

"Sort of." He glanced back at Tam and Josh's house.

She shook her head. "No way in hell, Vinh. I could've told you that over the phone."

He felt his heart sink. He should have known, really. He didn't know what perverse thought had convinced him that Emily would go for this. She'd told him that she'd unplug his life support systems to charge her phone, given the opportunity. Why would this be any different?

"Can I go now?" Emily said, crossing her arms.

To top it off, guilt needled at him. She'd looked so happy, if a bit tired, when he had opened the door—until she'd recognized him and then fled. "No, I should go," he said. "You stay here."

"You'd leave?"

He shrugged. "You belong here more than I do, at this point."

He didn't mean for it to sound self-pitying: it was nothing less than fact. He hadn't hung out with the Herd in any significant way since he and Emily had broken up. It had seemed the obvious play: she had been going home to Ponto Beach and dealing with so much. She'd needed them, far more than he had, and they could take care of her in a way he couldn't.

It was the best he could manage at the time, considering he couldn't be with her. As painful as it was, he was sure he'd made the right decision back then.

She frowned. "They are your friends too, Vinh," she pointed out. "Your *sister* is in there. I don't want to be the reason you feel like you can't hang with the Herd. It's been ages."

He shrugged again. "I don't want to make you more uncomfortable," he said. "I should have thought it through before coming here."

She looked at him, then shook her head. "Shit. It's been ten years, like you said," she muttered. "I . . . overreacted at the reunion, maybe. A little."

34

He quirked an eyebrow at her. "You told me to fuck off."

"You kinda deserved it," she said, and her impish smile surprised a rusty laugh out of him. "But seriously: I know Tam misses you. All the Herd does."

"All of them?" he asked, despite himself.

She scowled. "Don't push it. Let's just . . . we can be adults here. We can go in there and have a meal with our friends, right?"

He found himself nodding.

"Besides . . . Jesus, Vinh, you're out here in a shirt and socks! It's cold!"

He chuckled. "I've been living in New York. And I've been to Russia and Oslo. Even Montana. This is Southern Cal. I've been where it's actually cold."

"Okay, King of the North, fine. You're the tough ice guy. Now get in the house," she said, ushering him in. "And we'll just get through this as best we can, okay? Call a truce."

He nodded.

"But that means I expect you to drop whatever it is you wanted to ask my help for," she tacked on, with a stern expression.

He nodded, smiling wryly. "I figured that out for myself."

They walked back to the front door. She retrieved the pie, which thankfully had been in a tin pie plate and seemed relatively intact. "With any luck, nobody will make a big deal about this," she said under her breath, then opened the door.

"Happy Herdsgiving!" the numerous people crowded in the house called out happily. Then Hayden got a look at Vinh and Emily standing together.

"Holy shit, this is epic!" he crowed. "Are you two going to be okay together? Need a ref? Does somebody need to build an octagon?"

Vinh sighed heavily. Now, not only was he not getting help . . . he'd just agreed to have a meal with friends he hadn't seen in years, a sister he felt disconnected from, and the woman who had been the love of his life—and who, despite their temporary truce, still hated him. All this, in addition to the looming demise of his career.

He gritted his teeth and slapped his best, most placid face on . . . the one he used during tough negotiations, the one that didn't show a crack.

He would figure something out. He'd hoped for Emily, but as usual, Emily had always been a long shot—a dream that would never come true.

CHAPTER 5

The more Emily stared at him (without trying to, you know, *look* like she was staring at him), the more she knew: Vinh Doan was in deep, ugly, serious trouble.

She wasn't sure how she felt about that.

She might not have been in contact with him for years, but in the years they'd been together, first as friends and then as more than that, it seemed like she'd studied his face, listened to every note of his voice, until it was a part of her. She knew his tells as well as she knew her own. He looked calm, his expression neutral, for the most part. Sometimes he was chuckling over some silliness that Hayden was saying, or nodding in contemplation of something Josh and Tam were saying, or whatever. But she knew that there was something *wrong*.

The expression never matched his eyes.

Those dark eyes of his gleamed with an almost panicked intensity, and Vinh *never* panicked. Not even when Hayden had broken his arm on the playground and Vinh had martialed the surrounding kids to get help and stayed with him until adults and the ambulance got there.

Stop it. So what if he's panicked? You don't care.

But no matter what she told herself, she couldn't stop her heart from beating just a little bit faster every time she caught a glimpse of him . . . and she couldn't stop glancing over at him, even if she made sure he never caught her intense, if covert, scrutiny. She felt a mélange of emotions bubbling through her: a base level of simmering anger from their past history, a shot of startled fight-or-fight adrenaline, and that chemistry that didn't give a damn what he'd done—she'd still ride him like a ten-speed.

She peeked at him again. He looked handsome, serious, pensive as he talked with Josh. She could almost hear the gears in his head working overtime. He was frantically trying to figure something out, distracted. His muscles screamed with tension that he was forcing himself to ignore. She could tell because she knew that body of his almost better than she knew her own. He never put up a front like this unless he was dealing with something big—like, say, his nightmarish parents having yet another screaming, object-throwing fight.

She'd seen him like this just before he'd broken up with her.

Except this time, whatever his problem was, it wasn't a relationship. He'd asked her to work for him—a job. For his big-deal company.

Which, in and of itself, was . . . curious.

It wasn't that she was *interested* in what Vinh needed, or that she wanted to help him. But it was normal to be curious, wasn't it?

Aimsley & Company was a corporate behemoth. They could probably buy Norway or something. They also had a reputation for being ruthless (which fit Vinh to a T) and unforgiving (again, fitting). The thing was, they probably had hackers on staff, she'd think. Or he'd be able to shell out money to hire the best tech firms that could do whatever he wanted.

So . . . why her? What was the angle here?

Josh and Tam had regaled them with plans for their wedding the following year, with Asad designing the invitations and favors and overall aesthetic and Freddie doing the catering. "And you have to come," Tam said to her brother, punching him lightly on the arm. "No excuses, like . . ." She turned to Josh. "What was his last one?"

"Negotiating with a drug cartel, somewhere undisclosed," Josh said, chuckling.

"If you're going to come up with something," Tam said, shaking her head, "at least keep it in the same zip code as reality. Say that you have to solve an air filter problem on the International Space Station or something."

Emily looked at Vinh, noticed his smile was strained as everyone else laughed around him. Which was when it suddenly occurred to her: he really *had* been negotiating with a drug cartel.

Holy shit.

If he'd managed to play that off as dry sarcasm—if dealing with a cartel, where there was probably a good chance he could get captured or worse, was no big deal—what the hell kind of trouble was he in?

She felt her curiosity amp up a few notches.

"I promise, I will be there for your wedding," Vinh said solemnly.

"Maybe a few times before then too?" Tam nudged. "I miss you."

"We all miss you, dude," Hayden added. "Haven't seen you since the reunion, and that was for, like, five minutes."

Suddenly, an uncomfortable silence fell over the assembled group. The reunion had been last year, and he'd shown up, trying to talk to her. That time, he hadn't been trying to get her help. He had just wanted to see her, or so he'd said. She'd run from him then, too, cursing him like a sailor. He'd let her go, with a resigned look on his face, when she'd told him to go away.

He was good about that, she had to admit. When they had been together, if she'd set a boundary, needing alone time or wanting to do something on her own, he had respected that.

Of course, he was good at letting her go too, she thought bitterly.

"Yes, well, I'm here now," Vinh said, trying to smooth over the awkwardness.

"It's awesome seeing you," Asad added, helping to patch over the rough moment. "How long are you in town, anyway?"

Vinh went silent for a second, totally still. Then he shrugged. "I'm . . . not sure."

Silence fell *again* as they all gaped at him.

"What do you mean?" Tam finally spluttered, looking baffled. Which wasn't surprising, since Vinh not being sure of something was kind of like concrete turning into Jell-O. You didn't expect it, and it felt downright unnatural. "Not that I'm complaining! But what about your job?"

The tight smile again. "I needed a break," he said. *Lied.* Emily could tell. "And I wanted to spend time here."

"You're taking vacation?" Hayden yelped. "Jesus fuck. Satan's putting on a sweater."

"Hey, be nice," their friend Tobin said, putting his arm around his girlfriend, Lily. "Burnout is a real thing, you know. And sorry to say, but at the pace you've been running for the past . . . well, decade, I guess, it wouldn't surprise me that you're crispy around the edges. Taking a break is a good thing, and I'm glad you're realizing it's important."

There was a murmur of assent. Tobin had needed to take a break from his highly successful YouTube channel, GoofyBui, last year. Even though a lot of people had been shocked that he'd risk the momentum and lose income, he'd taken two months to travel and enjoy time off. And when he'd come back, he had been stronger than ever. He'd also managed to help his girlfriend and their type A friend, Lily, to ease up as well. Emily agreed with the principle: if you could afford to take the time off, if you had the cash and space to take care of your mental health, then you absolutely should.

She was looking forward to that, honestly.

Still, *Vinh* taking a break?

She didn't believe that for a minute . . . not the least of which because of that business in the driveway. He needed her help, as a hacker, *for his job*. He was here on *business*, and now he'd just lied and said that he was taking a break.

The question was: Was it Aimsley's business, or was it his own?

The curiosity grew. Even beyond any negligent, really nonexistent interest in Vinh and his life, she had to admit she couldn't stand not knowing what was going on. Her hacker senses tingled, and her fingers itched to get to a computer.

She didn't kid herself. She was good, but she was rusty. She'd tried to keep her hand in, reading through new information and studying security protocols for fun. She didn't breach security anymore—that had been when she was young and foolish—but she did sometimes participate in Pwn2Own, a competition where hackers competed to find previously unknown security breaches. It was how she'd won her laptop, actually . . . but that had been a few years ago, and the machine was now obsolete. And every now and then, she'd participate in some capture-the-flag hackathons. She was proud that she'd won a number of them.

Vinh hadn't told Tam about whatever trouble he was in, the trouble that required a hacker. Even though they were twins, Vinh always saw Tam as a little sister, much to Tam's frustration. That said, they were close, and if there was something important, he tended to tell her—unless he was afraid she'd freak out or it was really bad.

Curiosity was now burning Emily like a charcoal briquette. She took a bite of the blueberry-cheesecake pie, barely registering the gingersnap crust, even though it was her favorite.

Damn it.

"Hey, Tobin," Vinh asked in a too-casual tone. "Your friend, Skeptic . . . whatsit."

"SkepticSketcher," Tobin answered. "Also known as Shawn Rhodes. What about him?"

"He's good with computers, right? You knew him from computer science classes?"

Tobin shrugged. "Pretty good."

"Huh. How good?"

Tobin hadn't clued in to any change in Vinh's expression, so he just looked puzzled. "Depends on what you want. Obviously, he's a great gamer. He can build a great system. He's an excellent editor, and he learns software like a fiend. Why? What do you need?"

"Nothing. Work thing," Vinh said dismissively. "I'm always looking for people, possible resources."

Tobin shook his head. "Thought you were taking a break," he noted, with a gentle grin.

Vinh shrugged. "Oh, you know. You can take the guy out of the office, but you can't take the office out of the guy."

That did it. He was *desperate* if he was reaching out to Tobin. He could easily find someone, anyone. He had money—she knew how much they made at a place like Aimsley. So why didn't he just *hire* a hacker?

Her nose practically twitched. It was *killing* her not to know. Curiosity was one of her fatal flaws.

And Vinh knows that, damn it.

She got up, then rinsed her plate and put it in the dishwasher. She ought to go home. She had the weekend, but she was going to need to figure out how to take care of Greg's pets, and she was going to need to crunch numbers to figure out how much the property tax increase was. There were a million things she needed to deal with.

Vinh had retreated out to the patio, this time with shoes and a light jacket on. He had his hands stuffed in his pockets. She followed his gaze to the moonlight bouncing off the waves in the Pacific.

"It's a good view," he said. "I mean, it's kind of awkward, and you have to stand just the right way to see it, but just looking at the water— it's not the same in New York."

"Course it isn't," she quipped. "That's the Atlantic. This is the Pacific."

He sent her a smirk. "Ha ha."

She stared for a second too, careful not to stand too close to him. She could still smell the expensive cologne, something with bergamot and lemon or something, like the coziest cup of Earl Grey married to sharp citrus. She wanted to press her nose against the juncture of his neck and shoulder and just *breathe*.

Then maybe take one little bite.

She shook her head at herself. The rest of the party, still in full swing, was muffled by the sliding glass door. It was chilly, and nobody wanted to stand outside but Vinh— and now her, from the looks of it.

She knew what she was going to do.

"I'm not saying yes," she prefaced. He perked up immediately, ignoring the view, swinging his intense gaze to her. "But I'm open to hearing about your problem. If I can't help, maybe I know someone who can. I still have plenty of contacts, a network I trust." She didn't really hang with hackers at this point, but she was in contact online, here and there.

She saw the tension in his body release infinitesimally. "Really?"

"We'll see," she temporized. "But I'm gonna need details first."

He glanced over her shoulder. "We might not want to do this here," he said, rubbing the back of his neck.

"First detail: Why are you keeping this from Tam?"

"Because she'll worry."

Shit. So it was personal, despite being tied to his business. That ought to deter her.

It didn't.

"That's what I was afraid of," she said, then let out a huff of breath. "Fine. Are you crashing here at the house?"

He shook his head. "Nope. Got a room at that new hotel, on the beach."

She let out a low whistle. "Swanky. Well, you're going to leave now. I'll leave in about twenty minutes. Meet me at the Shack. Remember that? The diner by the pier? The one with the milkshakes."

He nodded, his eyes bright. "Got it. Can I have your phone number?"

She blinked. "Why?"

"In case you don't show up."

She couldn't help herself. She grinned. "If I don't show up, I probably won't want you to call me."

He rolled his eyes. "Nice."

"You're going to have to trust me," she said. "Get gone. I'll see you soon enough."

He nodded, then slipped through the door. Meanwhile, her head screamed at her: *What are you doing?*

Shenanigans, that was what she was doing. But she was going to find out what was going on. That didn't mean she had to agree to help.

Yeah. You keep telling yourself that.

CHAPTER 6

Half an hour later, Vinh found himself at the Shack, waiting for Emily. It had been an institution in Ponto Beach, one of the few diner-style places that was open late and didn't mind the hordes of teens that flocked there after football games or when the nearby movie theater let out. Even now, there were kids at various tables: a bunch of kids in letterman jackets that said **PONTO HIGH** with their mascot, the condor. They were tapping away at their phones, joking in loud voices. Considering, he'd bet they had just come out of whatever latest blockbuster had dropped this weekend. Another corner table had a couple kissing, so enamored and pure and wholesome that Vinh had to look away, uncomfortable with intruding.

He was hit with a wave of nostalgia. Back when they had been in high school, the Herd would hang out here every now and then too. They'd stood in line for hours to watch *Avatar*, then descended on the Shack to munch deep-fried "tot-chos" (tater tot nachos) and ice cream sundaes. They'd stay out as long as their curfews allowed . . . and he'd pushed Emily right to the last second, every chance he could, just to spend more time with her.

He wondered if she had a deeper meaning in asking him to meet her here.

"Vinh, right?"

He blinked, shaking off the memories, and looked over at the waitress. She was wearing a fire-engine-red T-shirt that said COME BACK TO THE SHACK and a pair of jeans. Her hair matched the shirt. He blinked. "Peggy?" he ventured, mining the dark recesses of his memory.

She laughed, the smoke-gravelly sound one he instantly recognized. She'd been a waitress when they were kids. She'd gained some weight and now rocked a pair of hipster glasses that she tended to glance over as she wielded her order pad. But otherwise, she hadn't changed a bit.

"How ya doin', kid?" she asked, with a broad grin accentuated by her heavy red lipstick.

He grinned back. "I can't believe you remember who I am," he said. "You must see thousands of high school kids."

She tapped her temple with her ballpoint. "I've got a mind like a steel trap," she said. Then she winked. "And you guys were good tippers, especially for kids. What did you call yourselves? The geek pack or something?"

"Nerd Herd."

"That." She held her pen at the ready. "You know what you want to order?"

"I'm waiting for someone," he said. "But can I have a coffee, black?"

She shifted onto her back foot and looked at him askance. "Black coffee."

He nodded, puzzled.

She frowned. *Really.*

"Yes?"

She tutted. "You were always the large mocha milkshake."

He laughed. "I had a better metabolism then."

"YOLO, kiddo," Peggy said. "It's still got that Turkish coffee in it, the good stuff."

He fought a smile and lost. It had been years since he'd had ice cream, he realized . . . and their milkshakes were awesome. "Okay, you win."

She laughed again, that happy sandpaper sound. "I'll get it out to you," she said, then turned and walked away, taking a moment to ruffle a football player's hair and give a hug to a girl who had just walked in.

He felt . . . odd being back, he realized. Of course, he was under a lot of stress. Losing a huge amount of money, watching his career circle the drain, and facing the threat of later prosecution would do that to a guy. It was exacerbated by the fact that he wanted to keep those details close to the vest. He was pretending to be all right.

Except, weirdly, for a few moments here and there tonight—he hadn't been pretending.

It wasn't like he'd *forgotten* the trouble he was in. But laughing at Hayden's ridiculous stories, or seeing Josh and Tam in love and talking about their wedding, or hearing Tobin tease Lily and having her chase him around the living room . . . it had been like bringing back the best parts of his past. It gave him a strange, sweetly painful ache.

And of course, there was Emily. Seeing her had been maybe the hardest part of all.

And the sweetest.

He clenched his jaw, closing his eyes for a moment. It was strange, how after all these years, just seeing her made his heart speed up. That had always happened. Ever since he'd seen her as a transfer in middle school. He'd taken one look, and his entire being had thrummed, saying: *that one.* His eyes had been drawn to her whenever she'd entered the room, even though he'd quickly looked away. It hadn't just been physical either. The more he'd learned about her, the more he'd wanted to know.

He'd thought her out of his league. Her family had been upper middle class, and while his family hadn't been hurting, their finances had tended to wax and wane, depending on his father's spending and his mother's college needs. And Emily had been a composition of opposites, the kind of girl who could rock a ball gown as easily as ripped jeans. She was like a punk Tinker Bell, fiercely unapologetic and yet somehow unbelievably idealistic. He'd been enamored. Enraptured.

And when he'd finally gotten the courage to kiss her, she'd made a soft, surprised noise that he could remember like it was yesterday.

Then she'd jumped him.

It had probably been the best day of his young life, that first kiss that had led to all the rest. If he was honest, it was still in his top ten.

But that's not why you're here.

No matter how badly he might want it to be, he realized, thinking back to seeing her tonight . . . the way she smiled at jokes, the way she unconsciously tucked her hair behind her ear when she was concentrating on something someone said. The way she bit the corner of her lip when she carved the turkey. He tried so damned hard to forget about her, burying himself in work, freezing any emotional attachment before it took root. But it took less than two hours at Herdsgiving, seeing Emily, and suddenly he felt like one big exposed nerve.

And it was the last thing he could afford at a time like this.

He frowned at his thoughts. Any lasting romantic chance he'd had with Emily had been a pipe dream at best, and then he'd guaranteed the loss when he had dumped her all those years ago. The important thing to focus on now was that he needed Emily's help. She still had skills—he knew it. She'd always been brilliant, much like Josh, or their friend Keith, or even Hayden, although his genius was more erratic. Emily had a technical mind. She easily could have gone to Caltech or MIT, but she'd chosen to go to NYU to be with him. Even if she'd dropped out freshman year, he knew her. Computer systems were in her blood. She'd read security manuals the way some people read mysteries or binged Netflix. She ate information like it physically sustained her.

She could help him. If he could only convince her.

"You falling asleep on me?"

He opened his eyes to see her looking at him with that sharp hazel gaze. She looked like a fae out of an urban fantasy, her hooded sweat jacket zipped up, thumbs hooked through the holes at the cuffs of her sleeves.

He was on his feet before he knew what he was doing. "Thanks for meeting me," he said, shifting into business mode. He felt stronger that way. He needed every ounce of strength he could get.

"Cut to the chase," Emily said, sitting down in the booth. She crossed her arms, looking very businesslike herself. "No bullshit. What kind of trouble are you in, Vinh?"

He froze for a moment, gripping the glass of ice water in front of him like it could somehow buy him time.

How the hell did he tell her? How much should he tell her?

You have to tell her everything.

Then he frowned as her words sank in. "Wait. How do you know *I'm* in trouble?"

She rolled her eyes and leaned back against the vinyl seat. "It's been a minute, but I *know* you, Vinh Doan. So spill."

He cleared his throat, feeling suddenly vulnerable. Which he should have remembered she tended to bring out in him. "I . . ."

"Emily, hon!"

"Hi, Peggy," Emily said, going from stern to sunshine in under a second. "How are you?"

"Can't complain, can't complain," Peggy said. "What'll it be? Totchos? Burger?"

"I ate a ton tonight. Just a coffee," Emily said, and Peggy made a noise. "Damn it. All right, a strawberry milkshake. But a small one!"

Peggy laughed, then put a large glassful of milkshake in front of Vinh, with an additional metal cup for the excess. It was a lot. "Wait a sec . . . Vinh and Emily. Wow! You aren't still together after all this time, are you? I never see him!"

Vinh blinked. Emily chuckled. "Um, no. We broke up forever ago."

"Oh." Peggy looked puzzled. "So . . . you got back together?"

"We don't even really like each other," Emily said, with a touch of smugness.

Peggy stared back and forth from one to the other. "Anger banging, then?"

"Peggy!" Emily burst out in scandalized laughter.

"What? That's the polite version," Peggy said. "And believe me, there's nothing wrong with it. Adds some spice, y'know?"

"Oh my God," Vinh whispered. Even as the thought of "anger banging" Emily . . .

Nope. No. Do not.

He couldn't start thinking that way. That was the path of madness.

"I'll have your milkshake out in a minute," Peggy said, then retreated with a knowing grin.

Emily rubbed her hands over her face. "So that happened."

He let out a low laugh. "I have missed this place," he said. "Ponto Beach, I mean. Well, the Shack too."

Emily sighed. "But that's not why you're here."

He straightened in the seat, centering himself. Then he looked around. No one was paying attention to them. Peggy was in the kitchen, getting Emily's milkshake.

He leaned forward, dropping his voice. "My company thinks I embezzled ten million dollars from my job."

Emily's jaw dropped. *"What?"*

"Best I can tell, somebody hacked into my accounts, into my computer, somehow. And then moved the money I was managing for my clients. I was supposed to transfer it out of crypto into a standard currency—it's a long story. But bottom line: I'm getting set up."

"Are they framing you for criminal charges?"

He felt a warmth in his chest. She might hate him, but she knew he wasn't capable of theft . . . that he wasn't responsible for this. "Not exactly," he hedged. "Again: long story."

"I've got time for this."

So he told her the high-level details: the crypto accounts. The need to clean up. The vanished funds. Even the short version had his chest clenching with anxiety.

"This is bad, Vinh," she breathed. "Really bad."

"Funny how people keep assuming I can't tell how bad this is," he muttered under his breath, before adding, "You see why I need you, then?"

"Not really," she shot back, sipping on the milkshake she'd finally gotten from Peggy. "What do you need me to do?"

"Figure out who broke into my computer. Figure out who took the money. Help me put the money back, and maybe get a little payback on the son of a bitch."

She was silent for a second, sucking contemplatively on the red straw. He forced himself not to stare at the way her pink lips closed around the plastic. Finally, she looked at him. "Even if I wanted to, Vinh . . . I am so slammed it's not funny."

He'd known there'd be some resistance. "Slammed with what?"

"My job," she said. "And, um . . . I might need to pick up some holiday work or more overtime. And take care of some stuff for my brother. Since he's fucked off to Antarctica with no notice," she added in a grumble.

That was easy enough to solve, he thought with relief. "I'll pay you."

Now her eyes glittered. "How much?"

"How much do you want?" he asked. She hesitated, biting her lip in a very distracting way, and he forced himself to stay on task. "You don't understand. If I'm lucky, all that's going to happen to me is the complete obliteration of my career. If I'm unlucky, they figure out a way to sic the cops on me and send me to jail. And the company who lost the account can afford to lose ten million, but they won't be happy about it."

She grimaced. "Of course, it's about your career. Hard to keep being the successful wunderkind when you're blackballed out of your chosen field, huh? When you're a disgrace?"

He should have seen this trap coming. He cursed himself silently but didn't let it show outwardly.

"I should tell you to go to hell," she mused, poking at the remaining milkshake with her straw. "You cared more about getting ahead than you did me. We broke up over it."

He felt the sharp cut of unfairness at her statement. That wasn't it—not exactly. But now wasn't the time to argue. He didn't have the time or the mental or emotional bandwidth for that conversation.

"Emily, I'm sorrier than I can say," he said, and he meant it more than she'd ever realize. "I'll let you punish me however you feel fit when this is over, I swear to God. But I *need* your help. There isn't anyone else I trust."

She stared at him, and for a second, he was drawn into the liquid pull of her eyes. And his traitorous heart did a double thump and sped up, just like always.

God, I miss this woman.

"All right," she said slowly. "You *will* pay me. And if you really want my help and you want to make it up to me, you're going to do exactly what I say."

He felt a bubble of triumph in his chest. "Absolutely," he said smoothly. "Whatever you say."

"Oh, and Vinh?"

He took a slug of his own milkshake. "Yes?"

"The stuff I'm going to ask you to do?" Her smile was small and evil, a pointed little grin. "I can *guarantee* you're not going to like it."

He nodded, even as he scoffed inside. He thought it was cute that Emily thought she could scare him. He'd negotiated multimillion-dollar deals, stared down CEOs, gone toe to toe with prime ministers and princes. He was pretty sure he could handle whatever she threw at him.

CHAPTER 7

Emily drove home, her car shuddering to a noisy stop in the driveway. It was late, and she hoped she hadn't woken her mother up pulling in. More to the point, she prayed that her mother was actually asleep, because after her discussion with Vinh, the last thing she wanted to do was try to pretend she was okay.

She quietly let herself in and locked the door behind her. The lights were out, which made sense, considering how late it was. She maneuvered through the living room, avoiding the creaky patches, skipping the third step on the staircase that led to the upstairs bedrooms. It was a lot like sneaking in after curfew, she thought with a bittersweet smile of remembrance. Although there was a big difference between creeping in as a teenager, fresh off a make-out session with the love of her life, and trying for stealth as a twenty-eight-year-old who was just wanting some sleep after a very trying day.

She washed up and got ready for bed, hoping against hope that she'd just collapse into bed and be asleep as soon as the light was out, but she knew better. As soon as her head hit the pillow, her eyes opened.

You should have said no.

Dealing with Vinh was like dealing with the devil. There were probably all sorts of pitfalls that she didn't anticipate, and God only knew what kinds of headaches she was letting herself in for. But there had been too many seductive elements for her to resist.

Getting to do what she truly loved—hacking into a security system for one of the biggest consultancies in the world?—was a dream being offered on a silver platter. Even the potential, real dangers were an adrenaline shot. It had been way too long since she'd done anything other than participate in fake tournaments and security tests.

But not just hacking. She would be *paid* to do it. And she knew the average salary for someone who worked at Aimsley. She wouldn't admit it under pain of death, but she'd kept a loose eye on Vinh's career, knowing that he'd gotten promoted, seeing him go from intern to vice president. He made more money annually than she'd made in her entire "career" working at the IT call center. He could afford plenty, and she wouldn't feel guilty about charging him as much as she thought he'd pay. Maybe even adding another 25 percent as an "asshole ex-boyfriend" tax.

Which brought her to the final pro on her pros and cons list: *getting some payback*.

He needed her, which meant that she could basically get him to do anything she wanted. The more unpleasant, the better.

There was only one item in her cons column: she would have to spend a lot of time with Vinh.

She pulled the blanket over her shoulder, flopping in her twin bed. She'd spent only a few hours with him, and she was already feeling hot, bothered, bewildered. He shouldn't be able to have this effect on her after all this time. That said, after all this time, she ought to stop pretending she was surprised that he did. She'd once mistaken a total stranger for him when she'd been at the Belly Up Tavern, and her heart had gone from zero to sixty in less than a second before he'd turned to show his full face, and she'd realized her mistake. Spending more time with Vinh would make that reflexive response only more pronounced.

She was *not* sleeping with him again.

Then she groaned.

That is easy to say . . . until you're faced with that gorgeous face and those sexy forearms—and I think he's been working out—and oh my God I am so screwed.

She sat bolt upright, huffing impatiently at herself. "Okay. Time to bring out the big guns."

She turned her light back on, then quietly made her way to her closet and dug around a pile of promotional tote bags, old blankets, and some storage blocks until she found what she was looking for. It was a beat-up little cardboard box that had once been covered in various colors of tissue paper. Gritting her teeth, she opened it, then sifted through the contents. A dried flower. Movie tickets. Purikura photos from when they had gone to Little Tokyo in Los Angeles. All memories from when they had been together.

Then, on top of the pile, there was a tearstained, handwritten list.

When she'd returned from New York with the last of her stuff from college, fresh off of being dumped by Vinh, she'd come very close to burning this box and all its contents, but she hadn't had the time. Shortly after that, her mother had had a complete meltdown, leaving Emily to make sure that the trains ran on time—and the bills were paid on time. Which led to the discovery that they were mortgaged to the hilt and that her father had racked up way too much debt. Which, in turn, led to Greg's ill-advised scam idea with his (now ex) friends. She'd applied to plenty of computer-related jobs, but no one had been interested in what essentially amounted to a high school graduate with one semester of general ed under her belt. She'd taken what she could get, stocking groceries and cleaning offices, all while keeping a watchful eye on her mother. Every day she'd gone to sleep crying before falling asleep under sheer exhaustion.

And she had hated Vinh with a fury that burned like phosphorus.

Months later, instead of burning the box, she had decided to keep it. Not out of nostalgia. As a *warning*. Because sometimes, after a hard workday, or a pointless date, or when she was feeling particularly lonely, she'd consider looking Vinh up or, worse, dialing to see if he'd kept the same phone number.

She had then written a list, in heavy block letters, and nestled it among all those positive memories.

WHY VINH IS EVIL

1. He dumped you after your father died.
2. He has never once called, friended, or otherwise interacted with you since. YOU could be dead, for all he cares.
3. He put his career before your relationship. All he cares about is success.
4. He never loved you the way you thought he did. All these memories are lies.
5. He will hurt you again, given the opportunity. DO NOT GIVE HIM THE OPPORTUNITY.
6. Don't call, text, direct message, Slack, or pass a message through friends. NO CONTACT.
7. He will never, ever pay for what he did.

She reread the list, even though she had it memorized.

This was just a job, she reminded herself. They'd find out who was framing him, they'd get the stolen money back, and then he'd pay her and leave her the hell alone for the rest of his life. Simple. She was attracted, sure. He was still exactly what she wanted, from a purely physical aspect. But she was older and too smart to just give in to sexual attraction. When she felt tempted, she'd just remember this list, remember what she'd felt like writing it. And then walk the hell away.

Her gaze ran over the last line.

He will never, ever pay for what he did.

She grinned slowly, remembering her conversation with him at the Shack. It was obvious that she had leverage here, and for once, she might be able to cross this particular line off.

Because if she was going to go through with this, she had every intention of making him sorry for what he had done. Just because she was helping him didn't mean he was forgiven or that it was forgotten.

She tucked the box away, then climbed back into bed. She might not sleep, but at least now she had visions of vengeance dancing in her head instead of sad memories of the past.

Tomorrow, Vinh wouldn't know what hit him.

CHAPTER 8

The next morning, Vinh felt confident, almost cocky, about whatever Emily might throw at him. At least, he was until he walked into Greg's place. He could feel his eyes widen as he took in the tiny one-bedroom apartment. It had a window in the bedroom, from what he could see through the open bedroom door, but that was the only one. The light was dim, and there were boxes everywhere.

It was also hotter than hell, felt really humid in a way that he didn't think had anything to do with the numerous plants spread around the place. There was a smell too—not terrible, just strange. It reminded him of the last time he'd been in the jungle, actually. And there were a lot of . . .

Boxes?

No. Not boxes.

Tanks. Aquariums. Enclosures. And a big cabinet-looking thing under a blanket, shoved in the corner. It looked (and kinda smelled) like a pet store.

He surveyed his surroundings with a growing disquiet. "Um . . ."

"We're going to use Greg's apartment as our war room," Emily said. She looked tired, with some dark smudges beneath her eyes, and she wasn't wearing makeup. Her chin-length hair was pulled back with a hair clip, and she was wearing a long-sleeved heather-gray shirt with **Pwn2Own** written on it. She'd been in the apartment for a little while, or at least he assumed she had from the way she'd put a dish away. The place was clean, at least. In fact, the tiny one-bedroom looked cleaner than he would've expected, considering Greg's room at Emily's house growing up had usually been a disaster area.

"Okay, that's fine." That was easy enough to agree to. If they were going to have one of those "red-string murder board" type things, with suspects ranging from coworkers to clients, the last thing he wanted was housekeeping or anybody from a hotel looking at it. Lack of security was what had gotten him in this mess in the first place, presumably.

"I'm going to need a new laptop," she said. "Mine is old and wonky, and you don't want any connection to yours, anyway, I'm assuming."

"No problem," he assured her, some of his confidence coming back. Buying equipment was easy, the least of his problems. "We can do that today."

She nodded, tucking some loose strands of hair that had escaped the clip behind her ear in an unconscious gesture that hit him like a club.

God, am I always going to react this way to her?

It might be better to limit his interactions with her, he realized. Maybe he could stay at his hotel suite and let her work here, then check in on her progress. It's not like he could help much anyway.

"Second condition," she said briskly. "You have to stay here, not at the hotel."

He goggled. "Wait, what?"

"Like I said: Greg just bounced off to Antarctica with no warning," she pointed out. "Somebody's got to take care of his stuff—water his plants, take care of his pets. Stuff like that."

He glanced around at the tanks, noticing the sheer number of ferns, cacti, and other plants he didn't have names for. "Um . . ."

"It's not that bad," she said. "He's had more, believe me. I had to stage an intervention when he tried to smuggle a baby goat in here. I think this all calms him down, honestly."

Now Vinh stared. "O . . . kay . . ."

"Don't worry. I'll write down the routines and stuff that I remember. Most of them are pretty chill, and a lot of them are reptiles, so, y'know, they don't have to eat as often."

He swallowed.

He'd never had a pet. His parents had had absolutely no interest in them, no matter how much he and Tam had begged for a dog or cat. He vaguely remembered having a goldfish in a bowl, something he'd won in a fair, but it had died in a month. He'd been hurt, but his parents had simply flushed poor Goldie, then washed out the bowl and tucked it away in the garage. He hadn't gotten another one.

"What . . . how . . ." He rubbed his temples. "How many pets are we talking about, exactly?"

"Let's see." She seemed almost gleeful. "There's Speedy, over here. He's a turtle. Or a tortoise. I always get them mixed up."

He leaned down to look at the turtle (tortoise?) in the tank. It was sunning itself on a rock under the heat lamp. He looked grizzled and grumpy, sort of cute in a Grand Master Oogway sort of way. There were pieces of lettuce and slices of bell pepper on the sandy-looking "ground." He seemed harmless enough.

"Then there's Sonic." She gestured to another enclosure. "And before you ask—yes, he's a hedgehog."

He peered into the enclosure. There was a light blanket and a running wheel, as well as a bowl of water. "I don't see it."

"He's in his house right now," she said, gesturing to a cute little wooden house that looked like a log cabin, with an opening in the front. "Don't worry, you'll see him later. Anyway, moving on . . . there's the fish, they're easy . . ."

He looked at the fish, a mix of brightly colored and silver-sided fish, zipping around their castle or getting lost among the plants.

She pulled a blanket off of a tank. "And this is Bastard. He's a Tokay gecko."

"Why is he called Bastard?"

"Put your hand in there, and you'll find out," she said easily. "For a little guy, he's got a surprising bite. Oh, and he sort of barks."

"Barks?" Vinh shifted his weight uncomfortably. He was definitely out of his comfort zone. But again: he needed her help. And if she was worried about making sure this was taken care of, handling it would help ease her mind so she could focus on the problem he was asking her to tackle.

"Finally," she said, going to the large cabinet, "here's our big boy. How are you, Herman?"

Vinh leaned over, glancing in. Then he recoiled, jumping back.

The fuck?

"He's a boa constrictor," she said. As opposed to the more accurate, "He's a large reptilian killing machine."

"How big is he?"

"Eh. About eight feet."

Vinh took another step back.

Nope. No. No. No way. So very much no.

Vinh gritted his teeth. "I don't think so."

"This is the only way I can help you." She looked like she was almost sorry, but there was a sparkle of mischief in her eyes.

"Don't worry. I'm going to hire a pet sitter," he said. "Somebody professional. Someone who's used to handling this kind of . . . menagerie." That was reasonable, right?

"Yes, but you agreed: you'd do whatever I said," she reminded him. "Besides, we don't want strangers in here looking at anything suspicious, do we?"

She had him there. That said, he sincerely doubted she was just insisting on this for security reasons. He glared at her. "You're enjoying this, aren't you?" he said.

Her answering smile was wicked. "I told you, you wouldn't like it," she said, leaning back against the wall. "You don't have to do this. Not any of this. But this is the agreement."

He took a deep, humid, fragrant breath. She was trying to see if she could scare him off or drive him away. Yes, on a certain level, she would be punishing him by making him do this, but she had a point. This was the best place to set up their war room, to get all the details, to do the work. He'd just have to suck it up and deal.

He'd dealt with worse, frankly.

"Fine," he said. "I'll take care of Greg's . . . stuff."

"And stay here. Sleep here, I mean."

He stared at her. "You cannot be serious."

"One of the animals might need something." Her look was completely innocent. *Too innocent.*

He grumbled, thinking of the material comforts of his hotel suite, then sighed. "And I'll stay here."

"As to compensation," she said. "I thought it over last night, and I came up with a number."

To her credit, her voice shook only a little as she quoted what had to be what she thought was an outrageous amount. Being a careful negotiator, he knew not to show that compared to the amounts he was used to dealing with, what she was asking for was almost laughably small.

She ought to ask for more. Was she helping him out, trying to offer him a better deal? No—she'd made it clear that she wasn't doing this out of the kindness of her heart. But even on-the-level "pen experts," cybersecurity people who broke into systems ethically, quoted higher rates than this.

Why didn't she think she was worth more?

"That's fine," he said. When she looked surprised, he said, "I'll even throw in a bonus if we can find out in the next three weeks." He figured he'd throw in a bonus regardless. Something that brought her up to the level she deserved, even if she didn't think to ask.

She blinked.

"Em, I'm trying to keep my job and possibly stay out of prison. Did you really think I was going to haggle?"

She startled. Then her expression turned grim.

"No. You're right."

"Anything else?" Vinh coaxed. "Now's the time. Otherwise, we can go get that laptop for you and get going."

"There is one more thing." The sharpness of the statement made him pause.

He motioned to her to name it, trying to not make it obvious that he was sidling away from the snake enclosure.

"After we do this," she said slowly, carefully, "we don't see each other again. Ever."

He stopped in his tracks. "Um . . ."

"I mean it, Vinh. I don't want you to be cut off from the Nerd Herd, obviously, but I'll make sure that we don't cross paths. I don't want to be surprised at your sister's house. I don't want to 'accidentally' run into you at Juanita's coffee shop . . ."

"I've never even been there," he pointed out.

"I know. You've hardly seen the Herd since you left," she said, her tone flat. "But this is a deal breaker. After this, it's going to be like I never knew you, okay?"

He couldn't help it. His heart clenched in his chest. It hurt way more than he thought it should, even after all this time.

"All right," he agreed. "It's a deal."

CHAPTER 9

Emily's brain was spinning that afternoon as they set up their makeshift "war room." She couldn't believe, after almost ten years, she was in the same room as Vinh and not trying to kill him. That she was actively trying to *help* him, in fact.

After this is done, you never have to see him again.

Although, honestly, it wasn't like seeing him was the torture she'd feared. He'd been nothing but polite, just this side of impersonal. Besides, as he'd mentioned and she kept reminding herself, it had been ten years since they'd broken up. Honestly, she ought to just get over it, right? That would probably be the consensus of most of the Herd, although they were too nice to say so. Hell, a therapist would conclude the same, if she could afford one.

But it still hurt. Not *stung*. Not *irritated*. It made her heart ache.

I needed you, and you dumped me.

That was the one-two punch, really. It wasn't just that he had broken up with her. He'd had every right, if he didn't feel the same, to walk away. But she had lost her father and had been moving across the country, and he'd said: *I can't afford to give up my career, my future. I can't be what you want.*

A clean break would be best.

She closed her eyes as the remembered pain sliced through her, an echo that was still so fucking sharp she felt tears prick at the corners of her eyes.

No. She didn't have time to indulge in that, not when she had a job to do. If she'd learned anything in the past ten years, it was putting her head down and getting shit done.

She cleared her throat, setting her new laptop on Greg's cleared-off kitchen table and slapping up some giant sticky notes on the walls. Vinh had suggested a full cork murder board, but for the simple sake of expediency, she'd just gotten the Post-its. This would work fine.

"What are we doing, then?" Vinh asked, crossing his arms. He was dressed casually again—a pair of jeans, a T-shirt that stretched across a nicely defined chest. "I mean, shouldn't you have the computer up and running? I can give you the account number. I made sure to write that down just in case what happened eventually happened. I knew they'd lock me out, probably without any chance to puzzle out how it all went down."

"That's fine, and yes, I'll need that," she assured him, pulling out some pens. "But hacking's not just all computers and numbers and a bunch of password stuff. It's about systems. The first thing that's hacked is always people."

He frowned, obviously puzzled.

"Do you think this is some random attack? That some high-level hacker would've just taken that account?"

"I don't *know*," Vinh said, his tone one of clear frustration. "Possibly. Although I don't know how." He arched an eyebrow at her, as if to say, *Which is why I came to you.*

"Hacking's kind of like murder," she said, and his eyes popped wide. "Let me clarify. There's the kind of hacking that's just trolls looking for a way in. There's the malicious black-hat stuff, where they're trying to install malware or ransomware, or steal account information to sell to the highest bidder. I don't think that's the case here."

"Why not?"

"Because if it was, they would've taken you for every account you dealt with," she said, with a shrug. "And not just you. Every single consultant you worked with would've gotten taken, too, more than likely. Unless . . ." Now it was her turn to frown.

"Unless?"

She didn't respond, mulling it over as she went to Greg's newly stocked fridge. She grabbed a cream soda, then popped it open and sipped thoughtfully. "Unless you were careless. Like criminally, foolishly careless."

As soon as the words were out of her mouth, she knew in her gut that wasn't the case. Not unless he'd had an entire personality transplant in the past ten years. His look of irritated amusement showed that he had the same thought.

"You mean, if I was careless enough to, say, put my passwords on sticky notes on my desk or laptop, or something ridiculous like that?"

She nodded. "Or used the same password for everything. Made it easy."

"Password123, with an exclamation point," he said derisively, then shook his head. "C'mon, Em. You know me better than that."

"Do I, though?" she murmured. "I haven't really talked to you in a decade, dude. And if you want me to get to the bottom of this, I need to ask, okay?"

He still looked irritated but then nodded, grabbing a chair and sitting at the table next to her. She whipped out a legal pad and grabbed a pen. "You work off of just one computer?"

He nodded. "My work laptop, yes. It's easiest, considering how much I travel."

"So you brought it with you when you traveled," she said thoughtfully, writing down *travel*. "Any chance that you left it somewhere that someone else could've accessed it?"

"Absolutely not," he said, cutting off that avenue. "Unless I was in the office, I always had it on my person, in my laptop bag, or locked in a safe at whatever hotel I was staying at when I wasn't working on it."

"Okay, that probably counts that out," she said, crossing out the single word she'd written. Then she felt her stomach knot as another possibility popped up. "You ever bring it home?" she asked carefully.

"Sure, all the time."

"So anybody who came to your house could've had access to it?"

"It's a condo," he corrected, and she rolled her eyes.

"Anyone who came to your *condo* could've had access to it?" she said. "Or were you locking it up in a safe there too?"

He blinked. "Who would be at my house?"

Damn it. She really needed to spell it out for him? Anger bubbled in her veins.

"*Women*, you doofus! A girlfriend? Some woman you picked up at a bar? Maybe you fell asleep and the laptop was there?"

Now he stared at her, his dark eyes warm with just a hint of amusement. "You asking me if I have a girlfriend?"

She growled at him. "I'm asking you if you got set up," she said.

Had she been asking him that? She was curious, sure. She couldn't help that: curiosity was her factory setting. But because she was interested or, worse, jealous? No, she reasoned. Of course not. This was strictly for business reasons.

You keep telling yourself that.

"I don't," he replied, his voice quiet. "Have a girlfriend."

"Oh." She made a note, just to give her hands something to do with all the nervous energy suddenly flooding her system. "And . . ."

"And I don't really, ah, hook up a whole lot," he said, and for the first time, there was a hint of color on his high cheekbones. "Either way, the laptop stays safely locked in my condo. And I don't take anyone home, period."

"You don't?" she said softly.

He shook his head. "Nope. Fortress of Solitude."

She felt both sad—and comforted, dammit. Which was utterly ridiculous and bugged the fuck out of her.

"Not that I'm home much," he added. "But no. I would say I haven't had anyone over of any gender, period, for . . ." He paused, doing mental math. "A few years, I guess. It's not like I have the time or the interest to entertain."

"All work, all the time," she noted. She saw his eyes flash. Then he shrugged.

"It's the job."

"Okay. You took the right security precautions," she said briskly. "So if one of your accounts got cleaned out, then you need to think about who else had access. Why you, and why now? Why not somebody else? Why were you targeted?"

"I don't *know*," he repeated, getting to his feet and pacing—as well as he could pace, given the cramped conditions. He stopped in front of the fish tank, and she saw him breathing deep, his eyes following the darting silvery fish. "All I know is, there should've been ten million in that account, and then there wasn't!"

"Could the client have taken it without warning you?" she asked.

"No. I was the only one who had access to that account," he said, and now instead of being angry, he just sounded weary.

"Why? It's their money, right?"

She could see the muscles in his jaw clench. Then he turned to her. "Just how much can I trust you, Emily?"

He was upset, that much was obvious. But he was also . . . desperate wasn't quite the right word. He was *struggling*. Struggling with trust, and the pain of being betrayed already . . . which, for someone who didn't trust, must've seemed like insult upon injury. He was no doubt beating himself up, assuming that ultimately, he was responsible for the disaster that had occurred on his watch.

She hated it, but she felt for him. She'd always hated seeing him in pain, and as much as she wanted to mess with him and give him some payback, apparently that hadn't changed.

She pantomimed locking her lips. "No matter how pissed I've been at you in the past," she said, "you know I won't tell a soul. I'm not going to use anything against you, and I'm not going to mess with you. You have to know that."

He stared at her, and his gaze was so intense it was like staring at a black hole. He finally straightened, looking like he was about to jump off of a cliff.

"The money was a slush fund," he said. "We were setting up factories in other countries for our client. Sometimes wheels needed to be greased, or local officials needed some tribute cash. Bribes needed to be spread around. Money expedites things."

She waited, but he stopped there. "That's it?"

"Yup."

"Well, that doesn't sound so bad," she said. "I thought you were talking, like, gunrunning or hiding dead bodies or something."

He finally smiled . . . a small smile, but still. "Nah. Just grift. The usual. But it's not the sort of thing that is necessarily strictly legal, and from a tax standpoint, the clients would rather it not show up in some books."

"I . . . see." She frowned. "Are you breaking the law?"

"No," he said. "Not technically. I am dancing right on the edge, though." She wasn't sure what showed on her face, but he looked . . . embarrassed? "That's why they pay me what they do. To guide them through the gray area."

"Wow. That's a commencement speech, for sure," she said dryly. "Or at least a cross-stitch. Maybe a T-shirt that says 'Wilderness guide for the gray area' or something?"

"Yes, well. You make a devil's bargain, this is what you get, I suppose." He shrugged, but tension screamed from every muscle. "I imagine you're thinking I deserve this."

She sighed. "No. I mean, karma's a bitch, but I wouldn't have wanted your career to go down in flames, Vinh."

"Really?" He paused a beat, then said, "Even after you said I'd be sorry for picking my career over you?"

She straightened. That moment was so indelibly etched in her memory, and it stabbed at her.

Fuck you, Vinh. Take your college degree, and your future, and fucking choke on it.

She sighed. "No. Don't get me wrong—I wanted you to hurt like I was. But I wouldn't want you to go down this way."

He studied her, then took a step closer. She could smell his cologne, something expensive, with subtle notes of spices she couldn't name. "Thank you for that," he said, and his voice almost vibrated with sincerity. "And thank you for helping me with this."

"In my defense, my fantasy was that you'd be super successful and rich, but then you'd look back and see how frickin' happy I was with, like, Jason Momoa, and you'd feel empty and cold and broken," she added. "So I wouldn't thank me that hard."

His eyes widened, and then he chuckled. She smirked back. "All right. Back to business. If this was done to you deliberately, the next questions are: Who are your enemies? Who would want something bad to happen to you and would go to some lengths to make it happen?"

He sank down on the chair at the table. "How much time do you have?" he groaned.

She laughed . . . then saw he was serious.

"Shit," she muttered, then got ready to jot down names.

CHAPTER 10

On Sunday morning, Vinh woke up at three, sandy eyed and irritated. He'd barely gotten any sleep. He'd slept on uncomfortable beds before, in much worse accommodations, so that wasn't a problem. He had never shared a room with a small lizard that apparently *barked*. And he would have to do something about the squeaky treadmill in the hedgehog's enclosure. Between that, the burble of the aquarium, and some other weird noises, it had taken him forever to get to sleep. Then, like clockwork, his eyes had opened at what should have been six o'clock eastern. That actually was sleeping in.

So he'd gotten maybe three hours of sleep, if he was lucky. And there was a laundry list of stuff he needed to take care of . . . somehow. He was still a little fuzzy on the details, since Greg had left in such a rush that he hadn't quite gotten a list together of who needed what care when, and Emily had only vague details that she'd jotted down on a Post-it.

After tossing and turning for an hour to no avail, he finally got up and powered up the new laptop he'd purchased when he'd gotten Emily her own. Then he texted Greg, hoping to at least find out what the heck kind of animals he was dealing with. It was twenty-one hours ahead at McMurdo Station, where Greg was working in Antarctica, so he doubted he'd get much of a response. Then, he figured out how to work Greg's coffee thing (a hipster glass pour-over contraption that took way too long to research when he was running on no sleep) and then puzzled out how to work Greg's TV. He dozed in and out of a few movies he'd previously caught on international flights, but his mind was still primarily preoccupied with two things: the missing money, and Emily.

The fact that he couldn't control what was happening around tracking down the cash and whoever stole it was eating away at him. The sense of powerlessness reminded him of his childhood, when he never knew which parent would be home, whether there would be a state of war as they screamed obscenities at each other. Never knowing if he'd have to try to protect Tam from the brunt of it, make sure she got fed, hope that she could go hang out with Josh or the Herd. He'd grown a psychic antenna that picked up tension and problems a mile off, and he was usually planning out three different solutions and strategies before anything blew up.

He knew it was a textbook response to become a control freak after a problematic (some might say *traumatic*) youth, but it'd served him fairly well, so he just rolled with it. In fact, it was part of what made him so damned good at his job: he had plans A through Z at the ready before his competitors entered the room.

Seeing Emily again, on the other hand, had hit him like a sledgehammer, and he hadn't been equipped with a single fallback plan. He had known it would be hard and probably nostalgic, even painful. But he'd been swept away by a wave of longing and loss that he, frankly, hadn't realized he needed to be prepared for. He didn't even know how he *could* prepare for something like this.

And he knew that he wanted her, sure . . . just the memory of her brought that back. But he'd forgotten how much he *liked* her—how much he enjoyed her company, her sense of humor, the way she listened, and the way she spoke her mind. There was just a *closeness* there that he hadn't enjoyed with another person in . . . well, ever.

Now, he didn't know what to do with that emotional overwhelm. His logic hadn't equipped him for these feelings.

After pacing, cleaning things that didn't need to be cleaned, and trying to figure out what sort of animals he was dealing with based on photos and Google, it was finally late enough for him to text Emily again.

VINH: When were you planning on coming back? We can grab breakfast.

He actually hadn't meant to mention that, but it made sense. They'd both need to eat. Maybe they'd avoid the Shack, though. They had phenomenal cinnamon rolls the size of a dinner plate, but he wasn't the cinnamon-roll type. Also, if he saw Peggy again, he wasn't sure what he'd do with another "anger bang" reference.

EMILY: Having breakfast with my Mom, then we're video calling Greg and figuring out what to do with his stuff. I want to make sure he's set up for paying rent and bills while he's gone, so he doesn't get evicted and the animal enclosures don't lose power. Won't be there until probably closer to late lunch. We can grab something then if you want.

Before he could answer, she tacked on:

EMILY: I'll ask Greg if there's any special instructions for what he wants done with his mini-zoo, but Hayden has pet sit for Greg in the past, I'm pretty sure? Here's his number. You might wanna text him.

While Vinh squelched an unreasonable sense of disappointment that he wouldn't see Emily till the afternoon—which was impatience, he told himself, because this was really important and they needed to get to work to get his cash back—he went ahead and texted Hayden, asking him if he had any notes on how to take care of Greg's various exotic animals.

Hayden's reply was immediate: a gif of Rapunzel in *Tangled* brandishing a frying pan, asking, "Who are you, and how did you find me?"

Vinh chuckled. The response was perfectly Hayden.

VINH: It's Vinh. I'm taking care of Greg's menagerie while he's in Antarctica. Help?

It took less than thirty seconds for the reply.

HAYDEN: Sure! Be right over.

Vinh blinked. That actually wasn't what he'd meant. He'd hoped that Hayden had, like, a list or some notes from the last time he'd taken care of the animals. He hadn't meant to imply that Hayden should actually *come over*. Not that he didn't like Hayden. Hayden was a great guy. And it wasn't that he thought Hayden might not know what to do. Hayden was possibly the smartest of everyone in the Herd—and considering the grades, SAT scores, and sheer mental firepower of their crew, that was saying something.

It was more that Vinh wasn't used to asking for help from anyone, for anything. And here he was, asking Emily for help, then Hayden.

How far the mighty have fallen, he thought to himself, shaking his head as he quickly tucked away the notes he and Emily had taken the day before. It occurred to him that they could've done this all along—he could be staying at the hotel, he could hire a pet sitter—but it had never been about security. It had been about torturing him, putting him in this ridiculous situation.

He grinned a little. It was petty, and spiteful, and he couldn't blame her for a second. Actually, it was very *her*. Were he in the same position, he doubted his "payback" would be as mischievous—or harmless. Tam said that vengeance was his love language.

She wasn't wrong.

The knock on the apartment door came faster than he would've thought. He answered the door to find Hayden there, looking disheveled but happy, per usual. He was wearing a T-shirt that said **CHAOTIC NEUTRAL: MIGHT SAVE YOUR LIFE, MIGHT STEAL YOUR WIFE** and a pair of cargo shorts that had, frankly, seen better days. He was also wearing sandals, despite the nip in the air. "Hey, dude," Hayden said, unceremoniously shoving a paper bag into his hands. "What's up?"

Vinh blinked. "What's this?"

"Cali burrito from the place on the corner. You still like those, right?"

"I can't remember the last time I had one," Vinh admitted, sitting down at the table and pulling out a torpedo-size burrito wrapped in foil. His stomach growled greedily in protest, considering he'd been up since three and had only drunk coffee. He dug in and groaned as the combined flavors of guac, sour cream, carne asada, and fat home fries exploded in his mouth—and almost down his shirt. He quickly moved to lean over the table.

"Whadya think? Still good?" Hayden said, with a grin, before taking a shark-size bite out of his own burrito.

Vinh waited until his mouth wasn't full before answering. "Still utterly unnatural," he said, shaking his head. "Like, ridiculously unauthentic. But yeah, really good."

"Even better when you're hungover. I think it's the potatoes," Hayden said, shrugging. "So you're on pet duty, huh?"

Vinh nodded.

"I thought Greg was going to Antarctica," Hayden said, tilting his head in curiosity. "How long are you gonna be here?"

"I'm not . . . I'm just . . . this is temporary," Vinh said, stumbling. Which, again—he was used to prevaricating with ease, especially when business was involved. Now, he could barely say even the truth without getting awkward.

Maybe it's because you don't want to lie, even a little, to your friends?

"Fair enough," Hayden said before demolishing his burrito like it was a competition. After wiping the residue on napkins, he rubbed his rail-thin belly contentedly. "All right, I'll walk you through the routines, okay? It's not hard, it's just not easy."

Vinh blinked, deciding not to point out the contradiction in that statement. He wrapped up the remaining half of his burrito, already feeling full, wondering where the hell Hayden put it all. "Um . . . okay. Sure."

Hayden handed him a yellow legal pad, one of the ones that Emily had been taking notes on. Then he escorted Vinh around the room, like a tour guide. "These fish? They're African cichlids, and they eat this pellet food, here, twice a day. I'd also check the temperature of the water—they're used to tropical climates . . ."

Vinh dutifully took copious notes on who needed to eat what, when, and how and when to clean their homes, and what temperatures they needed. "Mist the tortoise . . ."

"No! Don't mist the tortoise," Hayden corrected. "Mist the *Tokay*. Gecko. Oh, and be careful when you do."

Vinh frowned. "What, is it venomous or something?"

"Nah. Just . . . here, watch." Hayden then put a thick glove on, one that had been resting by the base of the aquarium. Then he reached in.

Suddenly, there was a *snap* sound, and he lifted his hand up. Hanging from the end of his index finger was a very fierce, very pissed-off-looking small lizard.

"Go ahead and change his water while I've got him," Hayden said as if he didn't even notice his new appendage. Vinh quickly did as instructed. Then Hayden eased the lizard back in the cage, waiting until Bastard released the glove and retreated to a corner of the tank before removing it and replacing the tank lid. "He's a trip," Hayden said with fondness.

"Any other challenges you need to let me know about?"

"Well, I'm pretty sure that you know that the hedgehog is nocturnal by now," Hayden said, tapping his chin. "Speedy the tortoise is pretty chill—although he should not be *literally* chilly. Keep an eye on his temp. And make sure he's got water."

Finally, they got to the portion of the program that Vinh had been dreading. "Ah, here's my baby," Hayden said, all but crooning. "Herman! How are you, sweetheart?"

Vinh fought not to shudder as he approached the big snake enclosure. He peered in, past the plexiglass. It was fat, a sort of greenish-tan color with darker bands, and had cold, lifeless eyes. He was the ultimate predator. He looked back at Vinh, probably sizing him up for food.

"How often am I supposed to feed him?" Vinh said. "And are there, like, snake pellets or something?"

Hayden burst into laughter. "Um . . . no."

Vinh's stomach fell to his shoes. "Oh?" His voice sounded reedy to his own ears.

"Don't worry. Greg trained him not to eat live prey," Hayden reassured him. "His dinner's frozen. You just have to thaw it out and warm it up a little. And always use the feeding tong things. *Never* use your hands."

Like there was a chance *that* was going to happen. Vinh barely wanted to open the door. "Do I want to know what his food is?" Vinh asked, feeling a little sick.

"Hey, if you're a carnivore, it's not really much different than grabbing a chicken out of the freezer or anything, trust me," Hayden pointed out. "You don't even have to cook. You just gotta put it in some hot water till it's thawed, then wiggle it in the enclosure till he chomps. Easy peasy."

Vinh cautiously sidled up to the enclosure, where the snake was wrapped up on itself, looking at him calmly.

Nope. No, no, no.

"You're lucky," Hayden said, with a chuckle and a shrug. "I had to take care of a Burmese python once. Fourteen feet long and thicker than my thigh, y'know? And it was *not* trained to eat prekilled prey," he said. "I had to go to a carniceria in Oceanside to get it, not like a pet store or anything, since I figured that way I knew it was gonna be dinner either way, y'know? Either some meat-eating person or the python. And there was a long line waiting for chickens. But when I picked out the chicken, they started to take it to the back to 'prep' it, and I yelled out 'No! *I need it alive!*' and everybody around me suddenly went silent and started backing away from me." He busted out laughing. "I can't even imagine what arcane rituals they thought I was gonna do with it."

Grossed out as he was, Vinh shook his head, laughing. "God, Hayden. Only you. And when did you take care of a python?"

"I've been an exotic-pet sitter before," Hayden said. "That's why Greg asked for my help. I actually helped him get Bastard."

"Videographer, exotic-pet sitter, surfing instructor, seat filler, construction demo guy," Vinh teased. "Dude, is there anything you don't do?"

Hayden grinned. "I don't punch a clock, and that's all that matters to me."

Vinh was still a bit baffled at how Hayden was able to survive cobbling together these various jobs, but obviously it was working for him. Considering his IQ tested at a scary-high level, he could've skipped five grades if he'd wanted, and he'd had colleges actively courting him like he was a star quarterback, it was more of a surprise that he'd never gone to college and never pursued any sort of career.

Even more baffling: Hayden was possibly the happiest person he'd ever met.

Hayden looked over his checklist (which, in true Vinh style, was set up with times, temps, and checkboxes so he could input it with alarms on his phone) and then nodded. "Pretty cool. Hey, wanna go hang out at Tobin's? We were gonna go old school, link up a bunch of computers and go whale on some noobs at Team Fortress 2. Want in? I'll let you be Spy or Medic."

Vinh couldn't remember the last time he'd played a video game, he suddenly realized. "I can't," he said. "Emily's gonna be back, and . . ."

He stopped short. He'd been about to blurt out what he and Emily were working on.

"You and Emily, huh?" Hayden said, waggling his eyebrows.

"It's not like that," Vinh said, cursing the slip. "We're just . . . she's helping me with a project. That's all."

"Suuuure," Hayden said. "Because you're well known for your collaborative nature, especially with her."

"Besides, isn't she dating someone?" Vinh said, almost desperately.

Hayden's grin widened to Cheshire proportions. "Now, that was smooth. You should totally play Spy," he replied. "And no, she isn't dating anyone. Hasn't for ages. Said that she doesn't have time for them."

Vinh felt buoyed by that—until Hayden followed it up.

"The way that girl works, I'm not surprised. She barely has time to breathe, seems like, except for when she gets to decompress with the Herd, and even then, she's fallen asleep on Tobin's or Tam's couch mid-discussion a couple of times."

"Why does she work so hard?"

Hayden smiled, but there was a tinge of sadness.

"You're gonna have to ask her," he deflected. "Anyway, I'm gonna bounce." He surprised Vinh with a one-armed hug. "Good to have you back, brother."

Vinh felt his throat tighten, and it took him a second before he could actually respond. "Good to be back," he said. And meant it.

CHAPTER 11

Emily was already exhausted, and it was only eleven in the morning. Still, she gamely knocked on Greg's door, strange though that felt, to help Vinh with his "project" and steal back slush fund money from God knew who so it could then be used for God knew what.

Her mind had been bouncing around solutions to his problem. While cryptocurrency *accounts* were completely anonymous, the ledger—the record of all transactions—was completely open to the public. It was part of how the whole thing worked. So as long as she knew the account number, she could see what transactions it engaged in and what accounts the money got transferred to. Then, it would be a matter of finding out who owned those accounts and how to get access to them. It would be hard, and possibly tedious, but for her, a hacker who had spent the better part of the past year asking, "Did you try turning it off and then on again?" it was a delicious brainteaser. She'd already come up with a number of potential solutions. It'd just be a matter of actually having the time to code them or backdoor into Aimsley's computers and do some sleuthing.

She kind of couldn't wait, if she was being honest.

Vinh opened the door. God, even casual, he looked like he ought to be in a photo shoot. How did he have the continued audacity to look so damned good?

"Hi," she said. "Sorry I'm late. The call ran kind of long. I swear, getting Mom and Greg on a conference call is like herding kittens. Together, they have the attention span of a golden retriever."

She'd pressed Greg to get his various bills on autopay and discussed moving his stuff out to the house and giving up his lease if he wound up staying in Antarctica for another season, which looked likely. Then her mother told her about "this funny sound" that was coming from the pipes. She worried it might be the water heater, which was probably on its last legs and would cost more than they'd currently budgeted.

"Everything okay?" Vinh said, frowning slightly. "Your mom, the house?"

"The usual," Emily said, with a brittle laugh. "Just repairs," she added to keep it vague.

"How's your mother doing these days?" Vinh asked.

Emily grimaced. "She's all right. Still misses my dad every day." Hell, the house had always been his dream. Sometimes she worried that her mother would chain herself to the front door before allowing anyone to try taking it from her.

"That's sweet," Vinh said.

You'd think. "How are your parents?" Emily asked out of reflexive courtesy.

"You knew from Tam that they got divorced after our sophomore year in college, right?" he asked, and when Emily nodded, he continued. "Dad went to Saigon with my grandparents. He started a company over there—computers or something. Seems to be doing well. I'm not sure of the details."

Which pretty much described his relationship with his father. Emily felt the familiar ache in her chest when she saw how he'd perfected the placid, I-don't-care attitude when it came to his father.

"And Mom is doing well in her medical practice. Busy, which isn't surprising. She and her husband seem really happy."

"When was the last time you saw her?"

Vinh looked surprised, then leaned back and studied the ceiling, as if he was doing the mental math. "A few summers ago, I think? I was in town for a convention, was able to grab dinner with them."

"You haven't seen them for holidays?"

He looked at her fondly. "You know that's not me. Or us, come to that. Mom's busy, and Dad's . . . well, Dad."

She nodded. She'd loved the Herd, just like he had . . . it had been their family. But at the same time, as frustrated as Greg and her mother sometimes made her, she couldn't imagine not spending time with them. Not just because they relied on her. Because they were family, and they meant the world to her.

"Well, now that we're caught up," she said, desperate to change the subject, "let's get cracking on this problem, shall we?"

"What can I do?"

She frowned. "I want to see if I can get into your computer through a back door."

His eyes narrowed. "Okay. Although—what kind of problems can you run into if you get caught? What kind of trouble?"

"Considering who it is? A good deal," she admitted. "But don't worry. I may have been out of the game, but I've kept my hand in. I won't get caught."

He looked skeptical. She found herself straightening.

"Other people might spend their time dating or binge-watching Crunchyroll," she said. "I spend my time reading security manuals and exploits on the dark web. I enter ethical hacking competitions on the reg. And I stayed up last night looking at who's taken on Aimsley. You guys might be dark mages when it comes to fixing corporate problems, but your security? Is for shit."

"I sincerely doubt that."

She grinned. "Then watch and learn, Padawan."

With that, she started typing. "Don't suppose you know any of your coworkers' passwords, do you?" She paused. "Unless you don't want to, in which case I'll try to find another way. This is one of the easiest, though. Still, I understand if you don't want to throw a friend under the bus. This will show up as a sign-in, and while I can cover my tracks, there's still the possibility that some of what I do points back to them."

"Honestly, *friends* is probably overstating it," he said. "Coworkers, absolutely. Peers . . . sure. But I don't think there's a person in that building that wouldn't give me up to the highest bidder, especially if it meant jumping my place in line for promotion."

"Promotion? I thought you just got promoted," Emily said, then reddened. "I mean, I heard Tam mention it to Lily."

His smile was sly, but he let it slide. "Yeah. But that doesn't mean anything. That is, it means *something*. I'm vice president of internal operations. But the org chart gets jumbled around like Scrabble tiles whenever they feel like it, and I figured out they just gave me the title because 'guy who cleans up our problematic publicity mess but still lets us get away with shit' didn't fit on a business card."

Emily looked at him, aghast. "Yikes on bikes. And you *like* this job?"

"They pay me an obscene amount of money," he said, like that explained it. "Besides, it's . . . what I have, you know?"

She swallowed, then nodded. "So. Passwords?"

He paced, very carefully avoiding the snake enclosure. "Maybe," he said. "The woman across from my office keeps her password on a sticky note, but I'm not sure I can remember it correctly. And there's a guy who works some of the big car-company accounts who tends to use cars as his password." Then he snapped, surprising her. "I know! Schmonk."

"Who or what is a Schmonk?" she asked, bewildered.

"He is Timothy Schmonk. The world's biggest Giants fan," he said, with a grin. "Also, he always uses the same password—bragged about it. His password is . . ."

And he wrote it down on the legal pad: *#1GiantsFan!*

"You are shitting me," she murmured.

"Not even a little bit," Vinh said. "Beyond that, he leers at the assistants and thinks women are chew toys."

"Wow. Yeah, I'm not gonna feel guilty about this at all," she muttered, then searched out Mr. Schmonk's account, typing in the password.

The damned thing popped open as easily as a soda can.

It took a few hours for her to do what she needed to do, and she realized that using a kitchen table with a rickety-ass chair was hardly what anyone could call *ergonomic*. She had gone deep into flow state, just connecting. She barely registered Vinh in the background, puttering around, talking at some point.

It took a knock on the door to actually shake her loose. "Wha? Wha?" she said, jolting.

"Don't worry, I got it," Vinh said. He opened the door, thanked the delivery guy, and then brought in boxes. "I got a pizza. Goat cheese, sun-dried tomato, and artichoke hearts. Also a salad and some bread-sticks." He grinned. "And those little chocolate cake things."

Her stomach yowled, reminding her that she'd ignored it for too long, but she latched on to a surprising detail. "You remembered my favorite pizza?"

"I guess I should've asked you if you still ate pizza," he said, "but I figured push comes to shove, I could just eat it later tonight. My body clock's all out of whack anyway."

She closed the laptop and pushed the notes aside, and they put the boxes on the counter. She grabbed plates, and they served themselves.

She groaned with pleasure when the first bite hit. "What the hell time is it, anyway?"

"Almost three."

She blinked. "What, really?"

"You were really fixating," he said. "How'd it go?"

"I got through. Dumbass really needs to change his password," she said. "I managed to use his account to get me through to IT to create a master account with all permissions."

He nodded. Then he said, "Let's pretend I understand what any of that means."

She laughed. "It means that I've got permission to check out your account and files, as well as anybody else's, to a certain extent."

He let out a low whistle. "I'm gonna have to give somebody a heads-up on that when I go back," he mused. "Maybe hire one of those, whatsit. White-hat agencies. What do they call them?"

"Pen experts," she said offhandedly, eating another slice of pizza happily.

"What does that even mean?"

"*Pen* means penetrative."

She swallowed, realizing the innuendo in the words. But he didn't laugh like a twelve-year-old, the way so many of the guys in the Herd would have. Instead, his dark eyes glowed, and his smile was . . .

Well. It was seductive. There was really no other word for it.

"You don't say," he drawled.

She cleared her throat, stabbing some salad on her plate with her fork. "Anyway, I've got access now. It's gonna be a matter of looking at the history of what happened in your account, and that's going to take a while."

That seemed to cool whatever his expression had been. He nodded seriously. They ate for a while in companionable silence. Then she sighed, taking her plate to the sink and then washing her hands.

"Guess I'd better get back to it," she said, feeling oddly nervous. She reached for the laptop and then yelped, wincing.

He'd also gone to the sink, but now he was at her side in a flash. "What? What happened? Are you okay?"

"Neck," she said. "I should've known better. Bad ergonomics. Stayed in the same place for too long. Damn it."

"You need to learn to take breaks," Vinh said, but before she could snark at him, he put his hands on her neck and shoulders. Then his thumbs pushed, gently but firmly.

She groaned, her head automatically falling forward as she let out a long, low moan. "*Ohmygodthatfeelssogood*," she slurred.

She felt more than heard the chuckle that was deep in his chest. He was giving off heat like a furnace, and she suddenly, inexplicably, shivered.

That means I'm cold, right? How she could be cold next to that much heat, she had no idea. Maybe if she just moved a little closer, she could warm up.

Let's hear it for justifications!

She scooted forward, just a millimeter. He kept rubbing circles, slow, soothing, drugging drags of his hands on her tight muscles. And she collapsed against him.

She felt his breath on her hair. And maybe . . .

Did he just kiss the crown of her head?

She pulled back enough to tilt her head up and look at him. He looked down at her, smiling, that gentle, fond, gorgeous smile that she knew was hers alone.

And her heart hurt.

Here he was, standing in front of her after all this time, looking at her the way he used to, the way she still sometimes dreamed he did. Part of her wanted to curse him for teasing her with this.

The other part of her . . .

His eyes studied her mouth, and that hunger, that glow, seemed to imbue all his features. He leaned forward, just a tiny bit. Leaned down, closer to her.

She stretched, ever so slightly, up. She thought about closing her eyes, but it was a train wreck—she couldn't look away. She didn't want to.

Suddenly, there was a loud, rattling *wheeze*. They both jumped.

"What the hell was *that*?" Vinh said, looking around.

She sighed, then walked over to the snake enclosure.

"That would be Herman," she said. "Looks like his asthma is acting up."

CHAPTER 12

Cockblocked by a boa constrictor. That's a first.

Vinh grimaced. No, not cockblocked. No cocks were involved here, he chastised himself, trying to ensure that the semi he was currently experiencing did not escalate to full mast. He'd asked Emily for help. She'd made it very clear that she wasn't interested in him. He had no intentions of sleeping with Emily, or making out with her, or even a small, insignificant, really-couldn't-hurt-anyone kiss. He took a very careful step back, releasing Emily. As if that made it easier. He looked at her as she bit her lower lip, studying him cautiously beneath her lashes. He remembered when she'd make that face just before breaking out with a mischievous smile.

God, he'd loved that smile.

He cleared his throat. "Sorry, I . . . sorry," he floundered, irritated with himself. "You're really tight."

Her hazel eyes rounded like saucers.

"*Shoulders.* Your shoulders are very tight," he quickly clarified.

"Oh. Yeah. This isn't the best setup," she said, with a groan, stretching out her arms behind her. "And there's a lot of typing in my job, so . . . repetitive. You know."

"Carpal tunnel?" he asked, unable to keep the note of concern out of his voice.

She shrugged. "Not diagnosed or anything. I wear braces, try to be careful. Don't want to go out on medical for the surgery."

He could feel his frown intensifying. What the hell? "That's a job-related injury," he pointed out. "That's why they have insurance."

She laughed. "You're cute," she cooed, patronization dripping from every syllable.

"I'm serious," he said. Well, kind of growled. "They're obligated to take care of you."

"Sure they are." She waited a beat, then smirked. "I'll bet they give you tons of vacation, let you take time off for doctor's appointments, and encourage both therapy and preventative medicine."

"They . . ." He stopped short. "That's different."

"Is it?" she challenged. "You're working for one of the richest companies in the world, and they aren't exactly putting health at the forefront, so maybe don't tell me what I ought to be doing here."

He clamped down on arguing further. She was absolutely right: this wasn't his business. Funny how, after a decade, it was so easy to snap into old patterns. How very, very badly he wanted to take care of her.

He found himself stepping forward. He reached out again, this time stroking her cheek as he studied the dark smudges beneath her eyes, the tension in her expression. Her whole body looked wound tighter than a garage door spring. "You look tired," he commented before he could stop himself.

Now it was her turn to take a step back. She shrugged again. "Late night," she said. "And I've been working kinda hard lately. Lots of overtime."

"Wanna take a break?"

She looked startled. "Um . . . isn't this kind of important?"

"You just need to sharpen the saw," he said, and she snickered. "Seriously. Sometimes you just need to take a break so you can come at a problem from a new angle. It reinvigorates you."

"I'm good for another few hours," she said mildly. "I just have to be out of here before ten or so. I'm working an early shift tomorrow, and I'll need to get a few hours' sleep."

That didn't sound good either. He clamped down on a protest. "How early?" he asked, proud at how nonchalant his response sounded.

"Five."

"In the morning?" He grimaced. "How long's your shift?"

"Should be eight hours—nine with breaks and lunch—but they've been having a lot of overtime lately. They used to just work IT support for a cell phone company but figured out they could provide outsourced IT support to a lot of different companies and charge by the call. So there's a lot of us, and we work around the clock."

He took a deep breath. *Keep it neutral.* "That sounds like a lot."

"It's not as bad as it sounds," she said, and it sounded like she was justifying it to both of them. "I've had worse jobs, actually, and at least I get as much overtime as I want, instead of juggling a few jobs—although I still sometimes look for holiday work, retail, if I need to keep my options open. Besides, it varies day by day. Sometimes, you're trying to help some baffled lady who's trying to figure out how to FaceTime her grandkids and who has no concept of technology. Other days, you're dealing with some dickhead who basically infected his cell phone with viruses by downloading porn from the wrong sites, and he yells and acts aggressive so it's somehow *your* fault. Those days suck."

"Why don't you get another job?" Vinh asked before he could stop himself.

She quirked an eyebrow at him. "I don't have a degree," she pointed out. "Have you tried applying for a job lately? They're offering a pittance and expect a master's. It's a dogfight out there."

He frowned. "I don't believe that's true." And he would damned well look into it as soon as she went home.

Not your business. Stay focused.

She shrugged. "Believe what you like," she said, going back to the table and opening the laptop. "Now, let me get back to what *you're* paying me for."

Like that, she ignored him, submerging herself into the tech. She'd make noises, her hands fidgeting when they weren't typing at lightning speed on the keyboard. She'd repetitively tuck the hair that fell in her face behind her ear, muttering to herself in geek speak that he couldn't follow despite being fairly tech savvy himself. She typed lines and lines of code. He wanted to ask her what she was doing but didn't want to distract her. And when he saw her rubbing her shoulders and the back of her neck, it was all he could do not to go back and massage them again.

That way lies madness, my dude. Leave her alone.

The thing was, when they had been in high school, and then in college, she'd always been so optimistic. Her family had been this shining, golden example of the American dream. Her father had sold yachts and sailboats, and her mother had stayed home and cooked things from scratch—with ingredients from Whole Foods, a store his parents had never set foot in, bemoaning ridiculous prices. Emily's family had lived in a ridiculously large house with a spare room just for guests. She'd gotten a fire-engine-red Miata for her sweet sixteen. Compared to his family, who had lived in a more modest house, with parents who had been known to yell on tame days and throw objects on worse ones, the MacDonalds had been a fairy tale, and she had been their princess. As a result, she'd dreamed big and pursued those dreams relentlessly, like it had never occurred to her that those dreams couldn't be accomplished.

It was part of why they'd broken up, honestly, although he didn't know how to tell her that. Or if he ever would. Too much time had gone by, and he wondered if opening up those scars would just make them even more damaging. Better to just let her embrace the idea that he was the bad guy. It would ultimately make things easier.

For her.

No, the problem was, it was as if all her previous relentless optimism was now flipped in a mirror, replaced with an equally determined pessimism. She didn't have dreams. She just seemed to stave off nightmares.

What the hell had happened since he'd gone?

He hadn't kept track of what had happened with Emily, avoiding her on social media and staying off the Nerd Herd Slack channel. At first, it had simply hurt too much. Then, he'd buried himself in work, and the feelings had lessened.

If he was honest—all his feelings had dulled, an advantage in his line of work. It was the perfect escape.

She finally stood up from the table, cracking her knuckles and stretching until he heard the pops work their way down her spine like Bubble Wrap. "All right. I've gotta go," she said. "I don't want Mom to ask where I was. She still doesn't like you."

"Fair," he agreed. Then another question leaped out. His mouth was really getting insubordinate. "Why do you still live at home?"

She sighed heavily. "I'm not getting into this, Vinh."

"I'm not trying to pressure you. I'm just trying to understand."

"Not all of us pull down mid six figures as a yearly salary," she said, with a bitter sort of pragmatism. "And you know Mom hadn't had a job since before Greg was born. She's doing the best she can, but the job market isn't exactly friendly. She's worked some retail, though she lost her job when the fancy cooking place shut down near us. Right now, she works at the fabric and yarn store, down in Carlsbad."

He hadn't thought about that problem—her mother reentering the workforce after so many years. His mother had been going to med school while he and Tam were in high school, and now she had a bustling medical practice. But Emily's mom had no such preparation when Emily's father, Jack, had died.

"Mom is having trouble keeping the house up," Emily said. "And a friend wanted to take over my lease, so I gave up the apartment. It really wasn't a big deal."

"Wait. She still has the house?" he asked, aghast. "*Why?* That's got to be way too expensive. That makes no sense!"

Emily reared back like he'd slapped her. "All right, I am definitely going," she snapped, grabbing her messenger bag and heading for the door.

"Wait, Em . . ."

"Just . . ." She made a cutting-off gesture. "You're paying me to figure out your little embezzlement problem. That does *not* give you carte blanche to judge my life, Vinh. Don't go there."

He gritted his teeth. "I'm not trying to judge. I'm trying to understand."

"Still feels pretty judgy," she pointed out. "So knock it off, or you're on your own, and fuck the paycheck."

He pinched his lips together, then nodded.

"All right. I'll be here after my shift tomorrow," she snapped.

"Emily?"

She looked over her shoulder from the open front door. "Yeah?"

"I am sorry."

She sighed. Then she walked out, shutting the door behind her. It was an echo of the last time she'd walked out on him, and he figured he'd earned the pain this time too.

CHAPTER 13

It was the Mondayest of Mondays to have ever Mondayed. It was the quintessential Monday. And it was the last thing Emily needed.

She'd tried to sleep that night. She really had. But all she could think of was resting her head against Vinh's hard chest, breathing him in. Feeling the warmth coming off of him in waves, after she'd felt cold for so long. She wanted nothing more than to cuddle in and let him tuck her against him, resting his chin on her head, wrapping his arms around her like a present. She'd never felt as safe, or as comforted, as when he cuddled her. And although he'd tried to hide the fact, he was a world-class cuddler.

Or at least, he had been. She wondered absently if he still cuddled like a champ—and if so, with whom.

Her call button lit up, and she sighed. "Help desk, this is Emily. How can I help you today?"

"Hi, yes, I'm having problems with my computer."

"Sure, let's walk you through it," she said absently, even as her brain whirred through Vinh's problem. She thought she had the answer pinned down. She couldn't identify the account yet—that was too hard—but she might be able to connect the dots in the business's computer system itself.

"I installed an update, and now nothing's working the way it's supposed to!" the guy on the phone carped. "And I've got a report due in two hours, and I'm going to tell them it's because *your* department told me I had to get my computer updated!"

She'd been hearing about the mandatory system update for the past three days. She bit back a long-suffering sigh. "We needed the security system updated," she said as patiently and kindly as possible. "There were too many exploits in the current system that needed patches. Getting everyone onboard, installing the updates, helps prevent viruses and malware and all sorts of bad things. Trust me: this is a good thing."

"Well, that's not my problem," he said. "Why don't you just . . . you know, fix it from your end?"

She closed her eyes. Not for the first time, she wondered if people thought there were just little elves or something that worked in the box on their desk. She didn't expect them to know Python or C++, but for God's sake, all they had to do was push a button to update and then restart their systems.

For a brief shining moment, she fantasized about pulling up the guy's computer account and plastering his desktop with a demonic clown. Or maybe she'd take a page out of Vinh's problem, and just take all his presentations and reports, wiping his own computer clean. That would show him instantly why system updates were important.

She stuffed the irritated feeling down. "So you *did* install the update," she prompted.

"I said that I did!"

He was a yeller. Fantastic. "Did you try turning the computer off, then waiting thirty seconds and turning it on again?"

There was a pause. "Do I seem like an idiot to you?"

Jury's still out!

She bit her lip, hard, struggling to keep her filter in place. "Can you do that for me now, sir?" The *sir* was like sucking on a lemon.

He huffed again. "Fine. You want me to turn off my goddamned computer? I'll turn off my goddamned computer."

There was a rustling sound. She looked at her screen, which was logging the call. She wondered, absently, if he felt the same about his personal computer security. She could probably get into his social media in a matter of hours, if not minutes. His privacy settings were probably nonexistent. Hell, if she really wanted to, she could probably get into his bank accounts.

She blinked at herself.

Stop that. You're not black hat. You're barely even gray hat.

But still—there was a rush. She loved the puzzle of it: beating someone else's security systems, seeing the flaws in an existing system. Ultimately showing how flaws could be fixed. It was a constant battle but one that challenged and excited her.

"Can I turn this back on or what?" the caller groused.

She glanced at the clock. "Yes, you can," she said, and he continued to mumble obscenities, presumably under his breath, as she heard him power it up again. "How's it working?"

Another pause, a long silence. "It . . . seems to be working," he grudgingly admitted.

"All right. If you have any further questions, please feel free to call us anytime."

He hung up on her.

She took off her headset, rubbing her temples.

Why don't you get a better job?

She'd wanted to punch Vinh when he'd suggested it, which wasn't like her. But seeing him, in his casual yet expensive clothes, buying her a top-of-the-line new computer like it was a pack of gum, had rankled.

She wondered if he'd felt like that when it had been her family that was rich. That, too, had kept her up the previous night.

There had been a moment, when they'd broken up . . . just a throw-away line in the fight that had led to their ultimate implosion.

"I can't be what you're looking for," Vinh had said, his eyes imploring. "You think that all we need is love, and money doesn't matter, and it'll all be easy. I can't do what you want. I wish I could."

He'd meant that he had to pursue the brass ring, of course. And that still hurt like hell. But she hadn't known, at the time. Not really. He'd made it through college with the help of his father's parents, who'd also paid for Tam's college tuition. But both twins had supplemented with grants and loans, and they'd both worked their way through as well. Vinh had waited tables and worked at the library, all while studying. It had been something they'd fought about, freshman year, before she'd left school.

In hindsight, she realized that she'd whined about him not paying enough attention, not spending time with her. Never getting to see him.

She thought about her job now. The holiday jobs, the constant overtime. The brief, unsatisfactory relationships that fizzled out because she had neither the time nor the energy to coddle somebody when she was so damned exhausted.

Was that how Vinh had felt?

She gritted her teeth. She could admit that she had been spoiled growing up. Her demand might have been unfair. But dammit, *her father had died*. And Vinh had simply told her that it was better that they stop seeing each other. Sure, she hadn't expected him to drop out of college and move home to Ponto Beach, but . . .

She frowned.

All right. She sort of *had* hoped for that. But he'd put an end to that, shutting her hopes down like a Spirit Halloween store on the second day of November.

Her phone rang again, and she forced herself to focus, helping yet another employee through the security update. She ate lunch in the break room, noodling through a bot she wanted to design to help "find" the account in Aimsley's system, how best to hide it from their security, how to find the connection between who had access and where it had been transferred. Half an hour later, she was back to her job.

By the time two o'clock rolled around, her brain felt like it had been bludgeoned into tapioca. And she still had to go to Greg's place and work with Vinh. She took a deep breath, turning her computer queue to "off duty" and packing up.

Her manager, Troy, walked up, fidgeting with his hands. He wore a pair of khakis and a baby-blue button-down with the sleeves rolled up, something she thought he did to show that he was "one of the gang"—but it really didn't make sense, seeing as it wasn't like he was lifting anything. Maybe he was just too warm?

"Um . . . where are you going?"

She blinked. "Home?" she asked tentatively in return, since it seemed like an obvious answer.

"But . . . it's only two o'clock?"

She nodded. She hated how he always seemed to make what ought to be statements into questions. "I've put in nine hours, with lunch and breaks." Of course, she'd wound up skipping breaks, but it wasn't like she was punching in and punching out, despite the fact that legally, she probably should have been. That was an HR problem, though.

"Yes, right," he said and laughed, running a hand through his slightly greasy red hair. He somehow managed to look both cheerful and nervous, and his habit of pushing his hair back made him look like he'd been electroshocked by the end of the workday. To his credit, he tended to put in long hours too. "The thing is, Gina called in sick?"

She blinked. Gina had seemed fine the day before, bragging about . . . *ah*. Bragging about going to a local concert.

Sick, my ass.

"So I'm going to need you to cover for her?" Troy continued.

"But what if I have something to do?" she parried.

"Um. It's kind of"—he coughed lightly—"mandatory?"

She blinked. "Overtime is *mandatory*?" She had no idea how that was legal.

"Yes," he said, finally breaking their question duel. "So . . . yeah. I need you to stay on."

"For how long?"

"Not a full shift. Just another four hours," he said.

"Four hours?"

He winced. "I'm sorry," he said. "But you're our best, and usually you love getting overtime. I really need you out there, okay?"

She closed her eyes. Vinh's job paid more, and it was a straight check. But as unassuming as Troy seemed, she also knew he held grudges. Or at least helped keep track of the higher ups' grudges, when they were irritated at someone's flightiness or lack of loyalty.

"I can stay," she ground out, putting her jacket back on the hook on her cube wall and sitting back down at her computer.

"Thank you." He sounded genuinely grateful. "I'll, um, get you a soda?"

She glared at him before she could stop herself, and he retreated. Then she grabbed her phone to text Vinh.

EMILY: Got called in for overtime, won't be there until after six. Will let you know if anything changes.

VINH: All right. See you when you get here.

She took a deep breath, then answered the phone. "Help desk, this is Emily. How can I help you?"

"This damned security update!"

She closed her eyes. It was going to be a long four hours.

CHAPTER 14

It was around three in the afternoon when Vinh finally made it to Tam's place. *Tam and Josh's place,* he corrected himself. A fact that continued to weird him out. He had barely slept the night before, between Bastard the gecko's "Tokay!" barking and Sonic running on his squeaky tread-mill-wheel thing like he was going for a world record. After a while, Vinh had given up, scrolling through the millions of offerings on the streaming services he subscribed to, which he mostly used in various hotel rooms. As usual, there were tons of shows and movies, and his brain didn't engage with *any* of them.

It did, however, seem to latch on to Emily.

He sighed. He didn't mean to think about Emily. But after the way she'd semistormed out of the apartment, he couldn't help but replay the whole situation in his mind. He'd gone too far into something that wasn't his business—that was for sure. He'd need to apologize; that much was obvious. And he'd need to stop sticking his nose in and making suggestions where they weren't welcome.

Even if it bothered him—really, truly bothered him—to see Emily dragging and hopeless.

He scowled as he parked in the driveway and shut off the Audi that he was renting. He'd spent the morning going through the notes Emily had left behind. He hadn't mucked around with the computer—his strength was strategy, not technical, and he knew enough to be dangerous, but that was it. Instead, he'd gone through the possible enemy list to figure out who might have done this to him. There were five pages—legal size—of people who might want him to fail. He'd developed the list based on people who he'd "crossed": people on the other side of the negotiation table, people who had beef with him, leadership at corporations who hadn't liked his suggestions, especially when it meant losing their cushy jobs as a result. There were plenty of people who would love to see him take a beating, metaphorically speaking.

Possibly literally, now that he thought about it.

And that didn't even include anybody at Aimsley itself. He internally groaned, not even wanting to start that list.

He walked up the neatly manicured path and knocked on the door. Tam opened it, then rushed forward and gave him a hug.

"Hey!" Her hair was up in a haphazard ponytail, and she was wearing a T-shirt that had what looked like a romance novel clinch, only both the hero and heroine were holding photoshopped wedges of cheese. The swirling script said: FOR-CHÈVRE LOVE.

He shook his head. "Only you would get a job at a cheese place," he said around a chuckle.

"Hey, I'll have you know, this T-shirt sold out of our merch shop in less than a week," she pointed out, then grinned. "Which reminds me: we have merch! Cloud City Creamery let me add that to the marketing mix. I'll make sure you get a T-shirt."

"Sure thing." He would never, ever wear it, he felt quite confident.

He sat on the chocolate-brown couch, since it looked like rain. She plopped down on the opposite end, tucking her feet under her and grabbing a lap blanket, bundling herself up.

"So what's going on?" she asked. "I'll be honest, when I called, I kinda expected you to blow me off."

He squirmed with guilt. "What, something needs to be wrong for me to see my sister?"

They stared at each other, then burst out laughing.

"Yeah, yeah, yeah," he said, when they'd collected themselves. "I set myself up for that. But in my defense, I'm usually halfway around the globe from wherever you are. That sucks, but that's the job."

"Which makes me ask why you're here in Ponto instead of Dubai, Tokyo, or Beijing," she said. "And you've been here for days. And what's this I hear about you staying at Greg's place and helping with the animals?"

His eyes widened. "Where did you hear that?" Had Emily said something? They hadn't said *not* to discuss anything, but this was top secret for obvious reasons. Of course, her loyalty was to the Nerd Herd, not to him. Why wouldn't she point out the little dig of vengeance she'd enacted?

"Hayden mentioned something on Slack," she replied, and he felt his heartbeat slow down a little. "Last I checked, you're scared of snakes. Not really fond of reptiles in general. Or . . . well, animals. Right?"

He shrugged. "How should I know? We never had pets."

"You freaked out *so bad* when we were little and there was that garter snake in the garage."

"They're not my favorite things, no," he admitted. "But these guys are in tanks and boxes and stuff. They're not free range or anything. It's fine. And I've stayed in tents in Bolivia, for God's sake. I can handle it."

She tilted her head, studying him. "You always say that," she murmured. "That you can handle it, I mean. Not the tents-in-Bolivia bit."

"That's because I can."

"So why are you home?"

He stiffened. He hadn't thought of Ponto Beach as home. Had he? Did he?

Was it?

Even if he hadn't, he had a lot of warm feelings for Ponto, more than he'd realized. It wasn't like he thought of New York as his home either, necessarily.

Did he even *have* a home, if it wasn't his job?

"The rest of the Herd might not notice, but I know something's up," she said bluntly. Then her eyes twinkled. "Although honestly, the Herd probably notices too."

"Doubtful. My poker face is legendary," he protested.

"Not with us," she countered. "And sure as shit not with *me*. So spill. You're not at work, and you're closed-door with *Emily*. Unless you're finally having an epiphany and realizing what you walked away from all those years ago and you're trying to get her back—a cause I fully support, by the way," she tacked on, "you're in some kind of trouble. And not the kind of trouble *I* get into, where you walk in on a significant other cheating or you rage quit your job. The kind of trouble that makes me nervous."

"Dammit." He grimaced. He probably should've thought this through more—not just visiting Tam but keeping his whole visit to Ponto Beach quieter. Still, given Emily's strictures, his hands were tied. "I don't want to get you involved in this."

She blinked. "What? Is it criminal or something?"

"No." But he'd paused just a moment too long, and her jaw dropped. "Not . . . exactly."

"Shit, Vinh. What did you *do*?"

"Why do you assume *I* did something?" he muttered.

"Because you're on Satan's payroll, you dingus." She crossed her arms, arching an eyebrow at him. "C'mon. Out with it!"

"There's been some things at work that look bad for me that I didn't do," he said, dancing around the subject. "So now I need to clear my name. I guarantee I didn't do anything. But I need proof of that. That's where Emily is helping me. And in return, I'm helping her with Greg's crap with the animals."

Tam took a second to process that. "That's all you're going to tell me, isn't it?"

"There's some confidentiality stuff," he said. Which was true enough. "And besides, I'd rather keep this as quiet as possible until the problem's resolved."

She sighed, resting her head on her hand against the back of the couch. "Can I ask you a question?"

"Sure. Why not."

"Are you happy?"

He blinked. He hadn't had anyone ask him that in . . .

Well, ever.

"I don't know," he said, his tone surly. Her expression fell, and he realized he was being an asshole. "I'm not—I'm sorry. It's just, I don't think about being happy. It's not on my radar. I'm too busy to be happy."

She shook her head. "And *that's* a crock of shit."

He looked at her, feeling indulgent. "You've always been way more emotional than I am," he said. "That's a feature, not a bug. I'm not bagging on you."

She sighed. "I know. I take more after Dad than Mom."

"Exactly." Their father was a businessman, but he ran on his emotions with little to no counterbalancing safeguards. He could buy champagne for the entire sales team for a closed deal, only to berate them the next day for a lost account. He was a roller coaster.

Their mother, on the other hand, was a guided missile. She knew what she wanted, she pursued it, and God help you if you got in the way. The two of them together were like pure sodium and water: utterly explosive, in a bad way.

"I mean, you're not exactly like Dad," he added, hoping that she wouldn't be hurt by his statement.

"I know what you meant." Her smile was fond but sad.

"Just like obviously I take after Mom," he pointed out. It had been a huge fight when their mother had decided to finish college, then go to medical school when they were in high school. She'd had to drop out of college when she'd become pregnant with the two of them, but she'd been determined not to change course, despite her own parents cutting her off and their father's parents strongly discouraging her. She'd gotten together the financing, she'd managed the time, and she'd ultimately left them to their own devices, care-wise. Meanwhile, their father had taken the time to have a variety of affairs and complain about being overlooked for promotion after promotion, never recognizing his own complicity in his "bad luck."

Her mother had finally divorced him when their father's girlfriend had shown up at the door, not because of the infidelity but because she had been studying for a final and could not afford the distraction.

"You are just like Mom," Tam agreed. "I mean that in the good way too. Although . . . sometimes, you both put work before people, and I don't think that helps you."

He needed to change the subject before he got even more uncomfortable than he currently was. "How is Mom, anyway? I don't think I've talked to her since . . ." He frowned, doing the math. "Her birthday?" His assistant had it as a reminder on his calendar, an alarm on his phone. They spent about twenty minutes catching up, and then he'd call again on Christmas.

Tam shrugged. "I actually invited her and Scott down here to hang out with Josh and me after we got engaged. I was surprised she came, but it was kind of nice," she said. "I feel like, now that we're adults, she's . . . changing a little? Although Scott's kids might have something to do with that."

He hadn't hung out with his mother's husband's family much. It felt too strange. He'd been about nineteen when their parents had divorced, and his mother had remarried just a few years ago. He didn't see Scott as his "stepfather," and he meant it with no disrespect. He just . . . didn't see it?

Thank God he'd never had to meet his father's new wives.

"You're not off the hook," Tam said, piercing his musings. "I think you're selling yourself short. You're successful, sure. Even Dad can't deny that."

"And yet he does," Vinh muttered.

Tam waved a hand. They both knew what their father was like. "My point is: you don't have to make your job your be-all, end-all. I remember what you used to be like when you were with Emily. You used to be happy. Even if it was a heckin' long time ago."

He swallowed, his throat suddenly feeling like sandpaper.

"You got anything to eat?" he said. "I had a granola bar with a questionable expiration date for lunch, and I'm kinda hungry."

She sighed, shaking her head. "Wait here," she said, popping up and heading for the kitchen. "This looks like a job for cheese."

CHAPTER 15

Emily was bone-deep exhausted by the time she shuffled to her car. It was only six thirty, but when you'd been working since five in the morning, that made a long day. Gina owed her, that was for damned sure.

"Good work," Troy had said as she'd made her way out the door. "See you at five!"

Not gonna lie, she kinda wanted to strangle him.

She took in Ruby, the car her father had bought her when she'd turned sixteen. It had been so shiny and sporty when she'd first gotten it. He'd even gotten a special paint job, a deep candy-apple red that made it look almost iridescent.

In the past thirteen years, a lot had happened. The paint job had dulled—knowing what she now knew about her father, she got the feeling he'd gotten a "deal" from a friend and cut some corners somehow, and the paint was never made to last. She knew the car was overdue for an oil change and tune-up, and she knew that the battery was on its last legs. She felt horrible. Maybe it was weird to anthropomorphize a car this way, but Ruby had gone through a lot with her, and she wanted to take better care of it, rather than relegate it to yet another to-do chore on her already long list.

She climbed in, closing the door gently—she'd had it stick before, forcing her to climb out the passenger window—and then put her key in the ignition. Then she took a second to just breathe.

She still needed to go to Greg's to see Vinh and work on *that* problem. She was actually happy with that, all things considered. It was challenging, and fun.

And you get to spend time with Vinh.

She bit her lip. No, she chastised herself. That was not why she wanted to go to Greg's. This was a gig, just like any number of other freelance jobs she'd done on various sites. It was a bit more dangerous, and harder, but it was ultimately just a job.

Her mind flashed to him asking her why she didn't expect better. Then to the smell of him, the feel of him, as she'd rested her head against him.

Stop it.

When they'd been together, she'd felt invincible. And he'd loved her so incredibly much—she hadn't realized just how precious, how rare, that feeling was. How much she'd taken for granted.

How broken she'd feel once she lost it.

She wasn't sure how much of that was them, and how much of it was her age. She knew she had been such a different person before her father had died and she'd dropped out of college.

She took a few more deep breaths, then rolled her shoulders. "C'mon, you can do this," she muttered to herself.

But before she could start the car, her phone rang. She glanced at the display, seeing MOM in bold letters. She groaned. She could ignore it, say she was driving, but she knew she'd hear about it later, and her mother might honestly need something. "Hey, Mom," she said, answering the phone and forcing her tone to be cheerful.

"Hi, darling," her mother chirped. "I had the most *awful* day. So busy. So I was thinking maybe we could have a movie night!"

"Mom . . ."

"Could stop at the Greek restaurant and get some takeout? That lemon-chicken-rice soup I like, and some dolmas? Ooh, and pita and tzatziki. I love that."

"Mom . . ."

"I know, I know," her mother said airily. "It's not in the budget. But it's like they say: if you can't enjoy yourself once in a while, what's the point?"

"They" didn't say that. Dad said that. And look where we wound up.

"I'm going to be home late, Mom," she said, when she could finally get a word in edgewise.

"What?" her mother said, finally registering her words. "But . . . why? You've been working since five!"

"I know. I had to cover somebody else's shift."

"You work too hard," her mother said, sounding agitated and worried. Emily could almost see her fidgeting hands, the way she puffed up like a harassed bird. "It's not right. They need to find someone else! They can't keep relying on you!"

"Mom . . ."

But her mother was on a roll, and once she got going, she was like an avalanche—impossible to stop, picking up speed on the way. "No. You should look for a new job. One where they pay you better and where you won't have to work these long hours, sweetheart. You think I don't know how tired you are? You think I don't see those dark bags under your eyes? You're twenty-eight, but at this rate, you're going to look forty!"

"Thanks, Ma," she drawled.

"You know what I mean. It's because you work too hard," her mother said. "I just don't want to see you like this."

Emily thought about the repairs, the property tax bill. Her car.

What else am I supposed to do?

She shrugged, forcing levity into her voice. "As it happens, I'm working on a freelance gig that ought to give me some breathing room," she said. "I'm going to be working on that tonight. And I'll be at Greg's for at least a while. I shouldn't be too late—I am beat—but I can't do movie night."

Her mother sniffed. "You've been out a lot lately."

"I know, and I'm sorry." She loved her mother to pieces. She also loved her flaky but ultimately well-meaning brother, who tried so hard to live up to what their father wanted, even though it seemed like it might not be a perfect fit for him. She usually had a good time hanging out with them, and movie nights or dinners were a frequent occurrence. The three of them had bonded to each other since her father's death, hanging on to each other like a lifeline.

"Listen," Emily continued. "When this gig is over, we'll have a proper movie marathon . . . a food one. *Big Night*, *Babette's Feast*, *Chocolat*. Even *Ratatouille*. And we'll order in something from French Bistro. What do you think?"

Her mother sighed. "All right. And I mean it: don't work too hard, okay? And drive safe."

"All right," Emily agreed. "Love you."

She hung up, feeling even more at a loss. She knew why she needed to get this money—why she was agreeing to work with Vinh.

She buckled her seat belt and turned the key.

Nothing happened.

She felt the cold tendrils of panic start to curl in her stomach. "C'mon, baby," she murmured, turning the key off, then back on.

This time, it made a low whining whimper . . . then went dead.

"No, no, no . . ." She clung on to the wheel until her knuckles went white. God *damn* it. This was the last thing she needed.

She tried a few more times, her subconscious whispering unhelpful things like "Trying the same thing and expecting different results is the definition of insanity" and "I think that continuing to do that is bad for the ignition." She was almost positive that it was the battery.

She found herself going back into the building, where the swing shift was hard at work. Troy stared at her, with a grin.

"Can't get enough, huh?" he said, with a too-jovial laugh. "What's going on?"

"My car's broken down," she said. "I think the battery's dead. Can you give me a jump?"

He reddened. "Um . . . I don't have cables," he admitted. "And to be honest, I wouldn't know what to do if I *did* have jumper cables. Sorry."

She looked at the pen. "Maybe . . ."

"No, you know they're working," he reminded her, with a little shake of his head. "But maybe you could wait for somebody to go on break?"

Her heart sank. God. That could be hours.

"You could always call Triple A," he said, not so helpfully, considering she didn't *have* AAA.

She sighed. "I'll get a ride."

She went back out to the parking lot, feeling defeated. She could call anybody in the Herd, she knew that, and they'd be there in a flash. She knew they had her back. Tobin and Lily had helped her the last time she'd had car trouble . . . Tobin had paid for a tow truck before she could stop him. Josh and Tam had provided her and her Mom with leftovers from Josh's various restaurants, saying that "they'd just throw it out" even though she could tell it was fresh. When a pipe started to leak from the upstairs bathroom, Hayden had fixed it. (Well . . . not exactly fixed it. His specialty was demo, not actual plumbing. But he'd gotten the drywall open to the point where they could find the problem and fix it, even if she currently had a sheet safety-pinned over it.)

She was tired of feeling helpless and mortified, reaching out to her friends, being the one that needed to mooch off of them yet again.

She sat in her car, feeling her eyes water until tears tumbled down her cheeks. She was really, really tired of things being this hard. Her shoulders started to shake, and she sobbed, softly, to herself.

After a few minutes, she took a few deep, hiccupping breaths. Then she shook her head, rubbing at her eyes with the heels of her hands. Then she squared her shoulders, grabbing her phone.

She called Vinh. After all, he was the one who needed the help. He could damned well come out and get her. And she'd figure out a solution from there.

"Hey," he said. "You okay? I was starting to worry."

She felt it like a razor across her heart. He sounded concerned. Not impatient, not irritated—just worried.

She hadn't realized how much she'd missed it.

"My car's dead," she said, her voice only barely wavering. "So I'm going to need you to pick me up."

There was a pause. Then he said, "Sure. Text me your address—I'll be there soon. You safe where you are?"

"I'm fine," she replied. "I'll be in my car, okay?"

"All right. See you soon." With that, he hung up.

She put down her phone, then pulled down the lighted visor in her car—which didn't light, because her battery was dead, so she turned on the flashlight on her phone. In the harsh light, she saw that what little makeup she'd been wearing that morning was now utterly wrecked, and she grabbed some napkins she had stored in the glove box to get rid of the worst of it. Now, she looked red, and puffy, and smudged. She looked like a train wreck.

Which pretty much matched how she felt.

CHAPTER 16

Vinh might've sped just a little bit on his way to the address Emily had texted him. He told himself it was because of the California freeway, the way that their drivers pretty much always pushed eighty when they could where there wasn't gridlock, the way you simply couldn't drive like this (or, often, drive at all) in New York City.

Still. He knew he was probably lying to himself.

He wanted to see her, make sure she was okay for himself. No matter how she might try to assure him, that little quaver in her voice told him that she was having a rough time. He knew that sound. He'd heard it when she'd thought she wouldn't get into NYU with him, when she'd worried that her family was going to move to Florida when she was in middle school. When her father had died.

He all but peeled into the parking lot of a nondescript-looking box of a building in a corporate complex, with names like Cynodyne and Brilliantech and whatnot. She was leaning against Ruby, looking at her phone.

He pulled up, then put the car in park and unlocked the doors. She walked up and hopped into the passenger seat. "Thanks for this," she said. In the harsh LED of the parking lot's lights, she looked washed out, but it was easy to see she'd been crying. The curse of an Irish heritage, she'd once joked, which resulted in "skin like sour cream" dotted with the world's palest freckles. He'd loved tracing those freckles, once upon a time, connecting the dots with his fingertip as she smiled, closing her eyes, letting her cinnamon-brown lashes rest on those cheeks.

He forced himself to look back at the lot. At this rate, he was going to write an epic poem in her honor. It was like he'd never gotten over her, for God's sake.

Did you, though?

He wasn't going to answer that. To himself. Because he didn't owe himself any answers, and as Tam would say, how very dare he call himself out like this?

Emily sat quietly after buckling herself in. "You want me to call a tow company?" he asked.

"I'll deal with it tomorrow," she said. "While I was waiting, I realized Greg left his truck at his place. I know where the keys are. I'll just use that to go to work in the morning and then sort out the tow truck stuff from there."

"Okay." He frowned.

"I'm not sure I'm going to have it taken to a mechanic," she continued, sounding agitated again. "Because I'm pretty sure it's just the battery. I can get a battery myself."

"Okay . . ."

"Besides, I can just drive the truck for a while. God knows Greg's not going to need it," she added on a mutter.

"Okay. So I'll just drive us to the apartment," he said. "You eaten?"

In response, her stomach yowled, and she laughed ruefully.

"I had buldak spicy chicken noodles at noon—does that count?"

It was going on seven o'clock. "Want to stop someplace? Eat something?"

When he glanced over at her, she gave him a quick shake of her head. "Maybe we can grab some takeout," she hedged. "I really need to get on writing that bot. I'm pretty sure it's someone that you work with. A bot would at least give us a start, narrow down who might have the account info."

"Just curious," he asked. "Why?"

"Remember when I said this stuff is like murder?" she said. "If it hit a bunch of your account managers, or vice presidents or whatever, I'd think it was a malicious attack on Aimsley. But unless other people were clearing out their desks the day after Thanksgiving . . ." She huffed. "Sounds like *you* were the target. And like murder, it's usually the people closest to you."

He nodded slowly, processing her words. They made sense. "You didn't used to be this cynical," he blurted out unconsciously.

She shrugged. "Yeah. Well. Life happens, you know?" She sent him a small sad smile. "And you always told me I was a dreamer."

He winced. He had, with reason. But the thing was, seeing her like this, he felt like he'd do anything to bring her back to the way she had been.

"I'm surprised you still own Ruby," he said, trying to change the subject. When he saw her scowl, he knew immediately he'd chosen the wrong topic.

"It's cheaper to keep her," Emily said. "She's pretty tore up. I got in a fender bender a few years ago, and it never got quite fixed correctly. The paint job's pretty wrecked, and it's not really a collector car or anything, so I'd get lowballed with all the work it needs."

He could see the sense in that. Still, even with all that, he imagined that she could get a decent enough amount to buy a newer, used working car.

But her father bought the car. She'd lose that connection.

He cleared his throat. "I'm sure there are a lot of good memories in that car," he said as kindly as he could. When she didn't answer, he added, "I didn't have quite the same memories of Buford."

She turned, then burst into laughter. "Oh my God. I'd forgotten about Buford."

Buford was his first car, one he'd bought thirdhand from a neighbor. It was what Emily had lovingly called "an Oldsmo-Buick Land

Cruiser," to the point where he didn't remember the actual make and model of the car.

"It was a behemoth," she said, around a giggle.

"Had suspension like a covered wagon," he remembered, with a grin. "And cornered like the *Titanic*."

"And shit brown, except for the rust spots," she said. "With that pea-green velour on the seats! Remember?"

"Hey, at least those seats were big," he protested. "We managed a lot in those seats!"

And just like that, tension hit the interior of the car. They'd both lost their virginity to each other in that back seat, he remembered.

Remembered *vividly*.

It had been a summer night, up in the bluffs off the coast. Not a soul around. And they'd laughed as they'd awkwardly fumbled, figuring out what they were doing by touch more than sight. Then laughter had been replaced by soft sighs and desperate panting, clinging to each other, moving faster and faster as they had very quickly learned each other's bodies. When she'd cried out against him, shuddering, he'd lost himself and held her tight and sworn to himself he never, ever wanted to lose this amazing woman he loved so much.

Obviously, he'd fucked that up since.

He glanced over from the road. Was it his imagination, or were her cheeks pink? Was she remembering too?

He cleared his throat. "I mean, we fit twelve people in Buford to go to DJ's Donuts," he said.

She laughed, even though it sounded strained, and shook her head. "We're lucky it was only five minutes away. God, we should've died."

"Hey, we could've been doing more foolish stuff," he said. "It's not like we were doing keg stands or mainlining drugs."

"You're probably right," she said. "I'm so lucky I still have the Herd around, you know? That we're still friends, after all this time. You don't always see that."

"That's true," he said. "I think it gets harder to make friends as you get older. There's work, which takes up all this time. And you can make work friends, but it's not always the same." Especially at a place like Aimsley, where every friendly gesture needed to be measured and evaluated: *Does this person like me, or are they using me?*

"I know. And going up to someone and asking, 'Will you be my friend?' is harder too. It's not like it was in school."

He felt a moment of deep, abiding loss. "I miss the Herd sometimes," he found himself blurting out.

For fuck's sake, what was wrong with his filter?

He heard her sigh softly . . . and then felt her hand touch his shoulder.

"You should see them more often," she said quietly, so quietly that he almost didn't hear her. "They miss you too."

He nodded, his throat feeling raspy.

"Don't worry," she said, her voice firm. "I'll stay out of the way when you're visiting. I don't want you to feel like you can't see your friends, people you miss, just because I'm around."

But I miss you too!

God, he was losing it. He'd just come here for help. For his *job*. For his career, which was hanging by a thread. He couldn't afford to lose focus at this point.

They swung by Wahoo's, grabbing fish tacos, ceviche, and chopped salads. Then they headed to Greg's and parked in the guest spot by his Ford F-150. At least she had a working vehicle—assuming that Greg didn't have the same bad vehicle luck that she had. At least it looked newer. And expensive, he thought, looking it over.

"When'd he get this?" he asked.

She sighed. "Two years ago. I need to make sure he set up autopay for the truck payments while he's in Antarctica. He's got a good heart, but I swear, he's got undiagnosed ADHD. Tobin thinks so too, and you know how hard *he* had it before he finally got his diagnosis."

He frowned. That made sense, actually. Her father, Jack, had loved his kids beyond measure, but he hadn't "believed" in ADHD, so Vinh doubted they'd have gotten Greg tested.

"Anyway, I'll scarf this down, and then we'll get to work."

"Don't worry," he said, carrying the food as they made their way to the apartment. "It'll still be there, and you've had a long day."

She smiled. "Don't baby me, Vinh. I can handle this and a lot more, believe me."

"But I don't want you to."

The statement startled both of them. She nudged him with her shoulder as they walked. "Careful. You're acting like less of an asshole."

He laughed. "Well, we wouldn't want that." He waited as she opened the door, then turned on the light. It was nice being with her like this. Lighter. Maybe they'd turned a corner.

Then she stopped short, and he walked into her, letting out a little *oof* as he collided with her back.

"Oh, shoot," she said.

"What is . . ."

He glanced over her shoulder, and lo and behold . . .

Herman was on the loose.

CHAPTER 17

It is a truth, universally acknowledged, that every single man fancies himself a gangster until a frickin' boa constrictor is loose.

Emily felt Vinh go completely stiff behind her, and not in the fun way. (*Stop that, subconscious,* she scolded herself.) He grabbed her arms.

"The snake is *out*?" he yelped. "How . . . what . . . how? How did it get out of its box?"

"How should I know?" she squeaked back, feeling her own heart rate rev up with adrenaline and fear. "This isn't my area! *You're* the one who's spent all day with it. Did you feed it or something?"

"No! That isn't until Friday!" Vinh tugged her backward, urging her outside the apartment. "Greg texted me his feeding schedule!"

"Did you open the enclosure, though?" She struggled against him as he stepped between her and Herman, all but shoving her out of the apartment. "Stop that!"

"But *the snake is loose*!"

She couldn't help it. It was so ridiculous, she started laughing. "That sounds like it ought to be a lot more entertaining than it is right now."

"If I felt safe enough to turn my back on it," Vinh said sternly, "I'd totally be scowling at you right now."

Which only made her laugh harder.

She saw his chest expand and contract, as if he were taking a deep, calming breath for patience. "I opened it just a bit to mist it and add water to the bowl and check the temperature," he said. "I did some googling and found out that boa constrictors need humidity and warmth so they don't get respiratory infections."

He sounded so matter of fact, but she couldn't help but hear the reluctant concern in his voice. "Yeah, Greg mentioned something like that," she agreed. "Herman was a rescue. His last owner really didn't know what he was getting into, and he kind of ignored Herman a lot. Herman got enough respiratory infections that he's kind of got permanent asthma now. It's amazing he's not dead, actually."

"Shit." Vinh huffed out a breath. "Well, now I feel sorry for him."

"I thought you hated snakes," she pointed out.

Now he did shoot her a look over his shoulder. "You *knew* I hated snakes," he pointed out, "and you insisted that I *sleep* here?"

She shrugged. "I'm petty. Sue me."

"We're gonna talk about that," he said, then turned back. "But first things first. What are we going to do about . . . this?"

She grimaced. Honestly, she wasn't all that eager to wrestle the boa back into the enclosure either. "You could just, um, lift it up and put it back in the enclosure. He looks big, but I don't think he weighs all that much."

"And what are *you* going to do?" he asked skeptically.

"Send lots of good thoughts your way."

He frowned at her, and she giggled again. Man, she was way too tired for this.

"Damn it." He groaned, then glared at her. "Stay right there. If it looks like he's going to move, shut the door."

She then watched as Vinh stepped forward, gingerly dodging Herman where he was stretched out on the floor. Then he walked to the nearby kitchen.

"What are you doing?" she asked, baffled.

"Washing my hands and arms," he said, doing just that. "I am not approaching a carnivore smelling like frickin' fish tacos, thanks very much!"

Good point, and one she wouldn't have thought of, but of course Vinh "King of Details" Doan would have. She took a half step back.

He then turned, approaching Herman with his hands out like some kind of hostage negotiator.

"Okay, buddy. We're going to do this nice and easy," he said, his voice low and comforting. It was surprisingly soothing. Hell, if he approached *her* like that, she'd probably fall right into his arms.

Wait. What?

Obviously, she still had strong feelings about him. Maybe not hatred anymore—she was too exhausted for anything as incandescent as the rage she used to feel when it came to him. But there was no way she was going to let herself go down the path of being *attracted* to him again.

And God forbid she feel lo . . .

She jerked, like she'd snapped a rubber band on her wrist. No. She was *not* going to complete that thought, damn it. Just because she was noticing how gentle he was being didn't mean that she was going to get all schmoopy about him.

Vinh stepped forward, reaching by the enclosure where there was a weird, crooked metal stick. "No sudden movements," he said, breathing softly. "It's probably cold and dry and uncomfortable out here, huh, Herman? And this carpet sucks. If we get you back into your enclosure, you've got your hidey house, and your water, and it's nice and tropical. It's like a five-star hotel compared to Greg's floor. Let's get you back there, huh?"

The snake let out a slight wheezy hiss.

"I know, my dude," Vinh commiserated. "Don't worry. I'll get you something for your enclosure, okay? And I'll make sure your cage is fresh and clean."

She watched, amazed, as Vinh took the stick and somehow managed to loop it behind the snake's head. Then, taking a breath like he was going to BASE jump off a cliff, he reached down and picked it up around its . . . waist? Was that a thing on snakes? The middle area, anyway.

"Nice and easy, nice and easy," Vinh muttered like a mantra. It seemed to take forever for him to move from the center of the small living room to the enclosure, when in actuality it was only a few feet. Then he placed the snake, still hissing slightly, back in its home.

"Wow," Emily said. "I am actually impressed."

Vinh's face was taut with concentration, and a bead of sweat was forming on his temple. "Hold on, buddy," he murmured, putting the stick back. Then he took a little shovel and a plastic bag and cleaned out what looked like muck. "Yeah, I wouldn't want to be in a little box with that, either," Vinh said, tying off the bag. "Okay? We good? You need fresh water or mist or anything?"

"You are taking this remarkably well," Emily noted. Ten bucks said he was internally screaming, though. She felt the teeniest bit guilty, especially since he was handling it with such grace. How? How did he manage to handle things he hated without losing his mind?

Vinh didn't even acknowledge her comment, all but tucking Herman in like a baby. "Okay, my dude," he crooned. "You just rest easy, okay?"

Then he closed the enclosure and tossed out the bag—and looked shaken, possibly vaguely nauseated, but determined.

Which didn't surprise her. If you looked up *determined* in the dictionary, his face would be the definition.

"You did good," she complimented Vinh, because he deserved it. She would probably be freaking out and calling Hayden if she were on her own, honestly, and even if she *did* wrestle Herman back in his box, she would've been cursing like a trucker the whole time. "Did you lock the enclosure?"

He blinked at her. "Lock?"

And just like that . . . "Didn't you have to unlock it to get it open?"

"No. Hayden helped me open and close it last time," he admitted. "He must've left it unlocked. I didn't even know it had a locking mechanism."

She shook her head. "I think I remember Greg saying Herman was a bit of an escape artist," she said as the memory slowly surfaced. "He almost named him Houdini."

"This information would've been more helpful when I first started sleeping here," Vinh said, his voice sounding strangled. "I am now going to take a shower in the hottest water imaginable. You can go ahead and eat without me."

"You sure?"

"I can't think about eating right this second," he said, doing a full-body shudder. She let out a laugh. "Be right back."

He beat a hasty retreat to the bathroom while she unpacked the food: crispy fish tacos and Maui onion rings for him, a citrus slaw taco and ceviche for her. She got out soda for them, then got things arranged on the table by the time he was done with his shower. He emerged from the bathroom looking much heartier. His hair was still damp and glossy as onyx. He was wearing a pair of sweatpants (gray, she noticed immediately, then cursed herself for noticing) and was pulling on a navy T-shirt. Since he was still in the process of dressing, she got an eyeful of a nicely defined chest before it was obscured by the cotton cloth. Her mouth watered, and it had nothing to do with the food.

They'd had sex back when they were dating, in high school and freshman year of college. They'd waited awhile, of course . . . but not *forever*. They'd been each other's firsts, with a chemistry so potent and explosive that even their fumblings had been intense. That said, it *had* been over ten years. She hadn't been celibate in all that time (even if she hadn't had a lot of sex that she'd consider noteworthy), and she doubted he had been either. Lord knew the man was intense and focused like a laser. What would it be like taking a decade of experience and applying that kind of focus to *her*?

She swallowed as the taco she'd been munching on threatened to lodge itself in her throat. God *damn*, she bet he'd be amazing. She could even hate him and still get off like a rocket with him.

Her body started to tingle.

He looked at her, grabbing his fish tacos and onion rings and tucking in. "Let's hope nothing else exciting happens," he said with a deep rumble.

"Sure," she echoed. "Nothing exciting."

Nothing exciting, she repeated to herself—even though part of her really, really wanted something exciting to happen.

CHAPTER 18

Emily was acting weird.

It had taken a little bit for Vinh to realize it, honestly. First, there had been the whole snake debacle, during which his skin had *crawled*, yet he'd kept his grip and managed to wrangle the boa constrictor back without screaming or doing anything that could've gotten anyone, including the snake, hurt. The thought of anything even potentially hurting Emily had helped, he admitted. He'd snapped into that cold, calm, emotionally numb place that he got into when he was in dangerous situations. He'd used that brave front a lot over the years, and it was a default.

But he'd shaken in the shower. In private. As it should be.

When he was confident the mask was back in place, he'd wandered back out to see Emily sipping on her soda, those plush lips of hers wrapping around the straw. Just like they had at the Shack. It made him fantasize about buying her a metal straw, just to watch her drink with one all the time.

Which . . . okay. Possibly creepy.

He'd settled down and started eating, and they'd made small talk. He wanted her to take a break and disconnect before trying to do any more work. But as the calming effects of crispy battered fish and only slightly soggy onion rings settled into his system, he realized that Emily was staring at him. She'd glance away quickly when he looked directly at her—which, considering they were the only two people in the room, felt really odd.

"Okay, what's wrong?" he finally asked.

"Nothing's wrong."

He was sure his look broadcast his skepticism, because she snickered, shaking her head and stealing one of his onion rings.

"It's just . . ." She munched thoughtfully, then swallowed, like she was marshaling her thoughts. "I'm really impressed at how well you handled the snake."

He grinned. "That feels like a sex joke."

She grinned back, and for a second, it felt like old times. "It sounds like a sex joke! Like, 'Whoa, that Vinh Doan sure can handle a mean snake.'"

He laughed, feeling some of the tension of the day and the whole reptile situation finally start to dissolve. "Well, I have some experience in handling large snakes . . . ," he said, in a deep, ridiculously cheesy voice.

"Don't I know," she said, then stopped abruptly, as if she realized what she'd just said.

He suppressed a smile, then closed his container of fish tacos, giving up on eating. "Not that it's a big deal or anything," he said, throwing out his trash and very deliberately not looking at her, "or even that you're interested. But my, erm, snake hasn't been handled all that much. Or at all for the past year or so. Maybe longer."

He wasn't sure what weird compulsion was forcing the words out. It wasn't like she had any interest in his sexual history. She hated him. She probably didn't care if he'd slept with all of Manhattan and half of Brooklyn. Or if he had a woman in every city he'd consulted in—which, admittedly, would've been a lot.

But when he looked back at her, her expression had softened.

"I don't handle snakes much at all myself," she said slowly. "I mean, if we're using euphemisms. Don't have the time. And most of the time, it's not worth the effort."

"I know those feels," he agreed, with a lopsided grin.

"That's kind of a surprise. You're still hotter than Arizona asphalt, no lie," she said, and he felt his body tighten up with pleasure. "But—and this is not a euphemism—you really surprised me with the snake."

"Because I wasn't a gibbering, screaming, terrified mess?" he commented wryly.

"Because you were *kind*," she said instead, surprising him. "You probably could have, and would have, wrestled him into the cage without being cruel, obviously. But you didn't have to be as gentle as you were. For God's sake, if you'd talked to me that way, *I* would've gone into a cage for you."

His mouth went dry, and he swallowed against it, unsure what to say.

"I'd always known you were hot," she said, her voice breaking slightly. "Hell, even when I hated you, I wanted you. But God damn it, I forgot that you were *sweet*."

Vinh couldn't help himself. He let out a creaky laugh.

"What?" she asked. "You are. Were." She huffed out a breath. "*Are.* Sometimes. Apparently."

"I promise you, absolutely no one I work with would think so." He could feel his forehead wrinkle as he mulled it over. "Or most of my family, come to that."

"It's not surprising. You wear this whole ice-cold persona like a mecha exoskeleton."

He shrugged. It was an apt description. "It gets the job done," he said. "I'm not trying to be Machiavellian or anything. I don't go out of my way to be an asshole, and I don't try to make people fear me."

"Bet they do anyway, though," she noted wryly, cleaning up the last of her meal's detritus.

"Yeah, well," he hedged. "That's on them, though."

She laughed, and he let a small smile escape.

"Hey, I can't help it if I have resting bastard face."

"The killer-robot/Vulcan impression you've got going probably doesn't do you any favors either," she said.

He cleared his throat. "Okay. So is there anything I can actually *help* you with tonight?"

She shook her head. "Nope," she said, and there was a weary note in her voice. "If there were, I'd have you working on it already. I think I've got the plan of attack. I strongly, *strongly* suspect that it's someone in your company. But getting that backdoor access and then getting a master account only gets me so far. I'm going to need to then link the account back to the IP address or the user, and that's going to be a bitch."

"Is that even possible?" he asked. He'd done some research too. "The whole point of using crypto was anonymity. That's why Silk Road was a thing; that's why drug cartels and other criminal organizations used it."

"And your company, apparently," she pointed out. He kept silent, since he'd admitted as much when they'd started working together. "Nice outfit you're working for, by the way."

He continued staying quiet.

She'd been typing away, doing something he couldn't begin to fathom on the laptop, and was still moving her fingers over the keyboard when she asked, "Doesn't it bother you? Keep you up nights?"

"What, specifically?"

"The stuff you do. The stuff they expect you to do."

He grimaced, glad she couldn't see him, since she hadn't turned away from the screen. "I don't do anything truly heinous," he said. "As you pointed out before, I'm not murdering people or anything."

"Do you think about the larger repercussions of what you're doing, though?"

"If I feel something's . . . beyond the pale," he said delicately, "then I don't do it."

Now she did look over her shoulder at him, sage-green eyes widening. "Really." Doubt was thick as frosting on her voice.

"I can usually come up with other solutions. Workarounds. Ones that work within parameters of budget and still accomplish the end goal."

"And clients are okay with this?"

"Usually. I can be surprisingly persuasive despite my, erm, 'robotic' exterior."

"Vinh Doan, song-and-dance man," she mused. "I would pay to see that."

"It's less entertaining than you'd think," he said. "Usually, I couch it as a disaster. I walk into a conference room, say, 'If you don't do things my way, your entire company will explode in a fiery hell of destruction not seen since Pompeii. Enjoy your chicken-salad wraps.' Then I walk out." He grinned. "They usually see things my way after that."

"And the ones that don't?" she pressed.

"There aren't many." He smirked. "But the ones that don't get a new consultant, and I get reassigned."

They also usually tended to fail, miserably. But disclosing that felt like bragging, so he kept his mouth shut.

She let out a low whistle. "You're even more successful than you said you'd be, I guess," she murmured, turning back to the computer screen.

It was like a slap. Not that she'd meant it like that, he felt sure. But suddenly, he could remember them snuggling in the back of his car, talking about their futures. She was going to be a premier computer science *something*—she had so many options she couldn't decide which. He was going to be a CEO or some big traditionally successful finance job. Sometimes, they talked about maybe doing a start-up together.

Every now and then, they'd talk about chucking it all and going to Bimini and living on the beach, but as they had the beach *right there* and neither of them could imagine "relaxing" for long stretches of time, it had usually been just a joke.

As she worked, he puttered around, cleaning things, watering plants, and caring for the animals—giving the tortoise his lettuce and spinach, giving mealworms and crickets from the fridge to Bastard and Sonic, sprinkling the fish food to the colorful cichlids who all but jumped out of the tank in their eagerness. He then made sure everybody had clean water and that their various habitats were the right temperatures.

It was weirdly soothing. Maybe he could get a pet someday. Not all *these*, and not a boa constrictor. He could get like a guppy or something, work his way up.

He should've stopped Emily. By ten, her head jerked, and he saw that she'd fallen asleep typing.

"Okay, that's it," he said. "You need to get some sleep, baby."

The *baby* had jumped out before he could stop it, feeling as natural as breathing. Fortunately, she was so tired she didn't seem to notice.

"Hmm?"

"You need to go home, get some sleep," he said. "I know you've got an early day tomorrow. And if you get called into overtime again, don't come here after, okay? You need to rest."

"Okay," she agreed, her words slurring slightly. She tugged on her jacket and grabbed her purse, then pulled out her keys.

"Uh, no." He gently nudged her keys back in the bag.

"Why not?"

"First of all, you'd be driving Greg's truck, remember? Your car's still in the parking lot, dead."

"Oh, right," she said, frowning. Then she grabbed what he assumed were Greg's keys from a hook by the door. "I'll see you tomorrow, then?"

"Again," he said, plucking Greg's keys from her hand. "Nope. I mean, you'll probably see me, hopefully. But you're not going to drive. You're too tired, and it's not safe."

She let out a frustrated sigh. "I need the truck," she said. "I can't get a ride at four tomorrow morning to get it."

"I'm going to drive you home," he said, and he couldn't help it. He reached out, stroking her cheek, downy soft, smooth, with those damned pale freckles he loved. "Then I'm going to Uber back here so you have the truck for the morning, okay?"

She sighed. Then she leaned into his hand.

"Like I said," she whispered. "Sweet."

Then she leaned forward and kissed him.

CHAPTER 19

She'd been exhausted, loopy, punchy. Drifting in and out of sleep. But by God, as soon as her lips touched his, her body jolted wide awake. Like, "mainlining eighteen twelve-hour energy drinks" awake.

She jerked away, but not far. She was still standing near him. He was staring at her, swallowing hard, his Adam's apple bobbing. She could see his pulse going a mile a minute in that gorgeous column of a neck. She could feel her own pulse racing, her heart beating like kettle-drums in her ears. She could barely breathe, barely think.

I didn't mean it!

But . . . she kind of . . . had?

He was looking at her with a hunger that she couldn't believe. His eyes practically *glowed*. Carefully, gingerly, he reached out, cupping her face in both hands.

And there it was, that cocktail of emotions. His fucking hotness, combined with his sweetness. Their history, both good *and* bad.

"This is an epically bad idea," she murmured before realizing she hadn't said it *would be* a bad idea. She'd said it *was*.

Because they both knew it was happening. She was just acknowledging it.

He smiled, catching the tense as well. "I'm not going to do anything you don't want to," he said. "But I feel like I'd sell my soul to take you to bed."

Well! If that didn't send pleasure zinging through her system, she didn't know what would.

She moved closer. So did he, until there were only millimeters between them, until she could smell his cologne and feel his heat, until she felt the brush of his chest against hers. The mix of apprehension and confusion and longing and heat, all shot through with a feeling of inevitability, was thick enough to choke on.

"This doesn't change anything about our deal," she said. "This . . . would be anger banging."

"I can live with that."

"And after tonight, we don't do this again."

He froze momentarily, then stroked her cheek as his smile turned cunning. "I'll leave that up to you."

Implying that she would change her mind. And if she were being honest? She wasn't sure he was wrong.

"God damn it, you are the king of loopholes," she said.

They stared for a moment longer.

Then, like they'd both been shot out of a cannon, they launched at each other.

She could barely keep track of what was happening with her body. He had her pinned up against the wall by the front door, and she was moaning, tugging at his hair, insistent, just this side of cruel. He growled against her lips (and how fucking *sexy* was that?) and held her up. Her legs went reflexively around his waist, and she felt his hardness through the sweatpants and through the denim of her jeans, rubbing against her center. She gasped, then arched a little, trying frantically to get some friction between them. His mouth pried hers open, but she was the one whose tongue darted forward, tangling with his. His body pressed into hers, his hips moving like a rolling tide. How the hell was he this strong?

He pulled away, and she couldn't help it—she whimpered slightly, even as she took gulping gasps of breath. "Bed," he said, apparently reduced to single words. "Naked. Now."

On some level, she wanted to slow it down, tease him, edge him mercilessly. Use her body and his to torture him for leaving her. But it would torture them both, and she had too much pent-up desire. She was running on pure adrenaline and lust at this point, and she didn't know how long it would last.

She wasn't wasting a single precious second.

She lowered her legs, then grinned as she sprinted to the bedroom, Vinh close behind her. He'd already tugged his T-shirt over his head, and she pulled her hoodie off, cursing when desire made her clumsy, catching her hands in her own cuffs. Then she popped the fly on her jeans and tugged them off with her underwear and socks. She pulled her T-shirt and bra off.

By the time she'd stripped down, she turned to see Vinh shucking off his sweatpants and boxers with just as much haste. And her mouth went dry and then very, very wet all in an instant.

She hadn't seen Vinh's naked body—specifically his cock—in a decade. And the whole package, no pun intended, had only gotten better with age, it seemed.

"See anything you like?" he teased, even as he looked like a jaguar ready to pounce.

Well, two could play that game, she thought. She held out her hand, then tugged him down to the bed, enjoying his laughter as he bounced on the mattress. The guy *had* to work out. He had a six-pack, and she couldn't remember the last man she'd seen who had one. He wasn't all "swole" the way some of Greg's gym buddies were, but he was defined, sleek, sharp. He even had those V muscles at his hips, the ones that were so mouthwateringly sexy.

She stroked her hand down his happy trail. His laughter quickly got cut off as she took him in her palm, enjoying the heated silk-over-steel of his body. She stroked him, loving the way he writhed and groaned. He finally grasped her wrist. "If we're only doing this once," he said, and his voice sounded strangled, "no way I'm coming that way."

"Oh no?" she challenged, squeezing slightly.

He flipped them so he was over her, his hot skin all but searing her, his eyes like molten black glass. "I'm not coming until you've come," he ground out, his voice sounding low and rumbly and—oh, God, she felt like if she listened to it enough, she'd get that orgasm he was promising. How had she forgotten this? "And when you've come, maybe a few times, then I'll let go. But not until I'm buried inside you. That's a promise."

She couldn't help herself. She shivered with sheer, unadulterated, uncut *want*.

"Yes," she found herself murmuring. "Please. Now."

He smiled, but it was that predator's smile, and she found herself wanting to be devoured.

He pressed another voracious kiss on her, drugging, seeming to go on and on. He stroked down her body, rubbing against her with his, and she felt the heat and solidity of his hardness teasing at her thighs. She spread them instinctively.

"Not quite yet," he said, shifting to the side, and she whined.

"But I want it *now*," she said, sure she sounded like some sex-starved Veruca Salt. He chuckled.

"Patience," he said and before she could strangle him, he leaned down, tracing a looping trail between her freckles, along her clavicle, down her chest. The sides of her breasts. Around her nipples.

She'd forgotten that he loved her freckles. He'd made them beautiful for her.

He looked at her, sheer mischief mixed with hotter-than-magma desire, and sucked his fingers into his mouth. She gasped, then arched her back as he reached through the curls at her opening, teasing and testing, until he finally found her rock-hard clit.

She was panting like a racehorse as he took a nipple into his mouth, swirling it around with his tongue, getting just the right pressure with his teeth, all while his fingers fluttered on either side of her clit. He was better than her vibrator, and that was saying something. She felt his cock pressing against her hip as he continued his single-minded pursuit, and she was shuddering and mumbling incoherently and tugging at his hair in the way she remembered he liked. Apparently he still did, if that raspy growl thing he was doing was any indication.

The orgasm surprised her, hitting her out of nowhere, and she let out a rippling cry, her whole body going taut and her mind temporarily blanking. She felt brainless and boneless.

He pulled back, removing his fingers after a few more loving strokes that sent aftershocks shaking through her. "Better now?" he said, his voice low and soft and so fucking seductive it ought to be outlawed.

"Almost," she teased, and he let out a laugh—a carefree laugh. Just like the ones she remembered. "I'll be better when you finally get inside me."

"Shit . . . ," he said, as if something just occurred to him. Then he made a face. "Wait a second." He rummaged in the side drawer, then produced a condom. After quickly checking the date on the foil, he shrugged. "We're going to pretend I bought this," he said.

She wasn't going to think about Vinh raiding Greg's condom stash at this point. She didn't care if he stopped a random stranger on the street and mugged them for a condom. She just wanted Vinh, to get as close to him as possible. To have him inside her, so close that she could feel his heartbeat, pressed together so tight that they could practically be one person.

She sucked marks onto his chest and his collarbone as he put the condom on but stopped when she noticed that his hands were actually shaking a little. She stroked his thigh. "Vinh?" she asked. "We don't have to do anything *you* don't want to do either."

"Baby, I have never wanted anything so badly in my entire life," he said. "I would give up every cent I have, everything I own, to be here with you like this."

Oh my God. With anybody else, that could easily sound cheesy as hell. But the way he said it, the tension in every one of his muscles . . . the way he hovered over her, his expression one of rapt concentration liberally mixed with longing and lust and more emotions than she could name . . .

She could see him doing exactly that.

That made this dangerous.

The thought fled as soon as he pressed forward, his body notching to hers, the blunt head of his arousal pressing against her still-sensitive clit as he stroked his way slowly inside. It had been a while since she'd had sex, but his previous activity had not only stroked her but also opened her and made her delightfully slick. He slid home, seating fully with a long, low groan, resting his head on her shoulder.

She clung to him like ivy, wrapping her legs around his thighs, her arms around his muscular shoulders, dragging him closer. They moved like dancers who hadn't danced together in some time . . . slowly experimenting, looking to each other for timing before finally hitting that perfect rhythm that had her breath catching in her throat and her eyes rolling back in her head.

She knew the moment he was starting to lose control. His body stuttered in its tempo, his hips starting to jerk harder and faster. She squeezed him, feeling the shocking beginnings of a second orgasm curling through her like smoke.

"Yes," she breathed, clawing her fingers down his back before dragging him down for a ravenous kiss. *"Fuck yes."*

"Gonna . . . oh, fuck . . . *Emily,*" Vinh muttered before slamming himself against her.

It was like hitting the blasting cap on a bullet. She exploded, letting out a cry of pleasure as her toes curled. He shuddered inside her, and she could feel him pulsing, releasing into the condom.

After a long moment, he pulled out, then took care of the condom and quickly used the bathroom. She felt floaty, weightless. And like someone had knocked her the hell out in the best possible way.

She found herself getting up, stumbling to the bathroom to clean up. Then standing in the doorway of the bedroom.

Vinh tugged at her hands. "Stay," he said. "It's late, you're exhausted. Please, stay."

That was a bad idea, some part of her seemed to believe. But God, she was so tired. Too tired to remember why this was a bad idea. So she shuffled to the bed, pitching face first into the bedding that smelled deliciously like Vinh. She sighed happily.

He laughed, climbing in behind her and spooning her, his warm body feeling like the best weighted blanket in the world.

"Get some rest, baby," he said, and she felt his lips ghost over the back of her neck.

"Jus' this once," she slurred before sleep dragged her under like a riptide.

CHAPTER 20

Emily woke up to the *Mortal Kombat* song playing softly on her cell phone, her usual morning alarm. She reached blindly for it, frowning when her questing fingers didn't immediately find it. She sat up. The room was pitch black, which wasn't too surprising at four o'clock in the morning. But what *was* surprising was the fact that her phone wasn't on her nightstand but rather in her jeans pocket. Which were on the floor, from what she could tell.

Where she'd hastily stripped them off before climbing Vinh like Mount Frickin' Everest.

She froze for a second, memories hitting her like a right cross.

Kissing Vinh, feeling like she'd been devoured by a bonfire, and eagerly hanging on tighter, wanting to be utterly destroyed by the sheer heat between them. Having some of the best sex she'd had in years. Possibly ever, if she was being honest with herself.

It's too damned early to be honest with myself.

As carefully and quickly as she could, she slipped out of bed, gritting her teeth against the cold of the air versus the warmth and comfort that she'd been enjoying spooned up to Vinh, breathing in that delicious scent of him. She found her phone and dismissed the alarm, then glanced in the dim light from her phone screen at the lump under the blankets that was Vinh's sleeping body. She was actually surprised that her motivational electronica hadn't woken him up.

I did wear him out, though. He might have been a light sleeper, but he slept like the dead after sex, she remembered.

Inadvertently, she grinned at the thought, then went about the business of grabbing her clothes. She had to rush. At this rate, she knew she probably smelled like sex and, well, Vinh. She grabbed her clothes and then sneaked into the bathroom, taking the world's quickest shower. She used some of Vinh's toiletries because they were *right there.* So despite the shower, she *still* smelled like Vinh. In the yummiest of ways.

But I don't smell like sex anymore. Small blessings.

She grimaced as she realized she was going to have to shame walk in yesterday's clothes on her way to work. She shut off the light and tried to navigate the darkened bedroom, biting back a curse when she kicked Vinh's suitcase. She shone her phone's screen at it.

Hmm.

She tugged out one of his Henleys. He wouldn't need it, she felt sure. And it was for a good cause.

She heard him murmur something in his sleep, and she froze again. Part of her would do anything to be able to call in, then climb back into bed and get some sleep. Wake up hours later in his arms and maybe go for another round. Hell, her thumb was ready to dial Troy's number, ready to leave him a message on his voice mail, complete with fake coughing, just so she could stay.

And then what?

That was the crux of the thing, damn it. She wasn't thinking. She was running on sleep deprivation and the aftermath of really good sex. She never thought clearly when it came to Vinh anyway, and now was not a good time for her to make decisions.

No. She had a job to do, and she was going to do it.

Retreat. Retreat. Retreat.

She headed out to the living room, which was illuminated by various heat lamps and aquarium lights. Herman surveyed her curiously while Bastard barked.

"Tokay! Tokay!"

"Shhh!" she hissed back. For once, Bastard did as he was told.

She pulled the Henley on over her bra, then tugged her jeans back on, commando, which was uncomfortable, but she couldn't find her underwear, and she was pushing it borrowing the shirt. She wasn't borrowing boxers either. Finally, she pulled on her shoes and her jacket, then grabbed her purse and Greg's keys. She thought about it for a second, then took the laptop and slipped it into her messenger bag. She'd have to be extra careful to make sure it never left her sight or her side. She wasn't even quite sure what she'd do with it, but maybe it wouldn't be the worst thing to take it home tonight. She needed time and space to think.

She glanced at her watch. She wished she had enough time to make a coffee, but she could make do with a K-Cup at work. She also didn't want to risk Vinh waking up and coming out because she was too flustered. She had no idea what to say.

She bit her lip. *Should I leave a note?*

What would she say, though?

No. They'd talk tonight, one way or another. That would have to be good enough.

With that, she quietly let herself out of the apartment, wincing at the chill in the air but walking with determination toward Greg's truck. This was what she did: the early shift, the shit job. Getting stuff done.

That was what she'd do once Vinh left.

I'm not thinking about that now.

The problem was, she could tell that her brain wasn't going to let her *stop* thinking about it for the rest of the day, no matter how hard she tried.

CHAPTER 21

Vinh woke up slowly and reluctantly. He was in an uncomfortable bed, and the sheets and blankets were all catawampus. His left foot was bare and cold. All this should have irritated him, yet he had a smile on his face and an unfamiliar feeling of utter contentment permeating his whole body. He reached blindly for his phone, then grabbed it and looked at the time. Then he almost fell out of bed.

"Nine o'clock?"

What the fuck?

He *never* woke up that late—ever. He normally got maybe four or five hours of sleep a night and woke up like he was in a foxhole, immediate and alert. Also, whether he was in New York or a hotel room in another city, he got up, worked out, and then had a small high-protein breakfast. Now, the idea of getting up, despite getting an unheard-of eight hours of sleep, made him groan softly.

He felt like he'd been run over by a train—only not in a bad way. If anything, the second weird thing was he was in a great mood. He felt like . . . dancing or something. Which was ridiculous, as he was not the dancing type. Or singing along with something. Or . . . eating an entire stack of pancakes.

He blinked.

Emily.

In a rush, all the memories from the previous night hit him, and he felt his body heat. And a certain part of his body plump up beyond his usual morning chub.

He hadn't expected to sleep with Emily, certainly. He'd *wanted* to since the moment he'd seen her at Tam's house, so he certainly wasn't going to complain. She had been everything he'd wanted in a sexual partner—fun and fiery, taking what she wanted and making sure that he was both glad and grateful that she did. She had been even more amazing than he'd remembered. He was pretty sure he had hickeys all over his body, and the thought of the sharp edges of her teeth nipping at him as she clutched him, her body tightening around him . . .

He groaned. God. He wanted to do that again. As soon as possible. *But it wasn't just the sex.*

The nagging little internal voice brought him up short. Yes, the sex had been energetic and amazing. But it wasn't because of technique. It was because of emotions, something he'd kept on a tight leash when it came to other sexual partners. The moment Emily had agreed, it was like floodgates had opened, and he'd gone from pursuing sex as a purely physical outlet to being overwhelmed, letting himself go, just focusing on being with her. That was what had moved it from incredible to transcendent.

His phone rang, and he picked it up, hoping it was Emily maybe taking a break. She'd be off at two. Maybe he could fix her a late lunch? Or fix her dinner? Yes, they had to buckle down to work. But if *The Shining* had taught him anything, all work and no play made Jill a psychopath, right?

So they probably ought to have sex again. Just to be safe.

His grin came out of nowhere, but it immediately fell when the display read: Winston St. John. It was an effective boner killer as well.

Still, this was important, so Vinh answered it. "Hey, Winston." Thankfully, his voice came out normal.

"Hey, Vinh." Winston sounded concerned. "How are you holding up?"

"As well as can be expected," Vinh said. "What's happening over there?"

Winston huffed out a frustrated sigh. "I'm not gonna lie. It's not looking good."

Vinh pinched his lips together. He had expected as much. "What kind of trouble am I looking at, specifically?"

"You're going to get fired," Winston said bluntly.

"Obviously." Vinh had known that was going to happen, even though the words still hit him like a crowbar. He'd never been fired in his life.

His father was going to be both humiliated and, potentially, a little smug. His grandparents were going to be simply horrified. And his mother—well, he wasn't quite sure how she was going to feel about it. She was harder to read.

He'd never thought about their reactions before, he realized. Because it had never been an *issue*. He'd behaved exactly as they'd expected him to. What happened when he no longer met expectations?

He swallowed against a wave of bile, calming himself as Winston continued.

"You were right—they can't bring criminal charges against you without incriminating themselves. And, as you so terrifyingly pointed out, you just know too much."

"But . . . ?" Vinh prompted.

Winston was quiet for a moment. "The fact that you were escorted from the building the day after Thanksgiving isn't helping. The rumor mill's just starting to spin up in earnest at this point, and people are sharpening their knives. We've managed to keep the details of what happened under wraps because the senior partners don't want word to get out that we lost ten mil in some kind of embezzling . . ."

"*I didn't embezzle.*" Vinh didn't mean to interrupt, but he couldn't help himself.

"Of course not!" Winston reassured him. "I know that. But you know what I meant. They don't want it to leak, so they're keeping a pretty tight lid. But that's not stopping somebody from letting the word get out that you somehow did something really, really bad. The rumors might even be worse than embezzlement, frankly. You've got a reputation for being ruthless. Now, it's coming back to bite you on the ass."

Vinh took his free hand and rubbed it over his face. "For fuck's sake," he muttered.

"And you know most of the hires around here are because Daddy's a millionaire or Mommy's a politician or whatever. They went to the best schools, they're in secret societies, they're networked up to their eyeballs. They're already gossiping about this. And once you're fired," Winston said, like it was a done deal, "that's going to taint every single job you apply for."

Vinh gritted his teeth so hard he was surprised he didn't crack the enamel.

"And the account? Tech-whatever?" Winston's voice was bleak. "They are going to be *pissed*. So far, we haven't said anything, but we're going to have to go over books with them next month."

"It's not their fault the money's gone," Vinh said. "Why wouldn't Aimsley cover it?"

Another beat of silence. "C'mon, Vinh," he finally said. "Do you really think that Aimsley's not going to just pin it on you?"

Vinh's stomach sank, forming a tiny ball of ice somewhere deep inside him. This was going to put a bull's-eye on his back . . . and spread the word that he'd stolen and gotten away with it to any prospective employer. He'd be lucky to get a job as a Walmart greeter.

Fuck.

The thing was, he *knew* all this. That was part of what he did, after all: predict outcomes, project possibilities. Develop strategies for preventing disaster.

Fixing disasters after they'd happened.

"Well, I figured as much," Vinh said, his voice holding only a touch of resignation. He didn't betray emotion on the job, and he sure as hell wasn't going to start now.

"I know it's hard," Winston commiserated. "This has got to be tearing you apart."

"It's less optimal than it could be," Vinh murmured. Because what else could he say? He also hadn't been raised to complain to his higher-up. Winston might've been a mentor and something of a friend, but he was also ultimately one of Vinh's bosses.

"I'd love to put a good word in for you, but . . ."

"But you don't want this shit blowing back on you," Vinh said. "Don't worry. I understand."

"Where are you on finding out who did this to you?"

"Who says I am?"

Winston's laugh was quick. "C'mon. I know you. You're not the type to take things lying down."

Vinh frowned. He hadn't really told Winston about his plans, possibly because they'd been nebulous at the time. He was also used to playing things close to the vest. "I'm progressing."

"Maybe I can help," Winston said. "I know people. I might be able to find out something for you, if you tell me what you need."

Vinh felt a little warmth. "You don't want blowback, remember? This is not something you should be involved in. Then we'd both be screwed."

Winston was quiet for a beat. "Remember: I believe you. I *know* you didn't do this. You are one of the most competent, downright dangerous guys I know. I trained you, and I know what you're capable of. Just . . . know that you don't have to do it alone, okay? I might need to work behind the scenes, but I'm not leaving you out in the cold. If there's anything I can do for you, I will."

"Thanks. I appreciate it." It was encouraging to know there was a resource he could tap if he had to. And Winston genuinely seemed to believe he had nothing to do with this. "I have to go. If—no, *when* I get this handled, I promise I'll let you know."

"Stay strong," Winston said. "Like you're anything but, right? Until then, I can try to put the brakes on, keep slowing down the firing process and the rumor mill."

"Thanks, Winston." Vinh hung up. His body felt like it was in a centrifuge—like he was spinning, almost out of control, getting crushed against the boundaries. All the good feelings he'd had from having sex with Emily evaporated.

He went about his morning routine, cleaning up, getting dressed. Taking care of plants and animals. He found himself slipping into a sort of meditative state. *Mist the boa. Feed the hedgehog. Feed the tortoise. Feed the fish. Water the plants.* It was soothing. More soothing than he would've believed.

Fuck it. When I go back to New York, I am getting a fern.

His phone chimed with an alarm, and he looked at it. Just when he'd thought the day couldn't get any shittier . . .

Dad's birthday.

He rubbed at his eyes with the heels of his palms. Because of course it was.

He talked to his father on only two occasions per year: Lunar New Year, and his father's birthday.

He opened up WhatsApp. This year, he was just going to message the man. It would be midnight where his father was, just turning his birthday. After his father and grandparents had moved back to Ho Chi Minh City, his father had pointedly "joked" that he "kept missing" the date and was late, all because of the fifteen-hour time difference. So he'd put the alarm on his phone for the day prior.

Ugh.

He tapped out: Happy birthday Dad. Hope you are enjoying yourself.

To his surprise (and dismay), his phone rang immediately. His father. Which was ironic, since his father *never* called—that was the responsibility of his children. That wasn't even an Asian thing, per se—it was purely his father.

"Vinh," his father said in Vietnamese.

"Hey, Dad," Vinh answered back, his Vietnamese still rusty from disuse, feeling awkward and strangely like he was twelve again. "Happy birthday. What are you doing up? Isn't it like midnight there?"

"Late call with a supplier," his father said. "He tried to claim that he'd sent the whole thing, but I showed him. Ha! He won't be trying *that* with me again."

Before his father could launch into one of his favorite genres of stories—how he berated a businessperson and had the upper hand—Vinh quickly intervened. "Are you planning on doing anything special for your birthday?"

"Well, your grandparents are throwing a party. It's not every day a man turns fifty," he said, sounding proud. "I'm sure it will be something elaborate. You know how they are."

"Yes," Vinh said, his voice flat. He thought of the people who had raised his father . . . and exactly what they were capable of, which he'd learned firsthand. "I know how they are."

His father didn't notice, continuing. "I'm sure that your stepmother will have spent a fortune, as well—new dress, the works."

"I'm sure."

"The company is doing so well, though, so I don't care. She could buy out four stores, and we'd still be in the black."

His father never asked about *him*, or about Tam. He never cared how his children were faring or what was going on in their lives. And while Vinh understood that his parents never should have gotten married, his father never said a word about their mother, unless it was to take potshots and point out how much better his life was than hers. The man's narcissism knew no bounds. After all this time, Vinh ought to be used to it. After all, two phone calls a year and an impersonal gift was a small price to pay.

Still, Vinh gritted his teeth. He wondered how Tam managed to talk to the man every few months without flipping tables. "Well, say hi to Cam for me."

"Not *Cam*," his father corrected, a snap in his voice. "Lan. Remember? I remarried last year."

Right. He was now on wife three. Possibly four. And no doubt had a girlfriend or two secreted away in various apartments in the city . . . much as he had when Vinh and Tam were in high school.

Vinh's sigh was audible. "Of course. Congratulations."

"Why haven't you gotten married?" his father asked.

Vinh frowned. That was a surprise. "I'm not even dating anyone."

His father snickered. "You take after me! Don't want to be tied down."

The thought that Vinh was like his father in that area made him feel ill.

"But you don't have to be," his father said, his tone dismissive. "As long as you're careful, there really isn't any reason marriage needs to change anything."

Oh hell no. He was not getting some kind of fucked-up marriage advice on how to continue being a player. "I'm too busy for all that," Vinh said in a tight voice.

"Must be busy at that firm of yours." His father sniffed. "Too busy to visit your grandparents, obviously, or your father! But they are proud of what you've made of yourself."

Vinh kept silent.

"Aren't you glad, now?" his father asked. "Glad you didn't drop everything for that blonde? You could have ruined your entire life, and at such a young age. Trust me, I know. Making a mistake that young is hard to come back from."

"A mistake," Vinh repeated.

"Marrying your mother at twenty because she was pregnant?" His father scoffed. "You have to admit, it was hardly the best move we could have made!"

And it produced us. There was nothing quite like hearing you were a mistake to bounce back from to really cement the family bond.

It was so, so hard not to be bitter. Which was probably why he'd never succeeded in tamping it down completely.

"But everything worked out in the end," his father continued. "The point is, you're not getting any younger, and your grandparents want to make sure the line continues. You know? I had a son—too early, but there you are. They would feel better if they knew you were on your way to getting married and having a son of your own."

Vinh felt rage bubbling up—at their expectations, at their coldness, at the sheer audacity of what they wanted.

Fuck them, he thought. *And fuck you.*

His father, as usual, was oblivious to any tension. He let out a yawn. "At any rate, it is late, and I've got a big day tomorrow. Thanks for calling. And I'll keep an eye out for my birthday gift—your assistant always picks out decent ones! Ha ha!"

With that, he hung up.

Vinh gripped the phone, if only so he wouldn't hurl it against a wall.

He could only imagine what they would say if his career was destroyed. His grandparents would be appalled—and if they found out Emily was even tangentially involved, they would automatically blame her. His father would simply be smug.

Vinh sighed. He'd spent his entire life, it seemed, trying to make his family proud, to prove himself to them. And if he was honest, he did it not out of love or even responsibility.

I do it out of spite.

He closed his eyes. Ever since they'd threatened his tuition and Tam's, he'd sworn he was going to be successful . . . and then ram it down their fucking throats.

The morning had started so well. Or at least it should have.

He was a fixer.

Why couldn't he fix his own life?

CHAPTER 22

You just fucked up royally. Now what?

Emily sat in the small break room at her work, barely noticing the spice level on her favorite buldak noodles. She could—and generally did—eat them every week, a little indulgence despite the fact that generic ramen was cheaper. She loved it, loved the heat on her lips, the way she'd have to take little panting breaths to try and cool the spreading fire. Some of her coworkers called her masochistic, but she just shrugged and kept shoveling them in.

Today, though, she was fixated on the laptop, surreptitiously getting her bot up and running. She was careful not to show anything that she and Vinh had been working on—not that a lot of the people she worked with would be able to understand what she was doing, even if they did look over her shoulder—but she'd promised Vinh secrecy. Still, after last night's scorching-hot lapse in judgment, she needed to pick up speed on the hacker side of things, so she wasn't tempted to fall back into the physical side. She knew that Vinh was desperate to get his name cleared and get his career and life back.

Now, she was just as desperate—for different reasons.

Why did you sleep with him?

She huffed an impatient sigh at herself. As she'd suspected, she knew that she wouldn't be able to think about anything else today. The best she could come up with: she'd slept with him because for a brief second or two, she'd seen the boy she had fallen in love with, all those years ago . . . and the man who had adored her before he then inexplicably hadn't, abandoning her when she'd needed him the most.

When they were still teens, he could be aloof with people he didn't know, which often read as coldness. It was something she chalked up to a mild social anxiety. But he could be charming with people when he had to be, like with her parents or when he'd interviewed for a school grant. And with her, he was more than charming. He was attentive and supportive. Often, he'd stared at her like she had somehow invented the moon. And he'd done little things for her, like leaving her little notebooks with pretty covers because he knew she collected them, giving her the last of his fries when they were at the Shack, or rereading her papers when she'd gone cross-eyed and lost all perspective. He'd taken care of her when she had been sick the first semester at NYU, even when her roomie had fled to her boyfriend's place. He'd gotten her NyQuil and soup and watched Disney movies with her, even though he had been hellishly busy.

His sweetness was her kryptonite, all the worse because she knew how rare it was—how so few people got to see that side of him.

She'd fallen in love with him in middle school, the first time she'd seen him, even if they hadn't done anything about it. When he'd made his first tentative move in high school, she'd all but devoured him. Maybe not *sex* but damned close. And he'd told her he loved her, and it had felt *right*.

Last night had felt right. But it wasn't.

Goddamned heart.

Well, she wasn't falling down *that* rabbit hole again, she chastised herself, typing rapidly. The bot had not helped, other than to show that the account user was definitely from Aimsley. She didn't have the time or computer power to tie a user to the account. It was time to call in the cavalry.

She used the laptop to log in to a private server run by one of her hacker friends, Banshee. The server was called the Lair, and it was where some hackers shared exploits or talked about upcoming capture-the-flag events where hackers tested their mettle against systems and each other. Banshee tended to run with ethical hackers for the most part, and Emily had felt comfortable there. That said, nobody was pure white hat there, either. Honestly, most of their alignments could be considered chaotic good at best, neutral at worst.

She didn't exclude herself from this definition.

Thankfully, Banshee was online and could provide at least a little help, fingers crossed.

> **BANSHEE: Long time, girl! What's brought you back to the Lair?**

Emily grinned, using her own hacker handle, MadMatter.

> **MADMATTER: Hey, sweetie. Got a job of sorts, need some help.**
> **BANSHEE: Well, you're in luck. We've got a good group lately, mostly.**

Emily slurped noodles and continued chatting, explaining her situation in the vaguest possible terms. She wasn't surprised when she got a variety of reactions, from "Finally, a real challenge" to "Yeah, that shit's gonna get you sent to jail."

> **MADMATTER: I don't have a lot of time to code something this significant. But I know big intelligence security firms like Elliptic are doing things already . . . they're collecting data from the ledger, and cross-referencing IP addresses**

to accounts. I know that some hackers have to be doing the same thing. I just need to figure out who.

More chatter. Then, finally, Banshee came through.

BANSHEE: Have you tried talking to Oz?

Emily frowned. She hadn't been on Banshee's board in a while, and she tended to lone wolf when she was hacking. She liked the banter and bullshitting, and she did share exploits and take notes when she could because no one was an island. Still, people came and went, and she wasn't always familiar with individual users.

MADMATTER: Who's Oz?

There was suddenly a chorus from the other people chatting on the board, again a mixed bag of positive and negative, making Emily even more confused.

BDE808: Not. Oz!
JANETHEUNVIRGIN: Actually, that's brilliant. Oz knows all and sees all. If anyone can get you into somewhere, or get you info, they could.
BDE808: if you sell your soul
JANETHEUNVIRGIN: Like you have a soul
BDE808: even if I did, I wouldn't turn it over to Oz. I'm not talking shit. Oz scares the fuck out of me.

Emily frowned, confused. Who was this person?

BANSHEE: Oz is Oz the Great and Terrible.
MADMATTER: Shouldn't that be Oz the Great and Powerful?

BDE808: Nope. Great and Terrible.

JANETHEUNVIRGIN: Self-named.

BANSHEE: They're new on the scene, or at least, I never heard of them, but it's obvious they're not new to the practice. They pop in every now and then, but they're more gray-to-black hat than we are. True old school, does-it-for-the-lulz kind.

BANSHEE: But they've got skills. If anybody could help you, it'd be them.

Emily typed out her thanks, and Banshee sent her their contact info privately. If this person could help her, then she needed to pursue it.

The sooner Vinh gets his life back, the sooner he can get out of mine.

She could still *feel* him, which was the worst part, and memories of their night together and the aftermath ambushed her throughout the day. She'd woken up with his arm around her, his head buried in the hair at the nape of her neck, his breath warming her skin.

Wanting him, after all this time, after all he'd done, was beyond foolish. It was self-destructive. She used to dream about them having a future, but she'd also dreamed of having a completely different life. She knew better now. She needed to get this taken care of and get him the hell out, ASAP.

She messaged the hacker on the new private server. She knew this was dicey. If they were as good as Banshee implied, then maybe there was a shot they could help. Then again, if they were truly black hat and just sort of vicious, they could also turn around and decide to mess up *her* life. She'd taken some precautions to keep herself anonymous, but she'd need to trust them to a certain extent at some point.

The message came shortly after, thankfully while she was still on break.

OZ: Who the hell are you?

So. No preamble there. She swallowed against the nervous lump in her throat and started typing.

MADMATTER: My friend Banshee sent me. She said you might be able to help.
OZ: With what?

She outlined the problem. That she'd had money stolen. That she needed to find out who and how.

OZ: Sounds like a job for the police.
MADMATTER: Prefer to deal with it myself. And get some payback.

There was a long pause, and she wondered, briefly, if she was about to get kicked and blocked from the server. But finally, they answered.

OZ: Why the hell not. Sounds like fun.

She blinked. *Fun.* Like breaking the anonymity of a crypto account could be fun. But the more she thought about it, the more she realized—it really *was* fun. The challenge, the puzzle, even the risk. If she didn't have the time constraints and the personal bullshit with Vinh, she might like to play around and create a program that collected data, like Elliptic had. Of course, she'd need some monster-big computers to pull that off. Which made her wonder . . .

MADMATTER: Are you sure you have the computer power to handle this?
OZ: I just said yes, and you're questioning my computer's dick size?

Emily winced, even as a surprised laugh burst out. A woman who was at the counter making herself a K-Cup coffee looked at her, startled. "Sorry," Emily said. Then she typed back.

MADMATTER: I mean no offense! It's just—the account's from a big place, and there are big numbers involved, and tracking the blockchain takes an insane amount of electricity and computing power.
OZ: Well aware. That's why I'm doing it. Been bored as shit lately, and this is right up my street. I'm no fan of crypto, but I understand it, and I think I know just how to crack this, and I probably won't have to do any heavy lifting. Don't worry, my set up can more than handle this.

Emily wondered again who the hell she was dealing with. Whoever they were, they sounded confident.

MADMATTER: I hate to add, but there's a bit of a time component.
OZ: You don't ask for much, do you?

She hoped they weren't pissed. She was asking a lot.

MADMATTER: We might talk in terms of payment . . . ?
OZ: Don't need payment. That's not what I'm in this for. I'll try to get you what you need by your deadline, okay?

Now she just needed to trust them. She bit her lip and sent over the account information. She didn't give them any hints toward Aimsley or any access codes there. But she told them which account it had been taken from, and what account it had been moved to.

OZ: On it. Will message you when I get the info.
MADMATTER: Do you need my contact info? Phone, email?
Or should I check here?
OZ: I already have your info. I'll contact you.

And like that, she got booted. Which was an unceremonious good-bye, but she'd take it. Most of her hacker friends were not known for their social graces, and she didn't really care.

It was out of her hands, but Vinh wasn't just paying her to code it all herself. He was trusting her to use her networks, to find people who were trustworthy. If Banshee gave Oz her stamp of approval, even somewhat qualified, then Oz was good. And if Oz said they could crack this . . .

Well. It's not like she had a lot of choices, but she was just going to have to see what happened. If they worked through it and got the information she needed, then she'd be able to hand Vinh his culprit as well as (hopefully) a way to get the cash back and put Vinh in the clear. Then Vinh would be back to his jet-setting life, wearing expensive clothes, wining and dining clients, kicking unholy corporate ass.

Never coming back to Ponto Beach.

Never seeing her, even if he somehow did visit.

She sighed. This was the route she'd chosen deliberately. It was the safest plan for her. No more kisses. No more sex.

No more love. Not from Vinh Doan.

CHAPTER 23

Vinh had done everything he could—which was a pitiful nothing, really. He'd contacted his assistant, Fergus, who had told him that he'd been reassigned. He trusted Fergus's discretion and loyalty, one of the few he could count on without question at Aimsley. He kept nudging Fergus toward going after a consultant job himself. Fergus had recoiled like he'd suggested skydiving naked without a parachute.

"I just work at this shitshow," Fergus had pointed out. "I don't want to, y'know, *live* it."

Vinh had always thought that was humorous. Now, he wasn't so sure. Fergus couldn't talk about it, but he'd texted that he'd been reassigned. The firing was imminent, from the looks of it.

Fuck.

Since he couldn't casually ask anybody else at Aimsley, "Hey, is anybody shit-talking me?" he decided instead to read a bunch of articles on cybersecurity, the blockchain, and cryptocurrency. He quickly learned that 1) he didn't have any sort of aptitude for the technical end, much like he couldn't service a car despite being a confident driver; and 2) doing research at this point was a lot like going on WebMD when you had a headache, only to convince yourself you had a brain tumor and less than twenty-four hours to live. He was now convinced that he was going to jail for life and that his clients would probably put a hit out on him.

It was an unpleasant day.

Feeling like the walls of the apartment were closing in on him, he'd gone jogging on the beach. It had been a while since he'd worked out in nature, normally using his spare bedroom, which he'd converted to a weight room, or using whatever hotel amenities were available when he traveled. After some exercise, he felt more grounded, at least. He went back to Greg's place. He vacuumed, changed the sheets, cleaned the enclosures, opened the windows (while still monitoring everybody's habitat temperatures), did the dishes, and took out trash.

Basically, he was keeping busy and killing time, waiting for Emily to come back.

He wasn't sure what he was going to say to her when she got off work. Obviously they ought to talk about last night . . . shouldn't they?

God. He didn't necessarily want to just talk about it. He wanted to *repeat* it. And the ball was in her court where that was concerned.

He'd showered and thrown in a load of laundry when the front door opened. Emily walked in, in fresh clothes, her hair damp. "You stopped at home?"

"Yep," she said, and her cheeks went pink. "Thank God my mother was at work—and that may be the most high school statement I've said *since* high school."

He chuckled. Then he walked toward her, stopping just short of touching her. She held a hand up.

"Nope. We aren't doing that again."

Disappointment hit him like a fist, but he nodded, taking a step back. He noticed that her eyes followed his every move. She was tense, tighter than a garage door spring. But her gaze roved over him, and he couldn't help some responsive tension of his own.

"I don't regret last night," he said. "And I'd love to do it again. But I told you: this is your decision. I'll respect whatever you choose."

She bit her lip, unslinging her messenger bag and putting it down on their war room table, then pulling out the laptop.

"You left early," he said, then remembered she started at five o'clock and felt like an ass.

Her laugh was rough and broken. "Yeah. I shame walked in there, but no one seemed to notice, except my manager, who of course said something," she said. "Anyway, I was careful with the laptop. I contacted some of my hacker friends. I think I've found someone who can crack this, figure out who owns the other account and maybe where they are."

"They're that good? And you trust them?" He didn't mean to sound skeptical, but his earlier "You're going to jail" visions kept dancing in his head.

"They seem to be. I trust the hacker who referred them," she said, rubbing her hand on the back of her neck. She fidgeted, toeing the carpet with her canvas sneaker. "I know that you asked me, and I love the challenge. With enough time, and maybe a stronger computer, I could maybe jerry-rig something. The problem is, you don't have that kind of time. I had to call an audible—hence, Oz the Hacker."

"There's still nothing I can do, is there?" he asked quietly, feeling helpless. Almost feeling hopeless.

"At this point, there's nothing even *I* can do, until this Oz gets back to me," she said.

He frowned. "Then . . . why are you here?"

She took a deep breath. "I . . ."

Then she took two steps forward, throwing herself in his arms.

He didn't question, just reacted. He held her tight, his mouth tilting over hers, kissing her fiercely. She made a soft sound of gratitude, all but climbing him in her eagerness, and he pressed her body tightly against his own. His senses were overwhelmed by her: her cinnamon-spice smell, the sweet-sharp taste that was uniquely her. The softness of her skin as his hands moved up beneath her hoodie and T-shirt.

He was startled when she shoved him away. "Damn it. *Damn it,*" she cursed, out of breath. "I . . . we . . . I swore I wasn't going to do this!"

He started to reach for her, but she glared, freezing his hand in midair. "I still want you," he said. "I still care about you. That's never changed."

"That doesn't matter," she said. "I *loved* you."

"I loved you too!"

Still do.

He tried desperately to shut down his expression before she could pick up on the truth he hadn't even wanted to admit to himself all these years. Instead, she shot him an anguished look.

"Then how could you just *leave* me all those years ago?" she asked in a tiny voice. "How could you dump me when I needed you?"

He grimaced. "I didn't want to," he said. "But it seemed like the best idea at the time."

"How?" Her voice broke. "I'd just lost my father. My mother was in freefall, just unable to deal with anything. And Greg was in shock. Hell, so was I. I had to *leave school* second semester, I didn't know what I was going to do, and I had to basically handle the executor stuff that my mother simply couldn't face. I needed help, Vinh. I needed *you.*"

Vinh felt guilt eating at him. "I know," he admitted in a small, sad voice. "And I'm so, so sorry."

She took a step back, tugging at the roots of her hair and closing her eyes. When her breathing evened out, she swiped at her eyes with one sleeve cuff, then surveyed him with intense hazel eyes. "Since we broke up, I might have a slightly better idea of what you were going through," she admitted. "Working a few jobs is no joke. Being worried about making ends meet. I get it now."

He nodded, feeling relieved that they seemed to be moving forward, but the relief was short lived.

"But you didn't just break up with me. It was how you did it. I mean, it was like a contract hit," she said, her voice small. "I wouldn't have ever talked to anyone the way you talked to me. Total ice, no emotion. Just 'We should have a clean break' and showed me the door. What the actual *fuck*, Vinh?"

He sighed. He hated this. Hated reliving it. But it was beyond time for him to have this conversation with her. He gestured to the bedroom.

"You *cannot* think I'm going to screw you after what I just said," she snapped.

"No. But your brother prioritizes animals over couches, and this is gonna take a while. Better if we're sitting down."

"No, it isn't going to take a while," she countered stubbornly. "What's left to talk about? I'm going to play with that master account, see if I can just poke around and find some things. I don't even need to be here . . ." She started to reach for the bag, but Vinh put a gentle hand on her arm.

"There are some things I didn't tell you," he said. "Things I honestly haven't told anybody. They're not excuses, but maybe they'll help you understand what was happening to me. Where I was mentally."

She looked like she was going to tell him to fuck off—*again*—but instead she gave a curt nod, following him to the bedroom, sitting on the edge of Greg's bed.

Vinh sighed, then rubbed his eyes with the heels of his palms. Where to start?

"You know we were having problems before we broke up," he said. "Pretty much that first semester. I was working two jobs—that job at the campus café and the one at the library. Plus a full course load. Remember? You hated how we couldn't spend that much time together?"

Her mouth pulled into a tight line. "Tell me you're not blaming this on me," she warned.

"No," he quickly reassured her. "But I was under a lot of pressure, and I felt like I was failing on all fronts. Then your father died."

She nodded, her eyes going misty.

"And I went home with you, and you started to see that there was no way your mom was going to manage with you on the East Coast," he said, remembering that horrible, hollow feeling. Her mother had been in hysterics, weeping. Emily and he had crashed at the house, only to awaken at three in the morning to her mother screaming at her father's photo in the living room, asking how he dared leave her, then sobbing, asking how she was supposed to manage. "You dropped out that week."

"I know," she said. "Then I went back a few weeks later to get the rest of my stuff and asked you if you'd come back to Ponto Beach with me."

He sighed. "Do you remember how that happened?"

She frowned, as if trying to recollect. "You were working," she said. "After classes. It was midterms, I think. You were at the café? Except you worked late. I didn't see you until close to midnight."

"That's because I wasn't working at the café," he said. "I lost that job when I gave them no notice and just vanished. Apparently going to my girlfriend's father's funeral wasn't enough of an excuse."

She hissed. Then her eyes narrowed. "Then where were you?"

"Starting my new job as a busboy at an expensive Italian restaurant," he said. "Over in Washington Square. La Candela."

She tilted her head. Then her eyes widened. "Wait, I . . ."

"Was there that night," he completed. "With Chris Werst."

She let out a long sigh. "Please tell me this isn't some bullshit jealousy thing," she said. "Because we both know I was *not* on a date with Chris fucking Werst. His father was a friend of my father, and he'd been kind of a friend since junior high, for God's sake. His father was doing me a favor and helping to get my stuff shipped back to Ponto Beach. It was just a friendly dinner!"

"I know this," Vinh said, and she settled down a little. "But he always wanted to date you. Not that it's relevant."

She scowled but kept quiet.

"The thing is, I was clearing the table. You were in the restroom, and it wasn't technically in my section. You hadn't seen me yet, and I'd planned to say hi. Chris knew exactly who I was, though. He pointed out that you could do better than a fresh-off-the-boat guy like me and that your parents knew that. Then he asked me how I felt about having a career in food service because it was obviously where I belonged."

"Shut. Up." Her eyes went wide. "Are you kidding me? I will kick his *ass*! That racist, arrogant dickwad!"

Despite the seriousness of what they were discussing, Vinh couldn't help but smile. "Anyway, that's where my head was by the time I got back to see you."

"But you have to know that wouldn't have mattered to me," she pleaded. "You weren't, what, 'fresh off the boat,' and even if you were, *I wouldn't care*. And even if you'd been a waiter all your life, I would've loved you! I know that you were slammed, but we could've made it work long distance if we'd tried . . ."

"There's one other component to this that I didn't tell you," he said. "That I couldn't really tell you."

She stared at him expectantly.

He swallowed, then let it all out in one breath.

"My grandparents told me, in no uncertain terms, that if I left college to be with my girlfriend, they were going to cut off the tuition they were helping with. *And* they were going to cut off Tam's as well. After she'd gone through so much shit with our parents, I didn't want to be the reason why Tam didn't go to college."

CHAPTER 24

Emily stared at Vinh in shock. *"What?"*

He sighed, throwing himself against the bed and putting his arms behind his head. She would've admired the way his lean body looked if she weren't, y'know, *freaking the hell out* over this new information.

"Mom had started the ball rolling on divorce proceedings, and she and Dad were haggling over the house," he said. "My grandparents knew that I'd gone back to Ponto Beach with you for the funeral. I think Tam mentioned it, since she wanted to come back, too, and she was already plugged in to all the stuff on the Slack channel. However it shook out, they actually called me and asked if it was true that your father had died and you were dropping out of school. When I said that it was, they asked if I planned on breaking up with you." He frowned, as if remembering the moment. "I told them absolutely not. In fact, I was considering trying to transfer. I'd gotten a partial scholarship at NYU, but I could probably get some financial aid . . . would've been hard, since I had a rough first semester, but I think I could've swung it. And even if it didn't, I could've maybe gone to community college or something until I could get into another school. I thought we'd make it work."

Emily swallowed hard, looking down at him. He told the story almost dispassionately, using his robot voice. Which meant that it hurt, and he had his shields up, full blast, even after all these years.

"Then they told me if I did, they were cutting me off without a dime. No financial help of any sort. In fact, as far as they were concerned, I wouldn't even be their grandson anymore. Wouldn't be a part of the family."

"Jesus," she breathed, unable to help herself. She stroked his arm, trying to comfort him.

"Yeah." It was the only acknowledgment that the incident had been painful. "As you might expect, I didn't take that well. I all but told them to go to hell. Said I'd make it on my own and that you mattered more to me than they did. Which *they* didn't take well."

Emily felt her heart stop for a brief second, then beat wildly at those words.

"Which is when my dad—who was also on the line, like some fucked-up team-meeting conference call—mentioned that it'd be a shame if Tam had to drop out of Vassar. Because it wouldn't be fair to pay for *her* tuition, especially since she didn't have a scholarship. She had a job in addition, but it wouldn't be enough to pay for room and board *and* school."

"No," Emily whispered.

"And my grandparents piled on. Said they'd disown her too. No help, no recognition, just fuck off."

The cruelty was breathtaking. She'd thought Vinh was cold. His father and his father's parents put Vinh to shame.

"So I told them I needed to think about it," Vinh said. "But you have to understand, I didn't want to hurt Tam. She'd had a rough time in high school with my parents. She was always more emotionally fragile. Also, I had you. She had Josh, but it was different then."

Emily nodded. That was true. Tam and Josh had taken years to finally figure out their relationship, beyond a rock-solid friendship that was still going strong. Now, it existed with a shiny engagement ring on top.

"And I did plan to talk to you about it," he said. "But then there was the dinner bullshit with Chris. And you were pissed because I had to work so late, and . . . I think I just lost hope. I couldn't see how we could make it work."

She blinked at tears that were dotting her lashes. "Oh, Vinh."

"D'you know that's what I do? My job, I mean," he said. "I look at problems, and I figure out strategies to deal with them. I come up with solutions that seem almost impossible but make them work. And that was the one time I couldn't see any way out for us. No positive one, anyway."

"Maybe *I* could have come up with a solution—did that ever occur to you?" she asked. "You had no right—*no right*—to make that kind of a decision for me. That was not okay."

He tilted his head to look at her. "I couldn't move to Ponto Beach. You couldn't stay in New York. And we barely had time for each other when we were in the same city . . . and were getting increasingly resentful of each other's expectations in that area. How do you think that would've worked? What solution do you think you could've come up with? Because even after all these years, I've never seen the answer to that one."

She felt guilt splash her like acid. She *had* been a little bit demanding of his time. She hadn't had to work while she was studying, and the computer science classes and general ed classes she had been taking were a breeze. She'd been bored, and lonely, and nervous. New York had been intimidating, not friendly like Ponto Beach. She'd clung to Vinh.

No wonder he'd felt trapped by their lack of options.

"But you were so harsh," she finally added, almost desperately. "It hurt so much."

"I know, baby," he said, and he stroked her cheek, his fingertips ghosting over her skin and tracing down her jawline, her throat, her clavicle. "And I'm sorry. But I figured it would be better to stop it quickly rather than drag it out. I was afraid the resentment would destroy us. At least with a clean break, it would hurt, but it'd be . . . you know. Fast. Surgical."

She laughed bitterly, shaking her head. "Yeah. That worked."

He propped himself up on one elbow, facing her. "I thought you'd be in pain. And I did suspect you'd hate me," he said. "But I thought you'd get over it. Get over *me*. Find someone else and be happy."

Her mouth felt like the Mojave, and her eyes stung. "Well, I did hate you," she said, with a wry grin that had him snickering. "So I guess you figured the same? That it'd hurt and you'd get over me? Find someone else who made you happy?"

His gaze was like a black hole, drawing her in.

"No," he said quietly. "I still love you, Em. And I knew, even then, that I was never getting over you. But that wasn't the point. You were. You always were."

She went breathless at the statement. Then she leaned forward, pressing her lips to his. It was gentle—a whisper, a promise. Then it unraveled into something deeper. It wasn't the fast and furious coupling that they'd fallen into the night before. It was sweet, almost bittersweet, and gentle. She let him undress her, and then she undressed him, until they were naked and facing each other.

"Emily," he breathed, and his hands stroked her skin. She reached for him, tilting his head back, kissing his throat, nibbling at his neck in the way she knew he loved, especially when his low rumble confirmed it. He held her hips, his fingers digging in a little before smoothing his way up her sides and over her back.

After what felt like forever, in the best possible way, impatience finally won out. This time, she was the one to raid the nightstand—the one to take the condom and roll it on Vinh's waiting form. He smiled at her.

"I'm at your disposal," he said, with that smile—the smile that was just for her.

"Damned right you are," she teased back. Then she clambered on top of him, fitting him to her and easing herself down until he bottomed out. She gasped at the sensation of fullness, enjoying the look of almost shocked pleasure on his face.

She moved slowly at first, rocking on him. He held her hips, not to guide but simply to continue the connection. She loved this.

She loved *him*.

But damn, if it wasn't terrifying, considering telling him that. Even if he'd said it first.

She closed her eyes, forcing herself to focus on the physical sensation like it was a zen practice. She wanted this, to be with him, as close as possible.

"Emily," he breathed, tugging her down until she could kiss him hungrily.

Their pace went from slow to hurried. He started lifting his hips to meet her downward thrusts, his cock dragging against her clit from the angle they were joined. When he moved slightly, the adjustment hitting her G-spot in a way that frankly none of her other boyfriends or hookups had come close to managing, she cried out, chasing the sensation. And Vinh paid attention, flipping them, driving into that point. The sensations were overwhelming.

"Vinh," she rasped, her hands clasping spasmodically on his shoulders, his forearms, his ass. Whatever she could reach. "Oh . . . *nngh* . . ."

"*Oh, fuck*," he said back. His thrusts were becoming more forceful, more determined. The bed shook. She could barely feel her feet. "Baby, I'm so close . . ."

"Come for me," she murmured and squeezed her internal muscles.

He let out a helpless, deep groan, and she moaned in response as her orgasm hit her like a train. It felt like all her synapses were being lit up like fireworks. She gasped and whimpered and shuddered, completely undone.

His hips snapped a few more times before he finally went still, a few little aftershocks of pleasure making him shiver and drawing a similar response in her.

"Emily," he said softly before kissing her.

She smiled back. "Did you take, like, a master class or something?" she said. "Because I have to say—I remember us being good together, but I don't remember us being *that* good."

He grinned. "Let's say I'm really motivated now," he murmured. "And lucky. I never thought I'd have a chance to be with you again."

She went quiet as he pulled out, then disappeared into the bathroom to take care of the condom. She pulled the covers over her. She knew she probably ought to go home, although she'd simply told her mother she planned to stay at Greg's and take care of the animals. Her mother didn't know Vinh was in town. She also didn't know he was staying at Greg's.

This was a can of worms she probably shouldn't open. It was enough she'd gotten closure on the past. It was enough to know that she wasn't so wrong, such a terrible judge of character, and that Vinh hadn't been the cruel, heartless bastard she'd once thought.

But that piece of information was enough for her heart to crack open, just a little. And Vinh was already squeezing his way in there.

She didn't know what she was going to do with that. And she knew that when their project was done, she was going to need to face it . . . one way or another.

CHAPTER 25

The next morning, Vinh vaguely registered when Emily left. He got up in that great mood again, only this time, it wasn't ruined by Winston or his father. He fell into what was now his "usual" routines: took care of the animals and plants, then drove over to Juanita's coffee shop to get coffee and some breakfast and say hi. He bumped into various members of the Herd there, since a lot of them set their own hours. He even went so far as to kill a little time playing the latest *Rainbow Six* with Tobin. It was more fun than he remembered, although he sucked and Tobin had gleefully killed him a number of times. It was gratifying to take out his aggressions on pixels on the screen, though. When Lily needed Tobin's help with a video, Vinh agreed to see them both later. He then drove a little farther south to Swami's Gardens in Encinitas. He took the time to look out at the waves crashing against the shore, then wandered the picturesque gardens, admiring the carp. It was tranquil in a way he hadn't experienced in a long time. It was a little brisk, but after New York winters, he was immune. Finally, he grabbed a bowl of chicken soup at Jorge's, which was arguably the best Mexican chicken soup in the world as far as he was concerned, and some taquitos. He'd gained a few pounds since coming back to Ponto Beach, but since he often ran on coffee and twelve-hour energy drinks and whatever packets of snacks he carried, he probably could've used it.

He was sleeping better, although he supposed he could credit athletic sex with Emily for that. Ever since he'd finally revealed everything, revealed the ugliness about his family's ultimatum and his own regrets, he'd felt lighter, freer.

He felt . . . weird.

He was used to going a billion miles an hour, strategizing the next move and then the next four. He was used to having his guard up, maintaining his game face while analyzing his opponents' true intentions. And he never forgot that was exactly what he was dealing with: opponents. At work, he didn't have friends. He didn't necessarily have enemies, but he was well aware that your career worked only when you proved your worth. If you proved to be a liability, you were cut off, kicked out.

Escorted from the building by Jake the Security Guy.

He grimaced, then ate his soup, which went a long way toward helping him feel better.

He was back at the apartment before Emily got there. He had washed the bedding and hoped desperately that she'd stay again that night. Even though she had all that week, the fact that she hadn't said she loved him in return weighed on him, and he didn't want to have expectations of her. That wasn't fair. He didn't know what was going on between the two of them. Maybe it was just anger hanging with a side of tenderness—maybe it was getting closure.

Maybe it's something more . . .

"Hey there!" Emily said as she strolled through the door. "C'mon. We're going to get out of here."

He blinked. "What? Why?"

"Juanita's going to have her holiday party tonight, remember?" she said. "At the coffee shop. The whole Herd's going to be there."

"But that's not for hours," he noted.

"Yes," she said, taking his hand and tugging it, "but I'm still waiting for Oz the Great and Terrible—true handle, I'm not kidding there—to get back to me on the details of the account. So since there's nothing *either* of us can do, I'm not letting us stay here and fixate. We'd both be bouncing off the walls before you knew it."

He couldn't help it. He leaned in a little, smiling wickedly. "I can think of other ways for us to channel our energy. Just thinking."

He saw her cheeks pinken, but she grinned. "None of that, Mister."

"At all?"

"We'll see how I'm feeling tonight," she said. "You know I hate being a foregone conclusion."

"*The Thomas Crown Affair*," he said, recognizing the quote. "That movie with the art theft. The new version, not the old version."

"I can't believe you remember that," she marveled, with that impish grin of hers.

"You made me watch it, all the Ocean's movies, *Tower Heist*, and *The Italian Job* like a million times. You do have a thing for heist movies."

"Guilty." She shrugged. "Bottom line: I'm not discounting anything, but *if* you get me back into bed, I'm making you *work* for it."

He wiggled his eyebrows. "Looking forward to it. Your car or mine?"

"Your car, since my car isn't even my car," she said. They locked up and took the Audi, heading back to the center of town where Juanita's café was situated.

"So we're just showing up early?" he asked when he finally found a parking spot a few blocks away.

"She can always use help," she said. "With decorations and such, if nothing else. But it's a nice stroll, and I like window shopping."

"Okay." He'd never window shopped a day in his life.

There were a number of little shops and funky boutiques on the way to Juanita's place. Emily cooed over a stained-glass place, remarking that she'd always wanted to make a piece. It was beautiful, he had to admit. She also got rapturous over pastries that were displayed in a nearby bakery.

"Want me to get you something?" he asked, feeling the need to spoil her. He got the sense she rarely got luxury or comfort in her life as it stood, and that made him want to shower her with everything that would make her happy.

That was probably a dangerous line of thought, but there it was.

"Nah," she said after one last covetous look at an éclair. "They provide baked goods for Juanita, so I can always grab something there. But she runs out quickly—she has *the best* coffee, and a lot of people don't want to make two stops."

They kept walking, passing a little Taekwondo dojang. It was after school, and there was a class in session . . . a bunch of little kids, all dressed in their white gi, most with white belts. They were trying their damnedest to follow along with the instructor, looking a bit like martial arts ducklings. One wandered outside, stumbling in front of them. Reflexively, Vinh reached down, brushing him off and making sure he was okay.

Unfazed, the kid looked up at them. "I'm gonna be a black belt," he informed them. "I make up my own moves!"

"Do you?" Vinh asked with a smile. Emily made a little *aww* expression, clasping her hands to her chest like she couldn't believe the cuteness unraveling in front of her.

"I do! Wanna see?" Not even waiting for an answer, he quickly did . . . something. Sort of a wriggle, a kick, and then almost a roll that would've landed him back on his butt, but he saved himself. "See? See?"

"I see," Vinh said. "Pretty cool."

"It's a cross between a duck and a kick," the kid said seriously.

"Awesome."

The kid beamed. "I call it a *dick*!"

Vinh could not help it. He barked out the laugh before he snapped a serious expression faster than you could blink. "I see," he repeated. "That's . . . wow."

A harried-looking woman popped out of the door. "Simon, I told you, you can't just run out and talk to people," she said sternly, then shot them an apologetic look. "Sorry. He's a raving extrovert and is very proud of his skills."

"As he should be," Vinh said, ignoring the strange, uncharacteristic impulse to ruffle the kid's hair. "He's good. You keep it up, you're going to be a black belt in no time!"

"Thanks!" Simon beamed, then turned and zoomed back into the dojang, the instructor shaking her head but smiling widely.

Emily burst out laughing. "Oh my God. That was both cute and hilarious."

"It's a *dick*," Vinh murmured as they walked away. "A lethal dick."

Which launched a fresh wave of laughter between them as they leaned against each other companionably.

Before he actively thought about it, his fingers tangled with hers. He held her hand. It occurred to him he hadn't really held hands with anyone since her. It had never felt natural with anyone else. It was a relationship thing. It was, weirdly, more intimate than sex to him.

He squeezed her fingers.

She squeezed back, then sighed and released him. He felt immediately bereft.

"We're probably going to need to talk about what's going on at some point," she said. "But not tonight. Right?"

He swallowed. "Yes," he said in a low voice. He wasn't sure if any of the other Herd were around, but he knew this was a private topic. "But since I'm not entirely sure what we're doing, I don't think tonight, no. Although—and forgive me if this is too horny—I do want to have sex with you again tonight. If you want to."

Her cheeks heated. "I . . . well, we'll see," she hedged. Then sighed. "But realistically, yeah."

His body started to go hard at the mere thought. He shifted in discomfort. Probably shouldn't have brought that up *before* they were going to walk into a holiday party with a bunch of their friends.

"The thing is, I don't want the Herd to know," she said. "You know how they are. They mean well, but they'll have *input*. Which I don't mind too much, but if they know, they're going to assume we're together. Which we don't know for sure. And if we don't work out . . ."

"It'll be like freshman year of college all over again," he said. He'd deliberately (and quietly) told the Herd that Emily needed their uncontested support. He had convinced himself that he'd be fine. And, while no one had "taken sides," they had clearly been there for Emily.

"Worse," she said, her expression bleak. "So maybe we just keep this quiet?"

He nodded, even though he felt like shit about it. Still, logically, it made sense.

Her phone buzzed, and she pulled it out of her pocket and unlocked it, her brow furrowing as she read the message. "Okay, I heard back from Oz."

He looked up and down the street. Still nobody he knew. "What'd they say?" he asked.

"They said that the owner of the account where your money got moved to is Mike Hanover," she said. "And that he's a dumbass who should've used a tumbler to spread the transactions out rather than move that much cash straight from one account to another."

Vinh goggled. "How the *hell* did they find that out?" He didn't know much about blockchain and crypto or any of that, but the whole point of the blockchain was that *nobody* could figure that out. It was anonymous.

She shrugged. "Well, there are big companies like Elliptic that monitor the ledger. They've been doing that for a few years," she said. "They've amassed enough data that they can largely figure out who owns what. More than most currencies want to let on, anyway. It's not perfect, but they've got the computer power and the man hours and the historical data to piece it together."

"And this Oz person can do that too?" Vinh said. "What, are you working with a supervillain with a supercomputer or something?"

"We'd better hope not," she said, typing away. Then her eyes widened. "Okay. I asked how they got the info, and their response was it's better I don't know. They also said 'Work smarter, not harder' and that they'd always wanted to crack into something that serious."

"What does that mean?"

"I suspect they decided to save time and just break into one of the companies that tracks that data," she said, sounding both impressed and horrified. "Which—and I can't stress this enough—is scary as fuck. Any hacker that can crack into an intelligence and security service of that caliber is someone who could topple governments."

Vinh made a mental note to never piss this person off, whoever they were.

"So do you know this Mike Hanover?"

He frowned. Now that the name had been confirmed, it made sense. "I do know Mike. We're . . . rivals, I suppose. I mean, technically everybody at my level is a rival when it comes to getting promoted and fighting for partnership. But Mike's close. We've had similar accounts, and he's got a decent track record. He tends to take shortcuts, and he goes a bit more in the gray area—and possibly further—than I'd ever be comfortable with." His brain whirred as he processed it. "Apparently he's going a *lot* further, from questionable ethics to outright theft, under the belief that he won't get caught and certainly wouldn't get punished."

She scowled. "What an asshole."

"Yeah, well," he said, shrugging. It was the nature of the business. "What now? Do we have his account information?"

"No. That's going to take a physical intervention," she said.

"What do you mean?"

"I think I figured out how he got to you," she said, sounding pensive. "You said that you always kept your laptop safe when you were traveling, and you didn't have any strangers at your house. But did you lock your computer when you were at the office?"

"I logged off," he said. "Every time I walked away from my desk." It occurred to him that he had known, on some level, not to trust his coworkers, even then.

"No, I mean physically locked it. In a desk drawer, maybe."

"No. Only our employees or clients were allowed in the building, and there are strict security measures in place. Nobody bothers to lock their laptops up when they're in the building, because they wouldn't be stolen. Why would I?" He was starting to have an uneasy feeling about all this.

"All it takes is a thumb drive and about five or ten minutes, and he'd be able to crack into your computer with absolutely no hacking knowledge. Totally turnkey. Five minutes alone in your office—hell, it could look like he was leaving you a note on your desk or trying to find a file or something—and he'd have access to your machine."

Vinh felt like he'd had the wind knocked out of him. *"Fuck."*

"Don't worry. You're going to return the favor. You're going to need to get to his laptop, which in your company sounds like it isn't that hard. Does he take it home on weekends?"

"No," Vinh said, disdainful. That was what made it worse. Mike had made it clear that he spent plenty of time at his family's "compound" in Sag Harbor, going sailing, playing golf. He was more about the schmooze than he was about the numbers, the details. It had frankly shocked him that Vinh had been promoted over him on sheer hard work.

"Then you go in when he isn't. He probably leaves the damned thing on his desk. Just hard reboot it with the flash drive in a USB port. It'll circumvent the password, load some malware . . . and, more importantly, a keylogger. That's probably what he hit you with. We'll know everything he types."

"What if he doesn't use a password or it's saved?"

"Then we'll send him an anonymous threatening email, he'll check his balance . . . and just like that, we'll get what we need."

"Sure, it sounds easy when you say it that way," Vinh muttered. "But one thing: I can't get back in the building, remember? I'm banned."

She frowned. "You have to know someone . . ."

He thought about asking Fergus, but as much as he trusted Fergus, he also knew that the guy wasn't going to go up against Aimsley. He could ask Carlos, maybe? But Carlos didn't know him like that. He might let him in the building, but there were security cameras . . .

Suddenly, the answer clicked into place. "You," he breathed. "It has to be you. They don't know you; you'll know how to handle the technology . . . it's perfect."

She looked startled. "I can't fuck off to New York on a moment's notice, Vinh!"

But he was determined. "I'll pay for any lost wages," he said, using his most persuasive tone. "I'll pay for the tickets. I'll pay Hayden to watch the animals. And you can stay with me in my apartment, or I'll pay for a five-star hotel room if you want."

He saw her throat work as she swallowed nervously. "It's a big risk," she said. "I've protected myself as best I can, but if I do this—this is big league if I get caught, and you know it."

He stopped short. *Shit.* He hadn't thought that through. He had been so intent on finally catching whoever had screwed him over he'd gotten tunnel vision.

Endangering Emily when she'd already done so much?

"No, you're right," he said. "There's got to be another way."

She blinked. "Just like that?"

"Well, yeah. I'm not going to put you in harm's way any more than I already have," he said automatically. "I know as a hacker you've taken risks, but this is a step above. And Aimsley would be furious—and vindictive—if they found out you did this. I don't need you to put yourself in even more danger."

Her expression softened, and she put a hand on his shoulder.

"Let me think about it, okay?"

CHAPTER 26

An hour later, the holiday party at Juanita's was in full swing. There was tinsel everywhere, it seemed, and a tree lit with blue and white lights and various ornaments from local artisans. The place was packed with people laughing and jostling. The Nerd Herd had taken over one of the tables and was playing a spirited game of Carcassonne, Hayden good-naturedly yelling at Keith for cheating. Juanita had outdone herself with over-the-top hot cocoa offerings with either mint, nutmeg, cinnamon, or simply "double-rich" and sinfully delicious chocolate. She also had an arrangement of holiday cookies decorated to look like presents. There was a huge holiday-themed cheese board, thanks to caterer Freddie and Tam's cheese-based job. Overall, there was a general sense of good cheer. There was even holiday music that Juanita's friend had pulled together, cycling between lo-fi mixes of instrumental classics and other unusual covers of well-known hits. As far as parties went, this one was a huge success.

Ordinarily, Emily would either be playing Carcassonne, cuddling Melanie's baby, or hitting the cheese plate like dairy products were about to be outlawed. But for the past hour, all she could do was fidget, barely able to pay attention to what anyone was saying as her mind tried desperately to figure out how she felt and what she wanted to do next.

Still reeling from Vinh's request, she had spent the past hour avoiding him. She could finally admit she had hit a wall.

She needed input from her besties.

She shepherded Lily, Tam, and Juanita into a corner. "Help," she murmured, looking over her shoulder. Fortunately, Vinh was nowhere in sight, probably tucked away in the throngs of people milling around.

"What is it?" Lily asked immediately. "What's wrong?"

"I'm in a . . . situation," she said, trying to figure out how much to disclose. "And I don't know what to do."

Juanita stepped up. "What kind of situation?"

Emily gnawed her lip. "The tricky kind," she said, then added, "and the private kind."

Juanita frowned, then gestured to them. "Let's go to my office. It'll be a tight fit, but nobody'll interrupt or overhear. Hey, Cyril! I'm gonna be a few minutes."

The massive, man-bun-wearing, heavily tatted guy at the counter nodded his acknowledgement with a smile. Juanita then ushered the three women into her tiny office, where they stood in a cramped knot. "So what's going on?" Juanita continued, looking concerned.

Emily wasn't sure how to start, so she just dove in. "I can't go into why, but Vinh just asked me to go to New York with him."

Tam goggled at her. "*My brother asked you to move to New York for him?* Like, *permanently?*"

"What? No, no," Emily quickly corrected. "Nothing like that! He just wants my help with a thing."

Juanita's eyes narrowed. "What kind of a 'thing,' exactly?" Her question was rife with suspicion. "Especially since last I checked, you—and I quote—'hated him with the passion of a thousand suns.'"

"My feelings have tempered somewhat," Emily allowed. She tugged at the roots of her hair and shifted her weight from one foot to the other. "Besides, it's professional, not personal. And I can't say what the thing is—it's a secret."

Lily looked pensive. "If it's professional, can you say why his request is freaking you out?" she asked instead, and before Emily could protest, she pinned her with a look. "And yes, it's obvious you're freaking out."

Emily rubbed her palms over her face. Of course it would be obvious. When it came to Vinh, she had zero chill.

Rather than answer the question and inadvertently admit that she wasn't able to keep things purely professional with Vinh, she decided to simply dodge it. "I should just say no," Emily said, testing the words. "Right? I mean, I can't take the time off work—they'd be furious. That right there should be enough . . ."

"You could get someone to cover your shifts," Lily said. Tam nodded in agreement, as did Juanita.

"I guess I could," she grudgingly acknowledged. "Gina does owe me some hours. And I've covered for other people too. But what if my mom needs something?"

"You know that we'd take care of it for her," Juanita reassured her. "Nothing to worry about there."

This was not quite going the way she'd planned. Emily had expected them to talk her *out* of it, not encourage her.

"I'm assuming this is tied to why Vinh is suddenly taking a 'break' from his job and hanging out in Ponto Beach," Tam said, sounding worried. "He hasn't told me specifically what's going on, but I know enough. Is he asking you to do something you're uncomfortable with? Something risky? Something you'd hate doing, but you're doing because . . ." Tam ran out of steam, looking puzzled. "Wait, why would you do it at all?"

Emily shrugged. "Actually," she said, feeling her cheeks heat, "I think I'd like it a lot."

"Now, *that* sounds intriguing," Juanita said with a grin, and Lily chuckled.

"Nothing sexy!" Emily said, rolling her eyes. "The . . . work thing is interesting. That's all."

"But you've slept with him since he came back, right?" Tam pointed out, then held up her hands when Emily started to splutter out protests. "Sorry! I don't want to comment on my brother's sex life, trust me. But like Lily said: it's pretty obvious that something is going on with *you*, and I can already tell something's going on with *him*. I haven't seen him this happy or healthy or *relaxed* in years. And he's mostly spending time with you. I don't think he's that happy just because he's been playing video games with Tobin."

Lily snickered.

Emily was sure she was red as a tomato by this point. "It's not like we're back together or anything," she said. "It was . . . a momentary lapse of reason." *Okay, a couple of lapses.* "Anger banging, maybe?"

Juanita cooed. "Ooh. That can be hot."

"I know, right?" Lily sighed.

"Still not talking about my brother's sex life," Tam said, sounding vaguely ill. "Gross."

"And maybe some of it was nostalgia," Emily admitted.

And maybe some of it was the fact that we have always been ridiculously attracted to each other and, beyond that, genuinely care about each other. Even when we weren't in each other's lives.

She didn't know how to get that across, though, especially when she barely understood it herself. Instead, she shrugged.

"So when this little 'project' is finished," Juanita said, cutting through the crap, as always, "where does that leave the two of you?"

Emily swallowed hard against the lump in her throat. "I told him after I helped him, he needed to make sure I never saw him again."

Tam's face fell. "Oh, Em."

"It sounds harsh," Emily said. "And yeah, I was pretty pissed when I made the ultimatum. But I don't know how else to do this. It's like we can't be together and not . . . *be together*. We keep falling into the same traps."

"You mean the sex?" Lily asked.

"No. Well, that, yes. But that's always just the springboard," Emily said. "It starts with the sex, and then it's suddenly cozy snuggles, and caring little touches, and then I think . . . God, I miss this, I miss *him*. And then I remember that he's all about the job. He's never going to put me first. And I can't even blame him—we've both changed a lot since college. I understand needing to go to work, needing to handle your responsibilities, in a way I didn't before Dad died. But that also means I have too many responsibilities now to turn myself inside out for a guy who's going to prioritize his career, who will never have time for me, no matter how good his rationale is. I am certainly not going to do it for a guy who's going to be three thousand miles away while he's climbing the corporate ladder."

The other women looked crestfallen. Tam finally cleared her throat.

"You need to have that talk with Vinh," she said. "See how he feels about it."

"Or you can cut the cord now," Juanita pointed out, then winced at Tam's look of betrayal. "Hey, I love Vinh too, Tam, and I'm not trying to slam him with that. But I was angry as hell when he and Emily broke up and then he ghosted us all."

"He had his reasons for not coming back," Emily said, then bit her lip again, not knowing if he'd ever shared with Tam what he'd done to protect her.

"Whatever his reasons were, he hurt you," Juanita said. "Then he vanished."

"Hey, so did I," Tam pointed out. "I didn't come back for years."

"Same." Lily nodded, looking guilty.

"It's not entirely Vinh's fault. And I'll bet he knew that he came off as the villain in that whole thing, and he wanted the support to go to Emily. That kind of thing's hard. I'm not excusing him for dumping you, mind you," Tam added, with a stern nod. "I ripped him a new one when I found out. That's when he pulled on this Iceman persona that I swear he's worn and only made colder every progressive year."

"How do you know it's just a persona?" Juanita said. "Sure, he's always been sort of quietly funny, and he's great with the Herd, but he can also be a cold son of a bitch. Again, said with love."

Tam sighed. "Say it's a twin thing. Trust me. I know."

Emily knew, too, which was the damnable thing. "That doesn't help," she said. "What do I do in the meantime?"

"I think you should go," Lily said, surprising her. "I got too in my head, and I thought that things could only work a certain way before Tobin and I got together. My life got better because I took a chance. Maybe things can work out with you two, if you give it a chance."

"If that's what you want too," Juanita said. "I'm not as forgiving, I guess. If it were me, I *might* stay friends with him, but not until he'd groveled, and I'd kicked his ass a little more. And I might have anger banged him, especially if we had lava-hot chemistry."

"Still my brother, ew," Tam muttered.

"But I wouldn't leave the door open for a relationship. And I certainly wouldn't be helping him with some work thing just because he needs help!"

"He *is* paying me," Emily admitted.

"Oh." Juanita looked shrewd. "Better than your current job?"

"Yeah." She squirmed. "By kind of a lot, actually."

Juanita's eyebrow arched. Then she shrugged. "Then maybe go and finish whatever the project is," Juanita said. "Afterward, see how he reacts. If he's just 'Thanks' and then shifts back into work mode, well, you'll know your answer. And maybe don't sleep with him again."

Emily was surprised her cheeks hadn't caught fire. "If I go to New York, I'm gonna sleep with him," she muttered, rolling her eyes.

"Okay. But make it clear: this is short term, temporary, just a fling."

Emily nodded, determined, even as her heart knew that was bullshit. She was half in love with him all over again, and she didn't even want to think about how long it would take to fall the rest of the way.

"I'm biased because he's my brother, and you're one of my best friends. I don't want to see either of you hurting anymore," Tam said, patting Emily's shoulder. "Whatever way you land, though, I'll support you and just keep my fingers crossed that it doesn't end in disaster."

"That's nice and hopeful," Juanita said, nudging Tam, who laughed. "But she's right. Go with your gut. We've got your back."

Emily thought again how lucky she was that she had the Herd. She just had to go with her gut . . . which was currently tied in nervous knots.

They exited the office and wandered back to the party. Vinh found her, smiling. "Didn't know where you'd went."

"Just had to talk to my girls," she said, indicating Tam, Juanita, and Lily. "What's up?"

He handed her a small pink bakery box. She tilted her head, puzzled.

"What's this?"

"Since they sold out of them here," he said, "I was able to jog to the bakery before they closed and got you . . ."

She opened the lid, seeing glossy chocolate on a fat éclair. "Oh my God. I can't believe you ran and got this!"

"You wanted it," he said, as if that was reason enough. Then he reached out, tucked a lock of hair behind her ear, and traced his finger along her jawline for a second, as if they were alone. It was so simple, a touch he'd done a million times.

She closed her eyes.

What does your gut tell you?

It told her that she was probably jumping off a cliff—and like a lemming, she'd go.

"All right," she whispered. "I'll go to New York with you."

CHAPTER 27

Vinh knew that it wasn't the first time that Emily had flown first class, but it had been the first time in a long time. From what he could tell, she hadn't done much traveling of any sort in years—too busy working or taking care of her family. She'd fallen asleep on the trip, making soft little whooshes, tiny adorable not-snores. She'd rested her head on his shoulder, and he'd cradled her. Pampering her was incredibly satisfying, he'd noticed. He was looking forward to doing more of that.

He took her to his place, making sure to put Emily on his approved-visitor list. Her eyebrows jumped to her hairline when he did, and as they waited for the elevator, she murmured, "Who else is on that list?"

"Tam."

"That's it?"

He shrugged. "Nobody else visits." She looked sad at that, and he quickly headed that off. "It's fine. I don't want anybody else to visit, frankly. Besides, it's not like I'm home much."

She still looked sad. "Not even your parents?"

His laugh was rusty. "Yeah . . . no. I mean, my dad hasn't left Vietnam in a few years now, and even if he did, he wouldn't want to see my condo. He'd want to be wined and dined and put up in a really ritzy hotel." Okay, that came out more bitter than he'd intended.

"And your mom?"

He frowned. "She's busy." He didn't have the same complex emotions with her as he did with his father. On some level, he felt like he missed her, but he'd closed it off . . . like so many other things.

He typed in his code, unlocking his door, then led her inside. It was evening in December. The tall windows muted the bustle and blare of the streets below, but the lights of the city shone outside. The apartment felt a little stale, the way it often did when he was gone for a while. It was also, to his embarrassment, a little dusty.

"This is nice," she remarked, looking around curiously. "Stylish but kind of stripped down."

He shrugged. There was a comfortable couch, a big-screen TV over a fake fireplace, a coffee table. A sleek glass dining room table with black high-back chairs. A few art pieces that he'd bought on Etsy simply because he liked them. It was sparse, now that she mentioned it.

"How are you feeling? Hungry or anything?" he said.

"I could eat."

"Want to go out?" he said. "I know a number of good restaurants close by. A hell of a lot better than La Candela."

He winced as the words popped out unbidden. He hadn't meant to say that, hadn't meant to *reveal* that.

She arched an eyebrow at him. "Trying to impress me, Vinh?"

He let out a huff of breath, a self-deprecating chuckle. "Apparently. Thought I'd put that whole episode behind me, but remembering it the other day . . . yeah."

"I don't blame you. I could still kick Chris," she muttered, and he grinned. "But you have to know you don't have to impress me. I never cared about any of that. You *know* that. Why would you think any differently?"

"Your family was rich. Comparatively speaking," he corrected when she protested. "Your dad was always taking you guys to restaurants and on fancy vacations. And his friends were all wealthy. You went to computer camps and had all these lessons. And yeah, there was the Chris thing."

She let out a soul-deep sigh. "It took a while to sort things out after Dad died. He loved my mom and us so much he wanted to spoil us, give us anything we wanted. Especially Mom. She'd come from a rich family, you know? And he didn't. So when she picked him over those country-club asshole types, he felt like he had something to prove. She wasn't used to doing much of anything, and her family was pretty pissed that she'd chosen Dad, and Dad didn't want her to ever feel like she was missing something or that she'd made the wrong choice. He thought she walked on water." Emily walked over to his couch, then sank down into it. Instinctively, he went and got her a glass of water and put it on the coffee table in front of her. She picked it up with a grateful nod and took a sip.

He sat down beside her, stretching an arm along the back of the couch and resisting the impulse to pull her against him. "So that's how he ended up in debt," Vinh said, connecting the dots.

"He had two mortgages on the house," she said. "Bad ones. We had to sell his car, first off, my mom yelling and crying the whole time. Greg had reenrolled in college by that point, but he dropped out again—although, honestly, I don't think he was heartbroken about that. Obviously I'd already dropped out, but I knew that I wasn't going back in the fall . . . that I wasn't ever going back to NYU, to be honest. But when I talked to my mom about selling the house, she lost her damned mind."

"Because your dad bought it for her?" Vinh asked.

"Yeah. Sometimes, I feel like it's a weird shrine," Emily said, looking embarrassed. She took another sip before turning the water glass around and around in her hands. "Anyway, it became clear that we needed to band together if we were going to pull this off. Greg and I moved home and got whatever jobs we could. My mom fought it initially, but she did finally get retail jobs, even though she hates it and hides it from her family back East."

"Where are they again? Massachusetts?"

"Connecticut," Emily corrected, with a rueful grin. "We've never been close. My mom's sister and mother still live there. I don't think they dig at her anymore since my dad died, though."

"When did Greg move out?"

"Two years ago. I'd managed to refinance the mortgage and get the payments reasonable; we'd cut out a lot of expenses, and she's on a semistrict budget. She still slides a little, but she's a grown woman. I can't treat her like a child."

You can if she acts like one, Vinh thought but grimly kept his mouth shut. It wasn't his family—and as much as he loved Emily, it wasn't his battle to fight.

"Anyway, I moved out too. But then there was a *string* of bad luck, and Mom lost her job, and . . ." She let out a long exhalation. "Yeah. I moved back."

He was quiet again for a long minute. "Have you considered moving someplace else?" He held his hands up when she looked irritated. "Just . . . if you could get a better job. More money would mean you could send more money to your mom and brother if they needed it."

"There'd be a bunch of other factors, though," she pointed out. "First, deposit for my own rent. My car would have to be more reliable. Besides I don't know many other places."

While they were valid reasons, he couldn't help but feel like they were excuses. She was talking out of fear.

"You used to have your own dreams," Vinh said quietly. "What about them?"

She looked at him, and the cynicism in her eyes, so different than the bright, confident sparkle that he remembered, broke his heart.

"Ever since Dad's death, I feel like I've been walking a tightrope between two skyscrapers," she said. "I feel like I'm constantly one step away from being a splat on the pavement, and it wouldn't just affect me . . . it'd affect my brother and my mother. I can't do that. I *won't* do that."

He hated the hurt and hopelessness in her voice. He wanted to sweep her up, take all her problems away. Make all her dreams come true. But even if he could, he got the feeling she was in no place to accept, because she couldn't trust them.

He swallowed hard. Why had he asked her about moving, anyway? *You know why.*

"I wouldn't want to leave Ponto Beach, anyway," she tacked on, unwittingly burying his own hope. "Ponto Beach is home. I love it there—the pace, the people. The Herd has been my family all this time. I have my routines . . . game night at Tobin and Lily's, Bastille Day at Asad and Freddie's. Big Cheese Party or new menu tests at Tam and Josh's. Herdsgiving and various holiday parties at Uncommon Grounds."

He smiled now, wistful. "That sounds good," he admitted. "I really need to come home more."

He didn't even startle. Ponto Beach was home, he realized. He hadn't appreciated it as much when he'd lived there, but this last visit, even with the boa constrictor shenanigans, had been one of the best times in his life . . . in no small part due to Emily.

He wouldn't want to lose that either. He *didn't* want to lose that.

She leaned forward, putting the glass on the coffee table, then shifted to look at him. "What're you thinking?" she asked, resting her head on his arm.

He stroked her face, then trailed his fingers down her neck and over her shoulder. "About how much I missed you," he said. "All the Herd, but you specifically."

She grinned. "Yeah, well, we missed you," she said. "Granted, I didn't realize how much until you pinned me up against that wall, but . . ."

He let out a bark of laughter. "Are you objectifying me?"

"I think objectifying you is pointing out you've got abs like a pack of Hawaiian rolls and you're cut like frickin' glass," she said. "*Ngh.* Seriously. Henleys with the sleeves rolled up, or gray sweatpants . . . holy crap, you are *hot.*"

He laughed some more, finally gathering her up the way he wanted to. "Yeah, well, you're still gorgeous," he said.

She blew a raspberry at him. "Dude, I hacked off my own hair, my skincare regimen is not wearing makeup and splashing water on my face, and all my muscle definition comes from clicking a mouse," she pointed out. "Also, I apparently have a terminal case of resting bitch face."

He laughed harder, and she lightly smacked his chest.

"Then we're a good match," he said. "And I like the faces you make."

Her eyes heated, and he knew she was thinking of exactly the same face he was.

"You hungry?"

"Yes," she said. "But not for food. Why don't you work up my appetite, and then maybe we could order a pizza?"

He smiled broadly. Then he got to his feet and tugged her to hers before tossing her over his shoulder and carrying her to his bedroom.

CHAPTER 28

This is it.

The next night was exactly what they'd planned. Vinh had made a call, and they'd gone around the city, pulling together the accoutrements of their plan.

Emily felt like her heart was going to beat its way out of her chest, that her pulse was probably cartoonishly obvious in her throat. She forced herself to slow her breathing before she passed out. She was wearing a surprisingly believable black wig, goth makeup, and a fake nose ring and some tattoos on her arms. She was wearing a cleaning person's jumpsuit, the flash drive tucked safely in an easily accessible pocket.

She didn't look like herself at all—which was the point.

"You're not going to get me in trouble, right?" Vinh's friend, Carlos, had said, looking nervous. He was taking a big risk letting her in the building with his cleaning crew. But Vinh and Carlos had known each other for years, and Vinh was going to pay his daughter's tuition for the first year or something. Emily didn't know the details, and she wasn't sure she wanted to know.

"I'll make sure you don't get in trouble," she promised. Hell, she didn't want to get in trouble either. Hence the racing heart and enough adrenaline to go up to the twenty-fourth floor via the stairs, if need be. Thankfully, she didn't need to.

Vinh had wanted to get those spy cameras and the earpiece-speaker thing, like they had in the movies, so he could guide her through the building and "talk her through." Unfortunately, that sort of thing really only worked in the movies, and they weren't in *Mission: Impossible.* Sure, there was technology that they could've used, but it was notoriously unreliable—and they didn't have the time to test and mess around. He was running out of time—she knew that.

She wanted to help. No: she was *going* to help Vinh out of this mess.

So instead, she'd had him draw a map of his floor, to the best of his ability. She had the man's name, which would be on his office door somewhere. And then she'd go in.

She shuffled, pushing the cleaning cart. Carlos nodded to her, indicating where she ought to work. She cleaned a few offices first. For the first time, she was grateful that she'd actually spent some time cleaning offices when she'd needed a second job. It had been exhausting work, mostly because of the hours and the lack of sleep with her first job. But she knew the drill, and after a quick glance at the checklist Carlos had given her, she found herself efficiently wiping down surfaces, vacuuming, dusting the large office plants that they'd plunked down here and there.

She noticed that there were some cameras in the main offices, where there were low-walled cubicles. But the actual closed-door offices, where middle management like their target sat, didn't seem to have any. Probably because upper management wanted the ability to keep an eye on the underlings to make sure they weren't fucking around all day . . . but they wanted plausible deniability and protection, especially anywhere a client might have a conversation with a consultant. It was for the client's protection, not necessarily the employee's.

Still . . . couldn't be too careful. Just because they wanted it to *look* like there were no cameras didn't mean there *weren't* any.

She finally made it to Mike Hanover's office. Her mouth felt like the Mojave, and her nerves jangled. She did the same thing: wiped down the surfaces, every single speck of dust on the dark-wood credenza and the wide expensive-looking desk. She also very carefully examined the picture frames, the pencil cup—the places where, if a spy camera was going to be placed, it would look the most natural and be the most effective. It's what she would've done. But no, everything looked like it was in the clear.

She finally allowed herself a small smile.

There, on the desk, was a sleek new machine . . . an HP EliteBook, last year's version. Just *sitting* there. Seriously. It continually shocked her how many top companies absolutely biffed it when it came to security.

She felt like something out of a spy movie as she carefully dusted (and, more importantly, *shut*) the privacy blinds to his office. Then she quickly moved over to the laptop, pulling a thumb drive out of her pocket. She jammed it in a USB port, then hard rebooted it. Just like that, it would prevent the need for a password—it would work around it and install the keylogger.

She vacuumed as her malware did its work. It would place the software that would record everything the guy typed, giving them access to any passwords he used. It also would require him to retype his passwords for everything, a little bonus feature she'd introduced to ensure they got what they needed.

By the time the drive had done its job, the office was probably cleaner than it had been in months. And his computer was completely compromised.

She pulled the drive, closing the laptop and then cleaning it for good measure. Then she opened the blinds.

There was a security guard standing there.

Her heart stopped, and she gasped.

"Hey," he said, gesturing to her.

She gathered her cart and tried to collect her thoughts. What the hell was *he* doing here? Carlos said that the security guards tended to stay in their little booth in the lobby, watching the cameras. Maybe this guy was new? Maybe he was suspicious? What the hell?

She stepped out of Mike's office, unsure of how to play it. A "go to hell" sort of attitude, to go with the whole alternative vibe she was rocking? Super humble and vaguely scared?

What the hell did he want?

"You're new, huh?" the guard asked.

She nodded and shrugged at the same time. She'd go with silent for now. Most people, especially when trying to avoid trouble, wound up getting themselves *into* trouble simply because they couldn't keep their mouths shut.

"I thought so." The guard was wearing a gray-and-blue uniform with a tie and a name tag that said SKIP. It looked very much like a knockoff police uniform—which, she supposed, it was. "I haven't seen you around."

She shrugged again.

"Skip" grinned like a circus clown. "I pay attention to these things, y'know. This is *my* building, and I keep track of what happens here."

This wasn't sounding good. She tried to look polite but also glanced around for Carlos, who seemed to be working the far end of the floor.

"I make a point to know all of the cleaning *ladies*."

She blinked.

Oh, for fuck's sake.

Was he *hitting* on her?

He leaned against a cubicle wall, his grin turning what she supposed was charming. "Yeah. I saw that you were doing a hell of a job. Better than even Carlos."

She sincerely doubted that.

"You're not like the usual cleaning women," he noticed. "Didn't think he hired white women. Ha!"

She did not like Skip. But so far, he wasn't accusing her of any-thing—and she needed to keep it that way. "It's a trial basis," she said finally, hoping to shut him up. He was taking her silence as invitation, and she needed that to stop immediately. "As a favor. I don't know if I'll stick with it."

"Oh, you should," Skip said. "I'd hate to have found you just to have you disappear."

Funny you should put it that way, she thought, tamping down a nervous giggle. No, no, no. She needed to keep her shit together for just a while longer . . .

"Although if you decided to," Skip said, "maybe you should give me your number. So I wouldn't have to wait for you to clean the offices to see you. And I *would* like to see you."

"I have a boyfriend," she said immediately, without thought. And then blinked at herself. Yes, it was an easy excuse to use, one she'd used plenty in the past . . . largely because "I have a boyfriend" tended to be more accepted than "I'm not interested," since that tended to only make them try harder. But in this case, it wasn't just a handy excuse. She had, on a gut level, recoiled.

Because she had *Vinh.*

Now her heart was thumping in ways that had nothing to do with the heist at hand. But of course . . . if she didn't care about him, have really deep feelings for him—why the hell else would she risk every-thing, *jail* time for God's sake, if she didn't love him?

"You guys, you know, solid?"

She rolled her eyes before she could stop herself, and he looked irritated. "Yes, we're solid," she said.

"Yeah, well, can't blame a guy for trying." Skip's smile turned sly. "Maybe you could give me your number and we could just be friends? Talk, maybe hang out sometimes?" She arched an eyebrow at him, and he laughed. "Hey. Worth a try. I shoot my shot. Good luck with the job thing."

He ambled away, whistling, waving a quick acknowledgment to Carlos. Carlos hurried over to her. "You okay? What was that? Did he suspect something?" Carlos hissed.

She shook her head. "No. He was just hitting on me."

"He *what*?" Carlos seemed scandalized.

"Sounds like he might do that to all the women you employ," she noted. "You might keep an eye on that."

Carlos's expression turned dark, and he muttered in Spanish. After a calming moment, he switched back to English. "Don't worry," he promised. "I will take care of it."

With that handled, she helped Carlos finish the floor, then another one. It was less suspicious. By the time she was done, her body was a little sore, but she still had adrenaline going through her like speed. She went out to Carlos's van to put away the supplies. Then Carlos drove her to Vinh's place and dropped her off.

Vinh was waiting, completely alert. "Are you okay? How did it go?"

She was exhausted but also wired.

"The program's installed," she said with a tempered caution. "Now, all we can do is wait."

CHAPTER 29

Vinh had felt like he was crawling out of his skin from the moment Emily had gone off with Carlos to pull off their caper. He wished he could've gone with them. He'd even gone so far as to suggest wearing a wig and fake mustache himself, but Emily had dissolved into peals of laughter, and he had to admit—she probably had a point. He was so tense he was practically vibrating like a tuning fork.

He'd tried to calm himself down by cleaning his apartment. He tended to do that when he got back from any work trip anyway. He didn't use a housekeeper or cleaning service—Emily would probably point out it was trust issues—but, like taking care of the animals and the plants, it was also meditative. With that in mind, he'd stopped in the middle of dusting to shoot Hayden a quick text.

VINH: Hey, how are the animals doing? Everything okay?

HAYDEN: Well, Herman got out, believe it or not.

Vinh winced, remembering his "snake wrangling" in the middle of Greg's apartment.

VINH: Yeah, I can believe it.

HAYDEN: He went great escape on you, too, huh? At least he didn't try to eat Sonic or anything.

VINH: I'm assuming he's back in the cage.

HAYDEN: Well, I let him hang out with me for a little bit . . . gave him a break from the box. But that's just cause he knows me, and it wasn't for very long.

VINH: He didn't get too cold or anything? How does his breathing sound?

HAYDEN: Awwww. Are you worried about your buddies?

Vinh frowned. Strangely, he was. He would've thought it'd be a cold day in hell before he got attached to a snake—especially an eight-foot boa constrictor—but here they were.

VINH: I feel responsible. That's just being a good caretaker.

HAYDEN: You keep telling yourself that. And it's like one o'clock out there. Why are you texting me? Go bug Emily! *wiggles eyebrows*

Vinh hadn't told Hayden why he needed to go to New York with Emily, and Hayden's expression had been full of mischievous speculation. He'd just said he needed Emily's help on something and ignored some innuendo. He wondered if Emily would ever tell them what had happened.

He wondered if maybe *he* should share with them, actually. It wasn't like he couldn't trust them. After all they'd done for Emily over the years—after all they'd done for him and Tam, for that matter—he suddenly didn't know why he hadn't before.

He could hear the code being entered in his door before it opened, and he was on his feet, rushing to Emily. "Are you okay? How did it go?"

She looked tired, but her eyes sparkled, reminding him of the Emily of old. "The program's installed. Now, all we can do is wait."

He felt a punch of triumph, even as he was chomping at the bit. "How long?"

"No telling," she said. "Not till Monday, at least, and we'll have to see if he does it himself or if we have to goose him. God! That was fun. It was like being in an Ocean's movie, or *Hackers*, except with accurate tech depictions. I fucking *loved* that!"

"I can tell," he said, smiling. "I don't think I've seen you this happy since high school."

"I haven't been this happy in a long time," she admitted.

"Maybe you could do it for a job," he nudged gently. "Certified Ethical Hackers are a thing, you know."

"Yes, I know," she said, rolling her eyes. "But that means training and taking the exam, and none of that's cheap, and who has time? Now let me get this crap off. This wig is itchy as hell."

He trailed her as she headed for the en suite bathroom in his bedroom. "And it went smoothly? Nobody stopped you? No cameras?"

"Other than a security guard hitting on me, it was fine," she said with a laugh, tugging off her wig and the fake nose ring and putting them on the counter. She ran her fingers through her hair.

He felt jealousy like a punch. "He hit on you?" he asked. "What was his name?"

She looked at him over her shoulder coquettishly. "Why? You gonna get him fired when you get reinstated or something?"

Since he'd been thinking exactly that—after the brief *I will pound him into putty* thought had been shoved out of his brain and more-rational thought had taken over—he stayed silent.

Her eyes widened. "Holy shit! Vinh the caveman. Who knew?"

He grimaced, looking away and feeling his face heat, adding insult to injury. "Who indeed," he muttered.

Once his face cooled and he felt more in control of his emotions, he looked back and almost choked on his tongue.

She'd been wearing jeans and a T-shirt under the cleaning jumpsuit Carlos had provided. Now, she'd stripped down to mismatched underwear that made his mouth water. She massaged her scalp, groaning and arching her body like she was stretching.

He went from zero to straight-up hard in less than a second.

"I know it's over, but I still have so much adrenaline in my system I feel like I could deadlift a hippo or something," she said around a chuckle. "I'm going to take a shower."

He nodded, not currently capable of thought.

She reached for the clasp of the bra between her breasts. "Join me?"

Now he was on his feet before his brain had caught up with him. "Hell yes," he breathed, stripping out of his own clothes and leaving them in a messy trail behind him as he rushed to the bathroom.

She giggled some more, taking the bra off, then wriggling out of her panties, leaving her gloriously naked. She'd lost some weight, her breasts slight, her body sharper angles nipping into her waist. She still had those freckles that he adored. The slight appendix scar. The tattoo of Bad Badtz-Maru, the pissed-off penguin, high on her right shoulder blade.

She turned on the dual showerheads, making a purring noise of approval, then stepped into the steamy cascade. He followed, reaching for her before he'd even closed the glass door fully behind himself. She tilted her head up and looped her arms around his neck, pressing her wet body to his, and he groaned.

"Let's get you clean," he said, his voice thrumming with promise, and he was rewarded with a playful quicksilver smile. He got the bottle of bodywash, then poured some in his palms and proceeded to rub every inch of her, slowly and thoroughly, lingering over her breasts, the nape of her neck, and between her legs. Her sounds, low and needy, like she couldn't help herself, went straight to his gut. And a bit lower, he thought with a grin.

"Your turn," she said with a wink, then got some bodywash of her own. She slicked it over his chest and shoulders, slowly and lovingly paying attention to his forearms, his hips. His ass.

"Missing anything?" he finally prompted, his voice strained.

She tossed her head back and laughed. "So dirty," she said, her voice pure seduction. Then she finally took him in hand, and he jolted forward involuntarily. Her soft palm and fingers felt so incredibly good around him he thought he'd lose his mind.

He reached down, finding her hard nub, and started stroking, guided by her gasps and pants of pleasure. She continued working him, a slow and steady rhythm. They moved together, sometimes awkwardly, but even that made it more real, more special.

He couldn't wait anymore. He leaned down, kissing her hard, his tongue fencing with hers as they shuddered and slid against each other.

He felt the rush of hot wetness between her thighs, felt her body wrap around him as she shuddered and leaned against him. She stroked him, and with one last perfect squeeze, he felt his orgasm hit him out of nowhere, like the damned Kool-Aid Man. The two of them collapsed against the smooth tile wall.

"You," she said when they'd caught their breath, "are a menace. I don't think I've ever had shower sex like that."

He grinned. "Same. Actually, I can't remember the last time I had shower sex." He frowned, his brain trying desperately to come up with any coherent thought, much less process memories. "I think it was you, now that I'm thinking of it."

"That trip to Big Bear?" she said, laughing.

"When we took turns freezing or boiling, and the thing was smaller than a phone booth?" He added, laughing too. They rinsed off and then stepped out. He wrapped her in a fluffy towel, then kissed her nose. "Yeah. This is definitely better."

She tilted her head, staring at him. "I think I had six orgasms that day. And night, obviously."

He snickered. "I was eighteen," he pointed out. "I had the refractory period of . . . I don't know. Something with a very short refractory period." When she burst into more peals of laughter, he shook his head. "Shut up. I can't think right now either."

"Ha. I haven't had that many orgasms since then either," she said. "Well . . . not with another person, anyway."

"Really." He was curious as hell. And his body was trying desperately to rally.

She wiggled her eyebrows again, then tucked the towel. "We've got leftover pizza, right? I am *starving*."

Which was how they wound up on his couch, naked, eating pizza and quarreling over what to watch.

"I've heard really good things about *Wheel of Time*," she mused.

"It is good," he said. "I binged it on a flight to Sydney."

"We should watch something you haven't seen, though," she grumped before chomping into the pizza. "Oh! How about that Korean zombie show?"

"Stressful," he said. "I don't really do zombie stuff."

"That's too bad. We watched *Alive* and *Train to Busan* as a movie night at Josh and Tam's, and it was fun. They had theme food." She grinned.

"I don't even want to know," he groaned. "How about action? Something with lots of explosions and very little story line?"

"Or we could go the other way," she said thoughtfully. "Animated. There are some really good movies."

They went back and forth until the pizza was gone and they'd run the gamut of choices. Finally, she grinned.

"You realize, of course, that we're not going to actually watch anything?"

He studied her with a matching grin. "Because it's almost two in the morning?"

She leaned forward, her breath whispering in his ear. "Because I'm about to jump you on this incredibly comfortable couch," she said. "And we're going to see if we beat that record, age be damned."

His body, which had been slowly getting back into fighting shape, quickly responded by tenting his towel.

"I am nothing if not competitive," he remarked, and she laughed before tearing off his towel and climbing him like a tree.

For the record, they conked out after two more, which Vinh felt pretty proud of. He nuzzled her that morning at nine. She snuggled back against him, cuddling his morning wood with her ass and almost making his eyes cross.

"Good morning," she said, her voice sleep rough and sexy as hell.

"Very good morning," he agreed, pressing small open-mouthed kisses between her shoulder blades and at the nape of her neck, which he knew were her erogenous zones. She was gasping and wriggling in no time. "Wanna go for four? See if we can work our way up to six?"

"I suppose I ought to let you."

Her phone buzzed, and he froze. "That's not the alarm, is it?" he asked. "Because I can't imagine Mike went back to the office to get his laptop. Do you think somebody else is using it? Like a dodge?"

She picked up her screen, then groaned, flopping back onto the pillow. "It's my mother," she said.

He winced. Well, that killed his ardor.

"I have to get this," she said. "It's six in the morning there, and I'm not supposed to be back until tomorrow, but . . ."

"Of course," he said.

She answered it. "Mom, you okay?"

There was a flurry of sound on the other end of the line, and he could feel all her muscles tense like piano wire.

"Slow down, slow down. Is there any water gushing or anything? Is there flooding?"

Now Vinh sat up, concerned.

"All right. Let me . . . it's okay, it'll be okay," she soothed. "We'll figure it out, okay? Let me call somebody, and I'll make sure that they're there as soon as possible. Just hang in there."

He heard her mother's voice, louder now. Something about coming home.

"My flight's Sunday," Emily reminded her, then sighed. "I don't know what it would take or what it would cost or if it's even possible to get a flight today . . ."

He grabbed a pad of paper on his nightstand and a pen, which he kept nearby since he was often hit with solutions to problems just as he was falling asleep. He quickly scrawled *If you need me to, I can make it happen.*

Emily read it, then nodded, looking grateful. "Okay, Mom, I'll come back. Might be late tonight, all right? And I'll take care of it. Yeah. Love you too."

She hung up, then looked at Vinh. "Apparently the house has no hot water, and she can't shower or wash dishes. She says that there's some water puddling around the water heater."

Vinh nodded, even though he'd never owned a house and had never done plumbing repairs. "You should probably call Hayden," he said. "And I'll make sure we get a flight back, if I have to get a private jet. I can pull in a few favors."

Her eyes widened. "Really? And you're coming too?"

"Why wouldn't I?"

"Because you don't need to?" she said.

"You and I probably need to do this face to face. Privacy, InfoSec, what have you," he said, totally pulling an excuse out of his ass because he was *not ready to let this go*. He didn't think that was what she wanted to hear, and he still hadn't figured out how to convince her to give him a chance. "Besides, I still need to take care of those animals myself."

She smiled, even though it was shaky and just a little bit shy. "Okay," she conceded.

He was running out of time. His career was still on the line, but in the course of saving it, he'd discovered something more important to save. Now, he just had to figure out a way to convince her to take a leap of faith.

CHAPTER 30

True to his word, Vinh had managed to get them a private jet, something Emily had never ridden in before. It was ridiculously opulent, and she would've enjoyed it a hell of a lot more if she wasn't freaking out about her mom. She'd driven to Greg's and dropped Vinh off there, and then she'd headed home.

It was late afternoon, and Hayden was still there. "What's going on?" she asked quickly without her mother around to hear.

Hayden rubbed his hands on his frayed, hole-ridden jeans. "Yeah, she's gonna need a new water heater," he said, sounding genuinely apologetic. "I hate being the bearer of bad news, but this is over twelve years old. There are leaks. And when was the last time you flushed the system?"

Emily's heart sank. "Um . . . never? I didn't even know that was a thing you were supposed to do."

Hayden looked perturbed. "Yeah. It helps, anyway, in prolonging the life of your tank. And see that rust around the spigot?" She nodded. "That's definitely not a good sign. It's making weird noises, and it's heating slow, and it should be replaced before it starts leaking. The last thing you need is a water leak *and* mold problems."

Emily winced. That was very true. "How much is a new water heater going to run us?"

"For a tank water heater?" Hayden shrugged. "Last I checked, somewhere between eight hundred and twenty-five hundred dollars."

"Thanks, Hayden," Emily said, even as her chest felt like someone had put a fifty-pound concrete block on it. "I owe you."

"You're Herd, you're family," he said with a wink. "How's it going with the animals?"

"I think Vinh's feeding Herman today," she said. She knew that he was approaching the whole business of thawing out the prekilled prey that he'd taken out of the freezer. He'd been prepping for it by watching lots of YouTube videos the whole flight home, in his usual intense, down-to-business way, and she could tell he was not thrilled.

"Then I'll go wander over there and help out," he said, with a grin. "For Vinh's sake, and for Herman's. Take care."

She hugged him goodbye, then braced herself and walked back in the house. "Mom?"

"In here, dear!"

She walked into the living room to find her mother eating some takeout. She'd loved cooking, loved entertaining, when they were kids, but since Emily's father's death, she hadn't done much of it, insisting that it was too much work. Unfortunately, eating out wasn't really great for the budget, which Emily had discussed with her. Her mother looked a little guilty as she quickly swallowed her dumpling.

"I was so stressed, so I got a craving for Chinese food," she said. "I've got tons of beef broccoli and that walnut chicken I like. And some fried rice. And there are fortune cookies!"

"I'm good," Emily said. If anything, considering how much the water heater was going to cost, she felt a bit nauseated. "Hayden says we need a new water heater."

"Ooh! Can we get one of those tankless ones?" her mother asked, her cornflower-blue eyes twinkling as she smiled. "I have always wanted one of those! They say you never run out of hot water with one, and you know I like long showers and the occasional bubble bath."

"Yes, I know," Emily replied, thinking of the last water bill. *Ugh.* She hated being the bad guy in this, absolutely *hated* it. "I think the tankless ones are more expensive. I'm going to have to do some research. But I can't right now. I'm still helping Vinh with his . . . project," she said.

Her mother sniffed. "Aren't you done with that? Isn't that why he dragged you off to New York?"

"Well, yes," she said. "It was part of it, anyway."

"He wants you back." Her mother sounded disappointed.

Emily scoffed. "I'm helping him," she corrected gently, even as part of her wondered: *Did* he want her back? And what would that mean?

What could that even *look* like, if it was possible?

She was too in her own head, so she missed her mother's next statement. Her mother's forehead wrinkled. "Sorry, what was that?"

"I said"—and her mother's voice was soft but sharp—"Vinh isn't good for you."

Emily reared back in shock. "What?"

"I'm not saying Vinh's not a good person," her mother said. "You know your father and I adored Vinh when you two were dating. That is, until he broke your heart. Then, I could've . . . brained him with my cast-iron skillet!"

Hearing her diminutive mother declare violence in her high voice was so ridiculous Emily couldn't help the shocked giggle that came out. Her mother rolled her eyes.

"Well, at least give him a piece of my mind," she conceded. "You'll understand when you have kids of your own, believe me."

"Yeah, I wouldn't hold your breath on that one," Emily muttered. That wasn't a battle she wanted to have anytime soon. She was more than willing to throw her brother under the bus if her mother started demanding grandchildren.

"The thing I was most disappointed about was that Vinh just left you in the lurch," her mother continued. "Your father would *never* have left me. Not if he had the choice. He would've stayed by my side, helping me weather all the ups and downs of life. He was that way about you kids too. He just loved us all so much." Her mother's eyes were damp. "You deserve that, Emily. You deserve to be with someone who puts you first, not his career, not his standing."

Emily had heard this before from her mother. Not about Vinh—or at least, not *just* about Vinh—but for the first time, Emily rolled the words over in her mind.

"Vinh had his own reasons for breaking up with me," she said. "Ones that had to do with *his* family. It's unfair of me to insist that he help me take care of mine when he had to take care of his."

Her mother's expression was skeptical. "I don't think . . ."

"And Dad did love us," Emily said. "But he loved his career too. He wanted to be a success. You can't blame Vinh for wanting that too."

Now her mother's expression turned mulish, and she jabbed her fork in the box of fried rice. "It's different."

"How?"

"It just is!" her mother grumbled, then sighed. "Let's not fight."

"We're not fighting, we're just talking."

"Well, then, let's stop talking," her mother said. "Oh, I know! We can watch a new movie. I wanted to rent that new rom-com movie—how about that?"

"Mom," Emily said, sitting next to her mother on the couch, "we still need to talk about the water heater. I'll do the research, but I think we've got to be ready to replace that sooner rather than later. We okay on the house-repair fund?"

Emily helped pay the bills, but she didn't have access to the accounts. She had to ask her mother—or in some cases, tell her mother—to pay things. This sometimes made her nervous, since her mother had left all financial matters to her father prior to his death and had been overwhelmed when she'd become executor of his will so unexpectedly.

Her mother squirmed. "How much do we need?"

"Probably around two thousand," Emily said, with a sigh. It was easier to ask for more, then look for something cheaper. If she told her the lowest amount, her mother would ask, "Why can't we get something less expensive?" even as she wanted the top of the line. It was a conundrum.

"Oh." Her mother paled. "That's . . . kind of a lot."

Emily grimaced. "How much is in the house fund?"

"I'm not sure."

"I'll look over the accounts, if you want."

"I can handle it," her mother replied, almost before Emily finished her sentence . . . which told Emily there was less than there should be.

"You didn't use the house fund for anything else, did you?"

Her mother now reddened. "There was a sale on Lancôme. I only got one bottle of my favorite moisturizer and that revitalizing eye cream."

Which would've been well over a hundred dollars. "That's it?"

"It's my money," her mother said, crossing her arms.

"Yes, but *I live here too*," Emily said.

Her mother's eyes filled again, looking like wet violets. "Please, let's don't fight."

Her mother was only fifty-five. Emily knew it was hard for her mom, after the life she'd led, to shift gears to this, going from coddled and, frankly, spoiled by Emily's doting father to suddenly being thrust into handling everything.

People do this all the time, though.

Emily didn't want to judge her mother. Her mother was who she was, and despite being somewhat flighty, she was sweet, and caring, and kind. But she was also sheltered, and she acted almost childlike sometimes. Greg was still working things out. Emily didn't have the same hang-ups. She was more like her father than either her mother or brother. When she decided something needed to be taken care of, she took care of it.

Unlike her father, she knew her limits and didn't get them even further in debt to do that, though. Instead, she'd worked to fix things, get them out of the hole. It was a tough thing . . . made tougher by the fact that her mother couldn't seem to get on the same page as her.

Emily took a deep breath. "No movie for me tonight. I'm going to go back to Greg's," she said.

"To Vinh," her mother translated.

"Yes." Emily tilted her chin up. "You don't have to be happy about it. And maybe I'll get my heart broken. But I want to do this."

"Well, I can't stop you," her mother said. "But when you come back here feeling miserable, I'll have ice cream waiting, okay?"

"All right," Emily agreed, then headed out.

CHAPTER 31

"This must be what a stakeout feels like," Emily murmured, snuggling against Vinh but keeping her eyes glued to her laptop monitor. It was five in the morning on a Monday. Ordinarily, she'd be starting her shift, so it wasn't that different. Being in her underwear and one of Vinh's T-shirts was different, though. He was just in boxers, heat radiating off of him like a sunlamp, smelling like a dream.

And, based on firsthand knowledge from last night, tasting even better.

"I think *stakeout* might be pushing it." Vinh laughed, smoothing her hair out of her face before cupping her chin and kissing just below her jawline. "Not unless cops have a next-level definition of 'This is my partner' anyway."

She grinned.

"But I get what you mean," he added. "I can't wait to nail this bastard and pay him back for getting me fired and possibly setting me up for jail. This guy is about to be the definition of fucking around and finding out."

Emily nodded, feeling the cold determination at odds with his cozy warmth. Of course this was important to him—she couldn't blame him. Still, she couldn't help but remember her mother's words.

You deserve to be with someone who puts you first, not his career, not his standing.

She bit her lip. Her mother was right about what she deserved—but wrong about Vinh. She had to be.

Wasn't she?

"You okay?" Vinh asked. She glanced over to see him looking at her with concern.

"Yeah. Yes! Sure," she said, frowning and focusing. "Just feels weird calling in sick."

"You didn't have to," he said.

"I kind of did," she pointed out, "since Mike didn't work this weekend, from the looks of it, and you're going to need me to help move that money quickly when we get that account log-in."

"True." Vinh sighed. "How long do you think it'll take?"

"Hopefully not that long." She started typing, her fingers flying over the keyboard. "It's eight o'clock over there. Don't you come in early?"

"I'm usually there an hour before he is, I think," Vinh said. "When I'm in the office. He travels, but not as much as I do. Did," he edited, his forehead creasing.

"All right. Looks like he's logging in," she said after about twenty minutes of waiting, during which Vinh made them coffee and she propped up pillows so they could stay in bed, laptops on a few bed trays she'd brought from the house. She felt those hacker senses tingling, a slow build of excitement. She cracked her knuckles. "Time to go phishing."

She logged in to the master account she'd created thanks to Mr. Schmonk's low-security password, then created another company email, this one now looking like it came from IT. She made sure it sounded apologetic but impersonal—she'd seen tons of those from the various companies her support center worked with—warning him that his computer no longer had stored passwords, so he'd need to reenter them all. She knew this because besides the keylogger, she'd added a tiny bit of malware that had cleared his caches. She even copied his assistant to make it seem official.

"Won't that give him more evidence to track back to you?" Vinh said, sounding worried.

"By the time we get the money, it won't matter." She was almost gleeful with anticipation. "We're going to see what he signs in to and do some digging. If he doesn't go into the account right away, I've got another way to goose that out of him."

Vinh immediately looked relieved. His trust in her made her puff up proudly as she drank the coffee he'd made for her—nice and strong with lots of sugar, just the way she liked it.

"What's he doing?"

"Cursing, probably," she said, her eyes scanning through the plain text lines that were scrolling quickly across the keylogger software screen. "Good thing there's practically no delay on this. You got your laptop ready?"

He nodded, opening the personal laptop he'd brought from his apartment in New York. "Got it."

"All right. Let's see . . . first thing is his email." She rattled off the log-in and password.

"Okay."

"Don't type anything," she quickly warned him. "You don't want to accidentally tip him off that there's someone else in there!"

"I got this," Vinh said, his voice sounding grim. "But I want to see what he's been dealing with."

"He wouldn't be foolish enough to document, would he?"

"Not him. Maybe someone else. Only one way to find out, and I want to know before we get the money in case we don't have much of a window."

As Vinh started sifting through the emails, making thoughtful little noises, she copied and pasted more log-ins and passwords. Social media accounts. *Bank* accounts. Then . . .

"Hey, do you make calls through your computer?"

Vinh didn't look over, too intent on scrolling through the folders on the screen. "Not really. We have satellite phones in the field, and if there's service, it's simply easier to use. I might if there's Wi-Fi but no cell somehow, but I doubt it. Why?"

"Because he's using a recorder," she said. "He's routing calls through his computer and keeping files."

Now Vinh turned. "What?"

"I don't even think he's talking to a client," she said, doing a quick search in another window. "That's a number for someone else in the office."

Vinh's frown deepened. "We're going to need to dig deeper into that. Jesus, I thought *I* was paranoid."

After Mike got off whatever phone call he'd been on (and she'd gotten the log-in for remote access to his recordings, downloading the latest), she waited to see if he'd go to the account. But no. After posting some photos on his social media (which was *set to public*—what was wrong with this dude?) of his "Holiday in Sag Harbor" with a plastic-perfect wife and two kids, he *then* logged on to another site—the tastefully named What She Doesn't Know.

"Eww," she said, shuddering with revulsion.

"What is it?" Vinh asked, finally looking over.

"He's on a . . . not a dating site, exactly. But a *cheating* site," she said. "An expensive one, sure, but I'd still bet that most of the 'women' he chats with are bots. The guy *literally* posted a picture of his wife not five minutes ago! That's just . . . gah!"

Vinh shook his head. "I knew he was an asshole, but I didn't know he was *this* much of an asshole."

"And I'll bet he has Tinder on his phone too," she said, "and lies about being single."

"Would not surprise me." Vinh rubbed his temples. "He's got some emails that suggest he's dipped his pen in the company ink, too, as it were."

"No." Emily looked over at an open email. Then she recoiled even harder. "What the *fuck*?"

"Yup. Looks like he's blackmailing a woman in contracts that he slept with, threatening her job if she didn't put a questionable deal through." Vinh looked a little green. "He took a video. She didn't know."

Emily felt like her hair was going to catch fire she was so angry. "Oh, this asshole is going *down*."

"He's got a whole folder here called 'Dirt,' and from what I can tell, it's stuff he's got on other people." Vinh's voice was cold as a glacier. "I can see how he's gotten some of his deals. It's not just that his family's rich. The man has been cheating the system from the jump and truly believes he will never get caught or get punished."

"Yeah, well, that stops today."

After an increasingly sickening hour, she finally sent one more email. This one was mocked up to look like the cryptocurrency wallet, telling him that there was a new computer logging in to his account.

"Won't he see through that?" Vinh asked, puzzled. "That's a pretty standard phishing technique. Also, won't it alert him to when we *do* break into his account?"

"Don't worry," she said, confidence ringing through her like a bell. "I got this."

"I know you do," Vinh said. "I just don't get it."

"Let me walk you through." She felt a rush as she typed. "This is going to reassure him: no typos—which are deliberate in phishing scams, by the way, to weed out gullible people—explicit instructions *not* to give his password to anyone and change it immediately, contact them if there's a problem. He won't. Because he'll be reassured that everything sounds just like what a real email would say. He assumes he doesn't have anything to worry about because you're out of the picture and nobody else is gonna touch him." She smiled viciously as she sent the email off.

Was it wrong, she wondered, that she felt so fulfilled, so damned *happy*, doing this? She felt like a combination of Moiraine Sedai (she'd wound up watching *Wheel of Time* after all) and just a cyber badass. She loved figuring out the puzzle. And she loved, loved, *loved* making sure bad guys got what was coming to them.

It's going to be hard to go back to the support center.

She swallowed. They were just about done. That meant that her time with Vinh was coming to a close too. He had a career to go back to. And she had . . .

What?

Her heart sank, and she shook her head. No. She didn't have time for that. *Focus on the job.*

It took fifteen minutes. Then she watched as he frantically typed in the account log-in and password.

"And now he's seeing that the money he stole is there, nice and secure," she said. "We got him."

Vinh nodded, seeming distant. "I've copied and downloaded a bunch of his emails, getting the details. Can I copy files straight from his computer?"

"He closed the account window on his browser. We need to move fast," she said. Then she proceeded to log in to the account, then use a Bitcoin mixer—which *Mike should have done in the first place*—to hide where the money went or at least make it harder to track. Vinh no longer had access to the Aimsley account where it had been originally since he'd been logged out, so they couldn't simply move it back. Frankly, after seeing the bullshit shenanigans that were being pulled, she wasn't sure if she trusted them anyway. If Vinh had access to the money, he'd have leverage when he talked to them. "All right. Money moved and hidden—there's no way he's getting his hands on it now. We do need proof that he's the one that planned this, though. Then you can move files, but again—move fast. We need to wipe our tracks."

"He didn't do this on his own, though." Vinh's voice was a low growl. "Not from the looks of what's in his Dirt folder."

Something in his tone was jagged, raw with pain. "Do you know who he was working with?" she asked.

"Yeah," he said. "Unfortunately, I think I do."

CHAPTER 32

Vinh had been growing colder and colder as he'd dived deeper into the mess that was Mike Hanover's Dirt emails. He found a similar file (did the man have no idea of information security?) on his laptop. Recordings. Photos. Videos. Email trails, text screen captures. Details of personal life, all ready for doxing.

Emily was right. Maybe it was his upbringing, his privilege, or the fact he'd never been caught, but it seemed to have never occurred to Mike that he might get caught, much less face consequences.

You, sir, are going to learn today.

But the thing that really bothered him—the thing that he couldn't admit, even to Emily—was the fact that the tactics that Vinh was witnessing weren't even that shocking, all things considered. He'd used blackmail before, fighting fire with fire when someone had tried to blackmail a client. He'd kept evidence on clients even after he was no longer their consultant. He'd called it "covering your ass"—but he hadn't reported it either. He'd kept it as a safeguard . . . just in case they tried something insidious.

Anger is great, but evidence is better.

His *ông nội* had essentially raised his father with that statement. While his father had never had the patience or emotional control to use his grandfather's sentiment, Vinh had absorbed it like a sponge. Vinh was just as cold and just as calculating as his grandfather had ever been.

He thought back to the way his grandfather had said, with no inflection, that he would have to take Tam's tuition away if Vinh did not do as instructed. No matter how his own father ranted and railed, his ông nội had stayed as calm as a funeral director. He'd made it clear: Vinh's duty was to his family. They were investing in him. They could make his life miserable. And without them, his life would be an abject failure for all to see. Vinh had taken it to heart, and then he'd learned to be an even colder bastard than either of them by using their playbook.

It was what had gotten him as far as he was. Now, he was about to unleash that on Mike Hanover.

There, in black and white, was a folder with Winston's name on it. It could've been run-of-the-mill trash, stuff to threaten him with, although it would take balls of titanium to try to trap a senior partner and especially one known to be as ruthless as Winston. Most of Mike's other "victims" were lower level—he was obviously a bully, used to punching down. He trapped people so he could use them later. Vinh seriously doubted he could get anything on Winston.

He opened it, his stomach already starting to knot. His pattern-recognizing, detail-oriented brain was already telling him what he didn't want to know, but he needed the proof.

There were emails. Phone recordings from the office phone, ones he felt sure Winston wasn't aware of. Texts. All showing that Winston had told Mike what to do and how to do it. Even providing Mike with the thumb drive that he'd used to crack into Vinh's computer—on a day when Winston had taken Vinh out to lunch to celebrate his vice president promotion.

You son of a bitch.

For a moment, Vinh felt hollow. Winston had been his mentor, the one who had championed him getting his first job there when there had been so many young, rich, well-connected graduates vying for the position like gladiators. Vinh—whose own family had been either distant or judgmental, offering the barest of conditional love—had never felt that kind of support. As a result, he'd taken his own cold nature and honed it as he'd navigated the treacherous waters of Aimsley. He had taken the jobs no one wanted. He'd made the miraculous standard. And he'd compromised, going more and more "gray hat," at Winston's gentle nudging and constant praise.

But Winston was playing you, and he used Mike as his tool.

Vinh found himself leaning over the laptop, pulling away from Emily.

"Vinh?" she asked, and it sounded like she was far away.

"There's no way that he can get ahold of the money now, right?"

"No. He only had a keylogger on your work computer, and they took that back," she said. "And we hid the trail the right way. He'd need to pay Elliptic or have a hacker like Oz to figure out where it went, and considering, I don't think he's going to go that route. Elliptic doesn't have private clients—they work with corporations. I don't care how rich he is—and judging by his bank accounts, he's got a good amount socked away in a private account in the Bahamas, but otherwise he's kind of cash poor—he's not going to be able to afford anyone by the time you prove your innocence."

Vinh nodded.

"Who was it?" she prodded, her gentle tone a contrast to her insistence.

"My . . . boss. My mentor," Vinh said, his voice lifeless.

"Oh," she said with a little catch in her voice. She wrapped her arms around him. "Oh, Vinh, I'm so sorry. That's such a betrayal."

On some level, buried deep, he wanted to howl. He wanted to scream with anger. He wanted to punch someone—Winston, or Mike, or both. He wanted to burn Aimsley to the ground.

He tapped into the cold.

"We have his social media accounts, his bank accounts, and control of his computer. Correct?"

She reluctantly released him. "Um . . . yeah."

"Right."

"But we need to wipe his computer down," she said. "And delete our emails. Erase our steps, make sure there's no evidence tying us to his machine."

"Not quite good enough."

She turned on the bed. "Vinh . . . what are you doing?"

"Choosing violence." He started typing. "You clean up our tracks. I've got some posting to do."

"What are you going to do?"

"I'm going to post his goddamned cheating account on his social media," he said, opening up his Instagram. "Gonna put his bank accounts on blast. And that blackmail shit? Yeah, that's going directly to HR!"

"Vinh, no."

"The guy is an *asshole*," he snarled. "I'm going to make sure I have his job, but I'm going to scorch the fucking earth under him for trying to screw me!"

"*Vinh.*"

He looked over, noticing that she was staring at him with uneasiness in her eyes. "*What?*"

"The guy is, without question, a dick," she said, and her tone was the kind you used to try to get away from a feral animal. "But think this through."

"You don't think he deserves it?" Vinh was shocked and angry.

"He absolutely deserves it," she said. "But his wife doesn't. You post that shit on his socials, she's the one that's going to catch the flak."

Vinh froze. "It's better that she knows what she's dealing with," he said.

"Not that way," she said, her hazel eyes—disappointed? "You don't have to hurt her to hurt him. Collateral damage is a thing."

He grumbled low in his throat. "I'll email her," he conceded. "Privately. From Mike's account. I'll give access to his cheating account, tell her to check his phone. And then give her access to his secret bank account in the Bahamas—the one he's trying to keep out of any prenup. There won't be any connection to me or what we're doing, so it won't trigger any warnings for the rest of the company. If anything, Mike will think one of his blackmail victims might've had him hacked."

"That sounds good."

It doesn't feel like enough, he thought as he quickly typed out the message, adding the pertinent information. But it would slow down Mike and hopefully save Mike's wife from staying shackled to that bastard. The rest would have to wait. He really needed to remember: revenge, done right, couldn't be rushed.

"You done?" she asked.

"Yes." He grimaced. "I want to take them all out *now*. But it'll have to do. I'll schedule an email to HR so that the rest of Mike's computer evidence comes out the day of the meeting."

"You've got this," she reassured him. "All right. Now, we disappear without a trace."

After a few keystrokes, she smiled, closing the laptop.

"Okay," she said. "Done."

"Now, time for the second phase of this." He opened his personal email account, speaking as he typed. "This is going to the senior partners. Per our earlier discussion, I wanted to inform you that I have resolved the problem of which I had been accused. Due to new evidence, there is an internal issue that needs to be addressed prior to rectifying the situation. I am setting up a meeting Wednesday morning, early, to discuss how we can fix this problem and ensure that there is no repeat. I sincerely hope we can put this behind us and close this chapter before moving on to a more productive future relationship." He glanced over at Emily. "What do you think?"

"I can't believe you made something so business-ese sound so threatening," she marveled.

"Lots of practice," he said, copying Fergus and doing one last check before sending it off. Then he called Fergus.

"Fergus. I just copied you on an email from my personal account. I need a favor."

"Of course," Fergus said eagerly. "Does this mean you're coming back? Because they've got me floating, acting as assistant for any number of ding-dongs. I'm mostly running for coffee."

"Well, that's ridiculous," Vinh said. "You could be a consultant, for God's sake. You *should* be a consultant."

"Yeah, except I have a soul," Fergus said cheerfully. "I'm opening the email now . . . oh, shit," he breathed.

"Yeah."

"I'll get you a conference room."

"One other thing," Vinh said. "I know you're the soul of discretion—it's part of why I hired you. But in this case . . ."

"You want me to start spreading some news and clarifying some things?"

"Just hearsay," Vinh said, pleased that Fergus had caught on. "But yeah. There are already rumors going around. We just need to put out some fires."

"I've been trying to keep a lid on things, but you know how the consultants are. They hear there's weakness or that some plum accounts are up for grabs, and they start howling like wolves." He could practically picture Fergus's eye roll. "Anyway. I'm on it. It'll be good to have you back."

"It'll be good to be back," Vinh said automatically. "This is what I've been waiting for."

"You're going to be in ass-kicking mode, aren't you?" Fergus's voice had a smile in it.

"I am going to be in shock-and-awe mode," Vinh said. "And yeah, I am going to fuck them up beyond recognition."

"That's the Vinh I know," Fergus said with approval. "You're going to be tackling million-dollar deals and claiming the biggest whale accounts ever."

"By the time I'm done with them, they're going to be begging me to take the billion-dollar accounts and handle them," Vinh said. "They train us to be ruthless. In a few days, they're going to learn what that really fucking means."

"Go get 'em, boss."

With that, Vinh hung up. Then he looked over at Emily.

She was staring at him like she didn't even know him.

CHAPTER 33

I am going to fuck them up beyond recognition . . . they're going to be begging me to take the billion-dollar accounts.

It wasn't like she didn't know who Vinh was or what he'd become. But there was a big difference between understanding something rationally and actually seeing it in action.

"What is it?" Vinh stepped up to her, reaching out for her, and she found herself stepping back.

"So I guess it worked," she said instead, her voice calm. She felt detached, like she was watching the whole scene from a distance, like an out-of-body experience.

"It was perfect. *You* were perfect," Vinh said. Now that the moment was over, it was like he'd never shifted into that Terminator mode. He looked concerned, stroking her cheek. How could a man so cold suddenly turn warm for her? Which one was the real face? "I literally couldn't have done this without you."

She frowned. She now wasn't sure how she felt about that. "I suppose our deal is done, then," she said, and her voice sounded reedy now, losing substance.

"Just because our deal is done doesn't have to mean *we're* done, Em. I thought we put that behind us. What's wrong?" he asked. "And don't tell me it's nothing. Come on, we know each other too well."

Her brain was still processing what she'd heard. It wasn't the sharpness. Hell, she'd felt similar feelings of vengeance and viciousness all the time. When someone cut her off on her way home. When someone was verbally abusive on the IT line. Certainly when Vinh had dumped her. But she'd never actually *done* anything about it. She'd dealt with it, cursed in her car or under her breath, and let it go.

Vinh had made a living in *not* letting it go. He was scary when he wanted to be, and it had obviously made him rich and, until he'd gotten in the crosshairs of his mentor in the shooting gallery that was Aimsley, powerful. Now, she'd not only helped him get revenge and clear his name but also put him back in a position where he would have the whole world on a platter, and he'd only go further from there.

"Is it the deal?" he said, and she let him take her hands. "Because I know what I agreed to, but I have to say: I don't want to walk away from this. From *us*. From the potential of what we've got."

"That's the thing." Emily felt her eyes prickle with tears. "There isn't really an *us*, is there?"

He reared back slightly. "There's something," he said. "You can't tell me you don't feel it."

"It's just sex," she tried.

His gaze pierced her. "Liar."

She sighed. There was no way she could make that stick, realistically. "Dammit. You know I still love you. There are times when I think I never stopped."

His eyes glowed, and he stepped up, kissing her hard. She wanted to melt into that kiss, wanted to let him sweep her away in emotion so she didn't have to *think*. But her brain kept on going.

She pulled away, gently but insistently. "It's not enough, though," she added quietly. "It never was."

"Emily, I explained why I broke up with you," he said. "If I could've done it any other way, I would have. But it wasn't just me."

"No, I understand. You were doing it for family—to protect Tam and give her the best shot at college. You acted like a parent for her when she needed it, and you didn't even tell her." She smiled indulgently. "Which you really ought to tell her about at some point, by the way."

He winced. "It's in the past. It'd only hurt her. What difference does it make?"

"Family should have honesty," she said. "My family's flaky and weird, they can't budget to save their lives, they have cockamamie schemes, and they still live in the clouds half the time. But we have each other, and we're honest."

His dark eyes were imploring. "I want you to come to New York with me."

Now she balked. "Wait. *What?*"

"I want you to move in with me," he said. "Be with me. I don't want to spend time apart again. And I certainly don't want to stick to the 'We never see each other again' clause. Do you?"

She bit her lip, then quickly shook her head. Before he could lay another mind-melting kiss on her, though, she sternly put up a hand. "But there's no way I can move to New York! Are you high?"

"Why not?" he asked, like he was proposing a quick trip to the grocery store. "You can live with me until we figure out what you want to do. Certifications or a college degree. Hell, if you wanted to make your own start-up or information-security business, you could, without any other hoops to jump through. You've got so many more options than you think."

"And who's going to pay for all that, Vinh?" she said. "Just move in with you? 'Don't worry, Sunshine, let Sugar Daddy take care of it for you' kind of thing?" She shook her head again. "I can't do that, and we both know it!"

"You could," he said. "I get paid an obscene amount, and I've never had the time or motivation to spend it. I've made some great investments. You could go back to school for the next three decades, and it wouldn't make a dent."

"That's not sexy," she scolded, wanting to smack him on the back of the head but refraining. "The entire time you've known me, you know that money hasn't been the driving force in my life."

He was quiet for a second. "Your dad sold luxury yachts," he said. "You grew up kinda rich, Em. I'm not slamming you telling you that. I'm just saying . . . I think I wanted to impress you when I started my degree. Maybe that was a bad idea, and I know that it's never been a status thing with you. But I'm also saying, having money and spending it wasn't a bad thing when you were growing up. Why is it bad now?"

"Because status is what got us in this position in the first place!" she said. "My dad was so intent on making his dreams come true, on living the high life, that he mortgaged us to the hilt. That included *sending me to school*."

To his credit, he winced. "But we wouldn't be like that. I can promise that."

"This time, it's my family that needs me," she protested. "You know how my mom is. She needs me. She and Greg both need me."

His expression was sad. "I love you, Emily," he said. "We could figure it out. I mean, I could give them money too . . . ?"

"You can't just throw money at this and fix the problem," she snapped. "I'm not abandoning them with a paycheck, and I'm sure as hell not asking you to subsidize me and my family. And I'm not walking away from the Herd, who have been my support and my strength for over ten years. I'm not leaving them."

Vinh took a deep, shuddering breath.

"You have to understand," she said, hating the pain she was reading in his body language. "I really do love you."

The hope in his expression almost crushed her.

Tightrope. She was about to misstep. She felt the sense of vertigo.

If she left her family and the Herd, she'd be making a mistake—she knew it. She wasn't ready for this kind of change. She needed the Herd. Her family needed her. What was she supposed to do . . . throw all that away? And there was no way that Vinh would do the same, nor should he. He'd worked too hard for too long to get where he was, and now, after a week or two, she expected him to just . . . put all their past aside?

She didn't have choices. There were no viable options, just painful ones. She forced herself to push on.

"What are you going to do while I'm staying in your apartment? While I'm in school? If I moved three thousand miles away, not knowing anyone there, without my friends or family . . . and you were running off to Taiwan or Melbourne or God knows where for months at a time?"

He frowned. "I could work around that," he said. "Get more domestic clients. I get the feeling that they're going to want to keep me happy once the dust settles."

"You're the best there," she pointed out. "That's why they give you the accounts they do. The prize winners, the high profiles, the hard cases. That's why you get paid an obscene amount."

"I'm going to make them make me partner," he said. "I know I can do it. And then . . ."

"And then you'll have other problems," she said. "You're going to have more challenges from inside the building. And I know you. You'll still be hands on, plenty."

"But—"

"I don't think you see what it's doing to you," she said, her voice breaking a little. "You said you wanted to be successful back when we broke up. I know you've got a lot of family shit tied into that. And I see now that I was tied into that too. But I think that maybe you've gone too far down that path—and if you're going to stay in the job, you're going to change even more. Maybe into someone—or something—that

I don't think I could live with. You wouldn't be the Vinh I fell in love with anymore. And given the choice between me and the job . . ."

"No!" He reached for her, wrapping her in his arms, holding her tight. "Damn it, *no*. I just got you back. You can't ask me to quit and ditch everything again. It's not *right*. It's not *fair*."

She gave him a hug, feeling tears run down her cheeks.

"I'm not asking you," she said. "Remember? When you broke up with me all those years ago?"

"Emily, don't do this . . . ," he said. Pleaded. And Vinh never begged.

"You said it'd be better if we had a clean break. It took me years, but I finally understand what you were saying."

He stilled, so quiet, like an ice sculpture.

"What are you saying?"

"I'm saying you were right," she said. "We wouldn't have worked then, and I don't think we can work now. I love you—but I think a clean break would be best."

CHAPTER 34

"Herman, Herman, Herman," Vinh slurred, kneeling and peering into the enclosure. "You got it *made*, dude. No lady snakes *anywhere*. No complications, amirite?"

Herman rose on his . . . well, his middle? Dude had crazy core strength. Anyway, he lifted his head and stared right back at Vinh, delicate whiplike forked tongue waving at him.

"Or other dude snakes, I guess," Vinh added. "Or nonbinary snakes. I'm not trying to make any assumptions about your sexual preferences. I'm just saying. You're *alone*. That's *awesome*."

Herman tilted his head, weaving slightly.

"Because other people *suck*." Vinh punctuated that with a too-emphatic wave of his hand, forgetting that he had a pilsner glass full of rum and Coke, all Greg had on hand. He was spending this last night in Greg's place before driving to the airport, returning the rental, and going back to Manhattan to wreak havoc on the people who had tried to ruin his life. After he'd had his quiet breakup with Emily—which was saying something, since he wasn't even sure they'd technically gotten back together—he'd holed himself up in Greg's bedroom and hadn't moved except to order food. He hadn't called Tam or anyone, knowing that he was in no state to keep it together. He'd checked on everything—the plants, the animals.

Then he'd gotten the booze out of the cupboard and ordered pizza and a liter of soda, and he was now trying to drown his sorrows into submission.

"I swear, I am never doing another relationship again," he told Herman. "And I'm not trusting anybody at work either. Can you believe this shit, Sonic?"

The little hedgehog immediately jumped on his wheel and started racing in solidarity. Good egg, that Sonic. Meanwhile, the tortoise, Speedy, slowly and meticulously finished the strawberry he'd gotten for a treat and then headed back to his hidey house. Still, Vinh felt like Speedy had his side.

He couldn't remember hurting this much, even when *he'd* broken up with Emily. Maybe because he'd buried himself in school. He'd had a cold fire burning in him, one that had scorched any feelings he'd had . . . everything had turned to ash in the face of what he'd needed to do. He'd held down two jobs and saved up money, and he'd set himself up for a career that eclipsed his own father's. His father and his grandparents hadn't been proud—they'd been *expectant*. They'd then bragged on him, the only and oldest grandson, to their friends.

He hadn't wanted to just succeed, though. He'd wanted to *shove their faces in it*. And he'd wanted to be in a position where he wouldn't be vulnerable again. He'd be able to help Tam if they tried throwing their weight around her too. And he'd gotten there, with a bloodless single-mindedness that had both scared and impressed his employers.

Now, he just felt empty and aching and wondering what the fuck he'd done all this for.

Maybe I should've told Tam, he thought to himself. About the tuition. About their grandparents' and his father's threat. But she would've immediately thrown her college career out the window. She was a hopeless romantic, and she was utterly impulsive. He knew that she would take a bullet for him. She'd feel horrible if she knew that he'd thrown away the love of his life for her.

And yes. Emily was the love of his life. He knew that even more now.

"Herman," he said, looking into the snake's eyes. "I miss her, my dude."

It was probably the booze, but Herman looked like he was commiserating.

"I think I'm always gonna miss her. And I don't know what to do about that." He felt a sob clogging his throat, and he swallowed hard before taking another slug of rum. "I hurt, buddy."

Herman nodded. Then, slowly, he nosed the glass. Vinh waited for a beat. Then, slowly, he raised his hand, putting it on the glass.

"You're the only one that understands me, Herman," he said.

He didn't know how much time had elapsed. He just found himself lying on the floor in front of the enclosure, the empty glass near his head. The door banged. "Whozzit?" he asked blearily. Maybe it was Emily?

He hoped it was Emily.

Then he looked down at himself. He had a pizza-stained T-shirt and a pair of *Cowboy Bebop* boxers.

Okay. He hoped it *wasn't* Emily.

"It's Tam. Open up."

"Tam?" he said, feeling utterly confused. Had he called her? Had he hit the drunk-dialing portion of the program? Oh, God. He needed to put his phone somewhere. Otherwise God knew what he'd be messaging to Emily. Or his work, come to that. He got up, then stumbled to the door and opened it.

"Hey . . . oh," Josh said, taking in his disheveled appearance. "Wow. Emily wasn't kidding."

"Emily?" Vinh asked. "What are you talking about?"

"Inside. Everybody inside," Tam said, ushering in Josh, Tobin, Lily, and Hayden. "Emily said that you were going to need some company tonight."

"M'fine," Vinh protested. "Got company. Herman and I were just talking."

Hayden chuckled, then tried to rein it in as Tam scowled at him. "What? We never get to see Vinh drunk. It's funny!"

"I should've come here myself," Tam said. "But I thought I might need someone to open the door if you'd passed out, and Emily didn't have another spare key."

"I learned lockpicking from YouTube," Tobin added helpfully. Lily shook her head, covering her face with her hand. "Also, I parkour. A little. I could've made it to the balcony maybe."

"I came to make sure he didn't try parkour," Lily added, smiling at her boyfriend.

"See? You two make it work. That's unbelievable," Vinh found himself saying. "You *hated* each other, but now . . . now you're all *schmoopy*, and it's a thing!"

The lot of them stared at him.

"This is worse than I thought," Tam said.

"Please let me record this," Hayden said, starting to pull his phone out.

"Do it, and I will cut you," Tam warned. Hayden quickly tucked his phone back in his pocket. "Vinh? Dude, how much did you drink?"

He looked around. "The rum . . . I'll owe Greg a new bottle, I guess. Gotta remember to buy him replacement condoms too. We went through a *lot*."

"Could've lived my whole life without hearing that. Aw, shit." She looked at the empty bottle. "You need to eat something."

He shrugged. "Actually," he said, "I don't feel so . . ."

Before he could stop himself, he found himself bolting to the bathroom. It was the one plus of the tiny apartment: it was a quick trip. And he did almost trip, slipping on the bathroom rug in his haste.

After that, thankfully, everything got blurry. He got sick. There were some comments of sympathy, a few hooting laughs (probably Hayden). He tried to apologize.

"We've all been there," Josh said.

"You're good for my sister," Vinh mumbled as he rested his head on the side of the toilet. "Better stay that way, or you'll deal with me."

"Ordinarily, that would terrify me," Josh said wryly. "But it's hard to take someone in anime boxers seriously."

"Fuck off," he said with zero menace.

Eventually, Hayden, Tobin, and Lily left, leaving him alone with his sister and Josh. Tam actually tucked him into Greg's bed. It was so weird. Not only because of their ages—and because a grown-ass man did *not* need to be tucked in—but because he was so used to being the one who did the caretaking. "I really wanted this to work," he found himself saying.

"Someday, I'm going to want all the details of what the hell happened to you," she said. "What all the business side was. But I know you can pull yourself out of that. You're a cat, except you seem to have unlimited lives when it comes to your career."

He grunted. She wasn't wrong, per se.

"But your personal life . . ." She let it trail off, adjusting the bottle of water she'd put on the nightstand by the bed. "Vinh, I know you think I'm a flake."

"No," he protested, but he knew that there wasn't a lot of weight there. He *had* thought she was a flake. "I don't think you are now. And I'm sorry I was judgy as hell."

She shrugged. "I know I'm not like you. Or Dad, or the grandparents, or Mom," she said. "But I'm lucky. I've been happier with Josh, and with my new job, than I've ever been in my life. I feel like that's made a difference."

He nodded. "I'm glad for you."

"That's all I've ever wanted for you," she said. "If you could change your focus, just a little . . . I think you'd be happy too."

CHAPTER 35

It was Tuesday, and Emily was back at work, logged in to her computer, staring at a never-ending queue of problem tickets as the air circulated sluggishly and the mustard-yellow walls seemed to close in on her.

She hated it.

It wasn't like she had much choice, though. She'd picked up the hours only because she'd bought the water heater, and it had wiped out the house-repair fund. If anything else essential broke or needed to be fixed, they'd be dancing into the red zone of their credit cards, and the last thing any of them needed was a bankruptcy if the interest rates rolled them over. At this point, she was tempted to simply take over the house-repair fund so none of it was used for "mood-boosting" takeout and cosmetics. She hated the thought of taking on yet another responsibility, essentially "parenting" her mother, but she was running out of options if they wanted to keep the house.

She was still heartsore from what had happened with Vinh. She'd never realized how hard it must have been for him to break up with her. She still didn't let him off the hook completely. They could have made it work. But he was right: it would have been hard, almost cripplingly so, and she didn't know if they would've survived long term as a couple. But the chemistry, and more importantly the love, was still there, so strong and so rooted that it felt like death to deny it.

But what choice did she have?

Vinh's treacherous words were like an earworm, something upbeat and bouncy and annoying in its inescapability. *Have you thought about moving? Why don't you get another job?*

Certified Ethical Hackers are a thing.

She opened a web browser to look at certification programs. Let some of the other staff pick up the queue for a few minutes. Not for anything specific, she told herself. Just as a way to keep her mind off of Vinh, as if placating the voice in her head would somehow soothe her heart. Instead, her spirit dropped more. As she'd suspected, the exam itself cost about as much as the water heater she'd just purchased. Not to mention the training—and while self-paced was cheaper, the more expansive authorized training tended to get trainees in better jobs down the line. But that was twice the cost of the exam. *And* it meant more of a time investment—time she'd have to somehow balance with her current work.

You could do swing shift or night shift.

She frowned. She'd done crappier jobs for longer hours, she realized. She could carve out the time. But the money . . .

You could save up the money. It would take a while. But you could. Maybe a second job. Or sell something? Do I have anything worth selling? Maybe . . .

She sighed, feeling a love-hate tug as her brain started providing solutions. She'd been too fixed in her focus, struggling to keep her head above water. But . . . what if she could pull this off? What if she could get a better job and get off this treadmill of making just enough only to get it wiped out again like a sandcastle at high tide?

What if she let herself dream again? Just a little?

It felt terrifying. But also alluring.

She just needed a little seed money to start, she realized. She just . . .

Her phone vibrated on the desk. She glanced around. It was a slow Tuesday, which had to make Troy tug his hair out. The other support staff were either on the phone or doing their own version of killing time—online shopping, playing games, whatever. She picked up the phone. It was an alert letting her know she'd received money electronically. Frowning, she opened it.

It was from Vinh, she realized. Then she gaped as she saw the total. It was for five times what she'd quoted him.

Oh my God, oh my God, oh my God.

She could pay property tax, all right. For the next *five* years. And sock away some for house repairs. *And* get certified.

She wondered if that was his plan all along.

Guilt twisted her, and she quickly texted him.

EMILY: You sent too much money! I can't accept this!

There was a long pause, the dots showing up and disappearing. Finally, he responded.

VINH: I told you I'd give you a bonus. You earned every cent of that. Also—you might want to look at what ethical hackers and cybersecurity people are charging. Your rates were way too low. I paid you what you deserve, and I'm happy to do it.

Emily wasn't sure how to reply to that. He kept typing, though.

VINH: Use it to make yourself happy, too, okay? I want you to be happy.

She felt gobsmacked. He wasn't making demands on her. He wasn't asking her to change her life. He was giving her what he felt she needed. Then again, if she decided to blow it all on clothes, or gambling, or whatever, she got the feeling he wouldn't judge.

He simply, genuinely, wanted her to be happy.

EMILY: I don't know what to say.

VINH: Don't say anything. Probably gonna love you the rest of my life.

VINH: But don't worry. I remember the terms of the deal. Take care of yourself.

She bit her lip, almost hard enough to draw blood, and had her phone in a death grip. He was giving her what she needed—and then walking away, no strings attached.

Just like she'd asked.

"You're not on your phone, are you?" Troy called out from the end of the cubicles. There was a flurry of activity. "Emily?"

"Just going on break," she said, talking past the frog in her throat. She got up and rushed to the restroom, ignoring whatever Troy was asking her. She slammed herself into a bathroom stall.

Then she started crying like she would never stop.

She kept sobbing until she heard a little voice outside the stall and a tentative tap on the door. "Um . . . Emily?"

She took a deep, hiccupping breath. "Yeah?" It came out as a whimper.

"You okay?"

Do I sound like I'm okay?

"Not really, no," Emily admitted, surprising herself.

"Do you . . . I mean, is there anything I can do?"

"No." Emily pulled out a bunch of toilet paper, scrubbing at her face and blowing her nose. "But thanks," she added, because it had been nice of them to ask. It sounded like Mindy, one of her coworkers, but might've been one of the other workers—Emily didn't work Tuesdays often, so she wasn't as familiar with the regular staff and their shifts.

She heard whoever it was use the bathroom, wash up, and leave. When the coast seemed clear, Emily left the stall and went to the sink. In the painful fluorescent lights, she looked even worse than she felt. Her eyes were red and puffy, her nose looked like Rudolph's, and her sprinkle of freckles stood out like cinnamon in a bowlful of salt.

I can't do this today.

She splashed water on her face, wincing when some water trickled down her sleeves despite her attempts to be careful, adding to her discomfort. She made her way out to the main call room. She could feel the gazes from the crew that was working this shift. They were looking at her without trying to be obvious they were staring. She didn't care.

She went to Troy's office and knocked on his doorframe (since he was proud to "always have my door open for you guys"). He'd been typing at his computer, so when he looked up and focused on her face, he visibly recoiled. "What's wrong?" he asked.

"I'm sorry," she said. "But I can't . . . I need to go home."

"Everything all right?" Troy asked. Because, as always, Troy asked questions. Still, it was to his credit that he sounded sympathetic.

"I'm having a crisis," she said. "Personal thing."

"Oh." He looked like he was stuck processing that for a long minute. Then he sighed. "Why don't we say it's allergies?" He looked pointedly at her face.

"Okay, let's go with that."

"And you'll be back for your regular shift tomorrow, right?"

She frowned. "I'll be honest—I'm not sure."

"Because you'll probably need a doctor's note if you're going to be out longer than that," he pointed out. "That'll be two days. Unless you can get someone to cover your shift?"

She gritted her teeth.

"Or," she countered, "I could quit."

"Quit?" His eyes bugged out. "That . . . doesn't seem proportional?" he stammered.

She sighed, rubbing at her eyes. "I have some things I need to work out. I wouldn't leave you high and dry, but I am mentally just not doing well right now, and I need to take some time. I never take PTO. I think I need to."

"Yes, but you need to apply for that in advance," he said. "Surely you understand why that's important!"

She crossed her arms. "I'm going whether you're okay with it or not," she said. "Think of it as mandatory overtime but in reverse. If you don't like it, you can fire me."

He was still spluttering when she walked out to the cube farm, signed out of her computer, and grabbed her stuff. She drove home, her head swimming.

She wasn't sure what she was going to do next. Vinh's money had given her options. Now, she didn't know what to do—and she was terrified of choosing wrong.

CHAPTER 36

Vinh had had a horrible hangover on Tuesday when he'd taken the flight back to New York. His apartment had had the ghost of Emily's perfume still lingering in the air, and it had made him grit his teeth. The only bright spot had been sending her the money she'd earned—and even that had been painful.

Saying goodbye always was.

He'd barely slept, too busy getting what would essentially be a presentation together. Throwing himself into work, his usual MO. By Wednesday, he was back to his old self—externally, anyway. He was wearing his best power suit and his sternest expression.

He felt like dry ice, unspeakably cold, able to cause irreparable damage if handled incorrectly. He got the feeling they'd figure that out soon enough. He hadn't responded to any private emails from the senior board other than acknowledging their agreement to meet him. He certainly hadn't answered any questions. Winston, especially, had been insistent that they speak prior to the meeting.

Winston can go fuck himself.

He was on the hook. He had to know it. He was, at this point, just trying to suss out exactly how much Vinh knew and how much trouble he was in.

"This way," Fergus said, leading the way, then lowered his voice. "I booked you in the main conference room—and left the blinds open.

Everybody knows you're on your way up and that the whole board of senior partners is there."

"Do they think I'm getting fired?"

"They don't know what's going on, although money is leaning that way," Fergus responded.

"Good." Vinh allowed himself a small smile.

Fergus winced. "God. You look like a serial killer when you do that."

"Thanks."

"Wasn't a compliment, boss."

Vinh didn't care. He walked into the conference room like he owned it. Like he owned the *building*.

Like he owned *Aimsley*.

"Thank you for meeting me today," he said, the pleasantry sounding distinctly unpleasant in tone.

Roger, the senior partner who had blustered when he'd initially disclosed the missing money, was red faced and breathing heavily. *He probably ought to get that looked at by a medical professional at some point,* Vinh thought. "I'm doing this under protest," Roger stated, his voice raised. "I can't believe they're letting you back in the building. And as soon as we have enough evidence, I'm going to ensure that criminal proceedings—"

"Are brought against the correct parties," Vinh snapped. "Which I can prove are decidedly not me." He put his Overland leather messenger briefcase on the desk, then took out the printouts he'd assembled and tossed them across the table.

"What do you mean?"

"It means I got the money back."

There was a moment of stunned silence. Then everybody talked at once.

"Well, where is it?" Roger demanded.

"How?" Sarra asked, looking dubious. "The whole reason we got into crypto was for anonymization and for safety. How could you possibly find out who did it, much less steal it back?"

Vinh's gaze met Winston's, and he could see the moment when his former mentor decided to save his own skin.

"There isn't any way," Winston said, managing to put a mournful note in his voice. "Unless he took the money himself and then transferred it back to make it seem like he had a skill set he doesn't have."

"Really, Winston?" Vinh asked quietly. "You want to go this route?"

"You are, undoubtedly, the best fixer we've ever had," Winston said. "I mean, I brought you up myself and pushed hard because I believed in you. But you've never been a hacker, and we all know it. The fact that you're trying this . . ." His face was a mask of tragic disappointment.

Vinh let him keep up the act. Then he cleared his throat. "I'm not a hacker," Vinh agreed. "But I know of several talented ones, and they did the forensic search to get the evidence necessary to figure out what happened. Then I took steps to get access to the account and then rectify the situation. I have copies of the ledger transactions as well as proof of where the account was accessed."

"Which you could have falsified," Winston continued. "Really. Do you want to keep up this charade?"

"I also have proof that the same owner has skimmed accounts of three other consultants," he said and saw Winston flinch, almost imperceptibly. "Didn't know about that, did you, Winston? I'm assuming it wasn't under orders?"

The rest of the board snapped their attention to Winston, who went pale as ultrabright copier paper. To his credit, he kept it together, straightening his tie as he gathered his thoughts to respond. Vinh knew the man enough to know it was one of his tells.

He was scared. He knew he was caught. He was also probably going to do a last-ditch effort to claw his way out.

"I don't know what you're saying," Winston said with exaggerated patience. "But if you're trying to pin this on *me*—"

"If you'll turn to page three," Vinh continued, steamrolling over his former mentor, "you'll see copies of the emails, text screen captures, and any number of details pulled directly from Mike Hanover's computer. As it turns out, Mike decided to build his own insurance policy by creating files on anybody he could use or who he might need leverage on." He grinned. "I would have put them up on the conference room screen, but I thought more discretion might be in order. The only other people who have access to his dirt—his words—are in HR. They were notified this morning, prior to this meeting, and they are probably scrambling to figure out how to fix this situation, as well they should."

They stared in shock at his chess-like move. It was decisive and incontrovertible. It also told them: *you can't just make this go away.*

"I have enough information, stored in various locations, that not only show that Aimsley was responsible for raiding its own accounts— but a senior partner was responsible for actually *ordering* it to happen. Detailing how to break into my computer. Which was foolish, by the way, Winston," he pointed out. "If you're going to have someone act under your orders, you need plausible deniability, and you certainly don't want an evidence trail as damning and easy to crack into as email and texts. Oh, and he recorded your phone calls, FYI."

Winston winced. "This is outrageous."

"That's one word for it. The other word would be *hubris*. You honestly thought I wouldn't challenge this or that I wouldn't fight it—or if I did fight it, Winston, that you'd covered enough of your bases that I'd never find out. You were so convinced that you were smarter than me, better than me, that you tapped a resentful, greedy incompetent to try and take me out."

He saw Winston's Adam's apple work and the tiniest bead of sweat appear along his hairline.

Vinh leaned forward on the table with both hands, glaring at all of them. "I was put on probation, humiliated, and barred from the office. My career here was all but terminated and any future prospects threatened *explicitly*. I was conspired against by my own employer. And unless you want every single major news outlet on the globe getting their hands on these details, you're going to make it up to me. *Handsomely*."

Sarra looked at the others. "You're right," she said. "Of course. This is . . . I don't understand why this would happen. What possible purpose would a senior partner have in doing something so criminal, outrageous, and ultimately foolish?"

"This wasn't me!" Winston said, desperation bleeding through, cracking his usually flawless façade. "If he can get someone to hack into a crypto account, don't you think he could . . . could create some fake email conversations?"

"And text messages," Vinh added. "And phone conversations. I told you, he kept everything."

"What?"

"You were texting his private cell," Vinh said. "You called his phone at work, and he ran it through a recording program. Yeah. I have all of it. Given that, I think that you could find . . ."

"Anyone could fake that," Winston added. "You've been thorough—that's for certain."

At this point, Roger grumbled out the name of a cell provider.

"I beg your pardon?" Vinh asked.

"We get all our cell business through that tech provider—it's one of our clients," he said. "They owe me a favor. I'm sure that they'd be happy to help us clear up this supposed misunderstanding by providing some messages."

Vinh knew that the legality of that was questionable, but then again, he'd hacked into a system to prove his innocence. He wasn't really able to throw stones at this point.

Sarra had been on her phone, and she looked up at Winston, her expression stern. "You're not touching your computer, any of them. I've initiated lockout through IT, and we'll see what evidence there is to corroborate this. The same will happen with your collaborator, Mike Hanover. In fact, he should be walked out by security right about . . ." She smiled, a tiny, cold, vicious smile. "Now."

"You can't be serious!" Winston flailed. "I'm a *senior partner*. You can't do this. You don't have the authority!"

"All in favor of Winston St. John being investigated for internal fraud and possible embezzlement, as well as conspiring against Vinh Doan, say *aye*."

There was a chorus of *ayes*. Winston looked floored. Roger looked resigned. And Sarra looked triumphant.

"But he's setting *me* up." Winston gave one last, pathetic attempt.

"Then he's better at this than you," Roger said dismissively. "So why would we want you in this position?"

Vinh had seen nature documentaries where a shark accidentally got bit and it became a cannibalistic frenzy. One bite was the difference between predator and prey. One show of weakness turned the big fish into sashimi.

Here in the conference room? It was just like watching that.

"We'll discuss how we can compensate you for this trouble," Sarra said to him. "And of course you're reinstated."

Which meant: *please don't sue us or leak this to the press.*

Vinh arched an eyebrow at her. "And that's enough?"

"We're also going to be discussing your partnership," she added, taking up Winston's leadership position before anyone else muscled in, smooth as greased glass. "I'd brought it up before, but Winston was against it."

Vinh shouldn't have been shocked anymore, but he still felt a little jolt of surprise.

"Personally, I think that he wanted to keep you where you were—high enough to be useful but still in place as his underling," Sarra added with a sniff. "Moving you into a partner position was threatening."

Winston looked sick.

Vinh nodded. "Partnership will go a long way towards making this right," he said, his voice quiet and firm. Then he closed his briefcase. "I'm going home."

He left the conference room with confidence, feeling the eyes of everyone in the outer room following him as he made his way through the cubicles, to the elevator, and out the building.

CHAPTER 37

Emily still felt shell shocked when she drove home that day. It was like the answer to her dreams, and the embodiment of her fears, had just fallen in her lap, and God as her witness, she had no idea what to do with it.

I should ask the Herd.

But it felt too personal, even for them. She'd relied on them for so long, and she loved them just as much as her own family. Maybe she'd been guilty of relying on them too much, using them as an excuse. Why grow when she had a nice cozy comfort zone right here?

Was she being complacent? Using her fears as an excuse to just . . . stagnate? Staying in a painful job and living situation, avoiding love, because it was too hard to change—it wasn't *quite* painful enough to actually *do* something about it.

She felt sick to her stomach.

Unfortunately, her mother had that day off. "How was your day, dear?" she chirped, then got a look at Emily's face. "Oh! Are you all right? What happened?"

"Rough day," Emily said, brushing aside her mother's birdlike fidgeting and avoiding details. "You still have the property tax bill?"

"Yes, of course." Her mother went to her "desk," which was actually the small breakfast nook. It was strewn with papers and envelopes.

Thankfully, Emily had set up most of the bills on autopay since the table tended to be an administrative black hole. "Here it is."

"I'll make sure it gets paid," Emily said, taking it.

"And the water heater . . . ?" her mother asked hesitantly. "That's . . ."

"Taken care of," Emily said.

Her mother worked her hands. "Well, that's a relief," she said. "Although I suppose the house-repair fund is gone now."

Emily thought for a good moment about her response. "Actually," she hedged, "that project I was working on? For Vinh? He paid me. It was . . . generous."

Which was an understatement. It was downright magnanimous.

You deserve to get paid what you're worth.

She closed her eyes as tears stung yet again. Anytime this emotional roller coaster wanted to stop, she'd be fine with it.

"So you're going to refill the house fund?" her mother asked hopefully.

Emily bit her lip. "I'll keep some money in reserve," she said. "In case the house needs it. Okay?"

"But . . ." Her mother scrunched up her expression, looking away. "You shouldn't have to deal with that."

Emily felt a moment's relief until her mother's next statement.

"Why not just put the money into that account? I'll take care of it—don't worry."

Emily sighed. "I've got it," she said, feeling exhausted. "It's not a worry."

Now her mother looked impatient. "But I've handled the house fund since your father died!"

"Mom, there *wasn't* a house fund when Dad died," Emily pointed out. "Because we were in debt. Remember?"

Her mother stopped short, staring at Emily.

"And he always took care of the bills, and the taxes, and calling maintenance people," Emily said. "He never wanted you to worry. He wanted to take care of you."

"You make me sound like a child," her mother huffed, but her voice did sound near tears. "And now you're *treating* me like one. In my own house!"

Emily shook her head. "Dad didn't treat you like a child," she tried to soothe.

"It was different," her mother said stubbornly. "He loved me. He'd do anything to make me happy—I knew that."

And in a glaring pop of clarity, Emily saw that her father had, indeed, done everything he could to make her mother's life easier. She'd never understood their finances because she'd never had to deal with them. When she'd realized she was executor of his will, she had broken down. Emily had never seen her mother in that state, and neither had Greg. He had had a freak-out of his own, retreating into himself and his private pain, since he and their father had been close. He would have done anything to please their father, or at least tried, and then he was adrift, lost without his captain.

Emily had quickly stepped in to fill the gap. She had done what she imagined her father would want. Take care of the family. Make up for the shortfalls.

Enable.

The term hit her like a wave.

She had been *enabling* them this whole time.

She blinked, looking at her mother. Her father had tried to shelter her mother from the harshness of life—and he'd done her no favors, as his unexpected death should have illustrated in stark relief. But Emily had picked up the torch, and now *she* was doing no favors for her mother or herself.

This had to stop.

"You say Vinh paid you?" her mother probed. "Are you two back together, then?"

"Does it bother you?" Emily replied. "Because he loves me."

"And he paid you enough to pay the property tax *and* for the water heater?" Her mother's eyes widened.

Emily sighed. "He paid me a lot more than that."

"He has that much money?"

Her mother had no idea. "He works for one of the most prestigious consulting firms in the world," she said. "He's one of their top people. He gets paid more in a year than I have in the past ten."

Her mother's mouth dropped open. "He does?"

She knew that her mother came from money. Her family lived in Greenwich, a ritzy part of Connecticut. They had been well to do since the time of the robber barons, from the sounds of it. Her mother hadn't gone back to visit since she'd gotten married because they didn't think Emily's father was good enough— and then, after her father had died, because her mother couldn't bear their possible scorn, especially since she was working retail.

"Are you two back together, then?" her mother asked. *Eagerly.* A far cry from her earlier complaints.

Emily stared at her for a minute. "No," she said. "I told him we couldn't get back together."

"What? Why?" her mother asked, sounding shocked.

"You didn't even like him!" Emily didn't mean to yell, but anger and despair were churning through her, and she wanted to lash out at the world. "You told me he was disloyal and bad for me. You said he was nothing like Dad!"

"Well, maybe I was wrong," her mother said. "He obviously feels like he can take care of you. Why not let him? Especially if he's as successful as he is?"

"Okay, *eww*," Emily said.

"What *eww*? You took the money, didn't you?" Her mother seemed genuinely confused.

"Because I earned it! Working!"

Her mother looked indulgent. "All I'm saying is, a successful man who wants to take care of you is no bad thing."

Emily recoiled. "Are you *shitting* me right now?"

Her mother's expression dropped. "Language, please. No need to be crass. And really, am I wrong? Your father was the breadwinner in our relationship for years, and I was perfectly happy. *We* were perfectly happy. What's wrong with that?" She crossed her arms. "Are you judging me for being a stay-at-home mother?"

Emily felt a headache brewing behind her eyes, thumping and insistent. "No. I am not judging you. But that's not the relationship I want to have with Vinh. I want us to be equals," Emily said. "I love him, and I don't want him to baby me. You said you don't want to be treated like a child. Why the hell would I want to?"

"I said it's different!" Her mother rolled her eyes. "Honestly. It's like you're deliberately trying to misunderstand me. With marriage, with love, it's different. You'd be taking care of him in your own way. And he won't mind. He'll like taking care of you."

"We'd take care of each other," Emily countered before rubbing her temples. "I love him, Mom. More than ever. But I'm not going to ask him to give up his life, and I'm not giving up mine just to wait for him to throw some scraps of time and affection at me. We both deserve more than that."

"You kids make things so complicated," her mother said, sighing. "Maybe I got that wrong. Your father would never abandon me, because he loved me. I told you that."

"And you said Vinh would, I remember," Emily said, glum. "But he didn't this time."

"No. You did," her mother said, and the sheer unfairness of those words shocked Emily into silence. "If you really love him, you need to think about what's so important about your life that it's worth giving up love for."

Another clarity bomb hit her. "You're right," she said slowly as her brain turned the matter over and over, exploring it from all sides.

Her mother grinned. "Glad you see that," she said, all conflict seemingly forgotten. "Now. You call him tonight, maybe, and make up. I'm sure he'll see reason. And then who knows?"

"What do you mean, who knows?"

Her mother shrugged. "He could help out with the house! It'd be perfect, and I'm sure for someone as rich as him, it's not an issue. Your father used to spend more than our mortgage is now on drinks for friends at the yacht club. I'm sure Vinh could be just as generous."

Emily sighed, not even sure how to start with how wrong her mother's view on her current situation was. Maybe she was judging, but she couldn't help but feel a bit sick at her mother's combination of airy optimism and shrewdness. "I am going to talk to Vinh . . . but not tonight."

Her mother frowned. "Well, that's one way to go about it," she said, stretching out each syllable, deep in thought. "Letting him wait for it is a . . . *strategy*. But if you love him, why wait? Men can be fickle. Not men like your father, but other men. And successful men especially have women throwing themselves at them left and right. Do you really want to risk—"

"I'm not going to talk to Vinh yet," Emily interrupted before she could get more upset by the conversation than she already was. "Not until you, Greg, and I have a serious talk."

She realized that she wanted to fix this. She didn't want to give up Vinh. She didn't want to settle for a job she hated. She didn't want to give up the Herd—but she didn't have to.

What she had to do was finally take a risk.

CHAPTER 38

"Congratulations!"

Vinh barely looked over at the man who had walked up to him, champagne flute in one hand and canapé of some sort in the other. He hoped that "Fuck off" was clear in his expression, but apparently, his expressive abilities were currently impaired. He couldn't even get up enough energy to be menacing.

Goddammit.

"You were *just* made VP, and now partner? Holy shit, fam, you're *lit*."

Now Vinh paid a little more attention. The guy who had just said that had to be in his late thirties, was white as mayonnaise, and was using *fam* and *lit* with no apparent irony or self-consciousness. He wasn't even using the terminology correctly, since Vinh was pretty sure that a thing could be *lit* as an adjective, but a person who was *lit* was, well, drunk. Not that he was an expert on slang, per se.

Vinh would've sighed, but even that made him tired.

"Thanks," Vinh finally said as the guy fidgeted, raising his glass in greeting to someone else, who joined them.

"This is my bro, Derek."

The new guy held out his fist for a bump.

Bro? Fam? Lit? Was this guy using a bot to pull stuff from Urban Dictionary? Vinh stared at the guy's knuckles until he withdrew them, shrugging and tucking his hand in his pocket.

"We heard that you're *the guy to know* when it comes to the new consultant assignments," the original guy said. "And there's a lot of rumors. A few really sweet telecom mergers . . . that satellite thing, you know what I'm talking about . . . and a few underdeveloped countries that are about to get developed with a quickness, amirite?"

Vinh felt his stomach turn over and knot. Good God. Surely it hadn't always been this bad.

Had it? Had it really, and he'd never noticed? Never cared?

He had the sudden, overwhelming urge to take a bath in Lysol.

"So . . . what do you say?" The first man's hunger was evident in his voice. "What's a guy gotta do to get in on, say, the telecom deal?"

Vinh took a half step back, finally mustering up enough anger to give the man a glacial glare. "Who are you?"

The man blinked. Then flashed a blinding megawatt smile "Right. Right! Robbie. Um, Robert. Birch." He held out a hand. "I worked on your team on the VitalTech deal. Well, after you shifted teams, but, y'know, with your people . . ."

So one of the deals Vinh had gotten himself reassigned off of due to excessive fuckery that they'd refused to address. That had been maybe a year ago?

God, that had been a shit show.

Vinh didn't shake the man's hand. He gave exactly zero fucks at this point.

"Well, Robert 'Robbie' Birch," he said. "If I saw any consultant speak with a client the way you just tried to schmooze me, I'd have you fucking fired."

Robbie blanched, his complexion going downright pasty.

"And now that I'm getting the promotion, I actually *could* have you fired," Vinh said with no inflection. "Come at me with that used-car-salesman, fraternity-bro bullshit again, and I'll see to it that you're out on your ass in less than twenty-four hours."

"You can't do that! That's . . . that's like wrongful termination or something! I'd sue the shit out of you."

Vinh blinked at him, then shook his head. Robbie must've realized his error.

"Suggestion two," Vinh said, his voice low and even, just this side of bored, like a high school teacher who hated his job. "If you're going to threaten someone, make sure you know what your threat is. And I mean *know* it. I promise you, I could have you fired for wearing shoes I don't like. Did you even read your employment contract?"

Robbie went from pasty to parchment. "Um . . ."

Fuck's sake. He could only imagine the kind of contract work this guy was cobbling together. "And even if I didn't have the legal standing to fire you, Aimsley has *billions* of dollars in its war chest, and it's not afraid to use them. I'm guessing that despite your salary . . ." He scrutinized the man in front of him, taking in the slightly too-flashy, obvious name brand, and current-season clothing, the too-ostentatious watch, the immaculate haircut. "You're living paycheck to paycheck and probably just a bit outside your means."

The man's jaw dropped. His friend's eyes bugged out like someone had hit him with a frying pan. "What . . . how . . . no, I'm not!" he finally spluttered.

Vinh arched an eyebrow at the man, who shut up immediately. "There's an outside chance you come from family money. A significant percentage of the workers here do." And many of them, like Robbie, were assholes who couldn't do their job. Vinh would bet his savings that Robbie absolutely *sucked* at his job, whatever harmless account they'd assigned him to. "But try finding a lawyer that'll take on a company like Aimsley for one wrongful termination, especially with no evidence. Even if you did find a lawyer, Aimsley could drag it out until we bankrupted not only you but any family you had. And you still wouldn't win."

Robbie looked green as key lime pie now.

Vinh took pity on him. "I'm not going to fire you," he said but held up his hand, trying to prevent Robbie from spewing any more conversation or, worse, apologies all over him. "Not now, anyway. But I'm going to keep an eye on you, and not in the good way. You fuck up, we'll be having a different conversation."

Robbie nodded.

Vinh dug deep, then unleashed one of his old, razor-sharp, unpleasant smiles—the kind that promised corporate violence if he was crossed. "Now go enjoy the party. *Robbie.*"

Robbie nodded again, then beat a hasty retreat, his dude-bro friend Derek by his side.

"Holy shit," Vinh heard Derek say. "That guy is an ice-cold *bastard,* just like they said!" He couldn't tell if Derek meant that as a compliment or not. He wasn't sure if Derek knew either.

This was supposed to be the holiday party for Aimsley. Not many companies had them anymore, but Aimsley was old fashioned enough to make it a big deal: catering, open bar, the works. Some clients were interspersed, but mostly it was consultants, management, and the partners.

Ever since he'd pulled off "the impossible" and gotten the cash back—and vanquished the senior partner, who was currently riding his golden parachute to somewhere in the Hamptons, "retiring" to a life of golf and rumors—he was the new unofficial golden boy of Aimsley. Not that anyone knew the explicit details of *why* he had originally been dismissed or subsequently reinstated. They just knew he had done what no one else had: taken on a senior partner and won. He was everything Aimsley purportedly wanted. He was brutal, brilliant, bloodless. There was literally nothing he couldn't do, and nothing that could stop him. It should have felt triumphant, effervescent, a pure victory.

It felt like Novocain. Or one of those sensory-deprivation float tanks.

He went to the bar, leaned on it, and ordered a whiskey sour. As he did, a woman sidled up to him. He smelled her perfume—a blend of yuzu and jasmine. Expensive and unusual. He glanced over to see a woman with a luscious tumble of chocolate-brown hair in Hollywood waves. Her skin was sun kissed, and her dark eyes were large with eyelashes that fanned out to ridiculous lengths. Like, Vegas showgirls' headdresses had nothing on these suckers. Her makeup was Instagram perfect, and she was poured into a New York black dress that made her look stunning.

"Hello there," she murmured. "Whiskey sour. That tells me you're old fashioned. Traditional."

"Does it." He didn't make it a question. He waited for the bartender to assemble his drink.

She wasn't deterred. "I wouldn't have pegged you for the traditional type, honestly," she continued. And then waited.

She was better at the game than Robbie—he'd give her that. But then, that bar was ridiculously low. He knew that she was waiting for him to take the bait . . . to ask what she expected.

Instead, he accepted his drink and then took a sip. Wasn't bad. He dropped a twenty in the tip bowl, then nodded at the woman and started to walk away.

"You're Vinh Doan," she breathed, stepping up to him and smiling. Her lipstick was a deep bloodred, and she deepened her smile seductively.

He nodded. And, again, didn't take the bait.

"Oh, c'mon," she said. "It's a party. Why so serious?"

He wondered if she realized she was quoting the Joker.

The Herd would've known. Hell, it would've been a deliberate quote from any of them.

A little twinge of pain hit him in the chest. He set his jaw, pushing the sensation back down into the float tank.

She huffed, crossing her arms—which, not coincidentally, plumped her breasts up in her sweetheart neckline. Less subtle than she could be, but it was a nice dress. Expensive, tasteful. Vintage, possibly.

He'd had a fashion-house client at one point and remembered some really weird things, he realized clinically. There was so much information from this place that was crammed into his head, all of it jumbling together.

None of it *mattering*.

"Now that you mention it," she said, although he'd mentioned literally nothing, "this party *is* a little dull. I mean, what's up with those appetizers? Did they have to put cheese on everything? And the liquor . . . well, obviously somebody's economizing."

He wondered how long she'd keep talking despite his obvious non-participation in the conversation. A macabrely fascinated part of him thought about checking his watch to time it.

"Maybe we could go somewhere else," she said, her voice dropping. "I'm sure we could figure out something more interesting?"

Okay, that was clumsy. Like, Robbie-level clumsy. He looked over at her, surprised.

"Don't worry," she reassured him. "I don't work at Aimsley. I'm Delilah Raya. My family owns the fashion house Raya, as well as a number of European conglomerates in consumer goods. My company works *with* Aimsley, not for it. If anything, you work for me." Her laugh was bright and whimsical.

It kind of made his skin crawl.

He slung back the rest of his drink, then put his empty glass on a passing waiter's tray. Thankfully, his phone buzzed. "I'm sorry," he finally said. "I have to take this. Have a great evening."

She was silent in obvious shock as he hurried away, heading to a quiet corridor. He might as well go home. Everyone here was swimming in the shark tank, same as him. Now that he'd been accepted back into the fold, everyone wanted to see if some of his redemption magic would rub off on them. They wanted to charm him, or size him up as competition, or look for weaknesses. Or, in the case of Delilah, they wanted to try him on, try him out. Keep him or use him as a prize.

He glanced at his phone screen. He'd possibly never been more grateful that his mother called rather than texted than he was right now. He answered. "Hello?"

"Vinh," she said. He let out a dry laugh. Her tone, cut and dried and businesslike, was just like his. "What's funny?"

"Nothing," he said, then surprised them both by saying, "it's just good to hear from you."

"Oh." She sounded nonplussed. "It's, ah, good to speak with you. What are you doing for Christmas? Are you spending it with your sister?"

"Hadn't planned on it," he admitted.

"Well, what are you doing on December sixteenth?" she asked. "I know it's sort of last minute, but Scott and I are going to be in New York that day. I was wondering if we might have dinner."

He found himself feeling something again. This time, he didn't tamp it down.

"Unless you're busy," she amended quickly. "I don't want to—"

"Sure," he said instead, swallowing hard. "Sure. I'd love to have dinner."

CHAPTER 39

Emily had the new laptop propped up on the kitchen table in her mother's house. Her mother looked puzzled, a little irritated, a little nervous. They connected with Greg, whose scruff had grown long. With the beanie on his head as well as a thick red-and-black plaid shirt, he looked like a hipster lumberjack, but he grinned, which was nice to see. Greg went through cycles of happiness and anxiety, usually depending on where he was and what he was doing. He'd never quite "landed" in life, and Emily hated seeing him struggle. It seemed like Antarctica was good for him.

"Hey!" he called out.

"Greg!" her mother said, waving at the screen. "Baby boy, how are you? Are they feeding you enough? You're not too cold down there, are you?"

Emily sighed. It was going to be tough to stay on task, she realized, as her mother chirped questions and her brother answered them cheerfully. She let them talk for a bit, then decided best to get the tough part out of the way . . . maybe they could use the rest as a way to decompress afterward, because she got the feeling this talk wasn't going to be pleasant.

Because it wasn't going to be pleasant. But it *was* necessary. She kept telling herself that.

"Hey, how are the animals?" Greg said.

"Fine. I've got Hayden taking care of them now," she answered, and he looked pleased.

"Not Vinh?"

"Not Vinh," she said, even his name making her chest hurt. "He went back to New York."

"I'm glad that Hayden's helping, anyway. I should've asked him myself, but everything happened so fast. I'm glad that you remembered," Greg said. "But I figured you'd come up with the solution. You always do."

"He's right," her mother said, with her quiet, sunshiny smile, looking at Emily with a little nod. "You always do. My smart girl."

Emily took a deep breath. But before she could continue, her mother plowed forward.

"Did you know that she helped Vinh with something? Some computer thing?" her mother asked Greg conversationally. "She flew to New York with him and everything, and he *paid* her! She says that property tax is taken care of because of it. They might even get back together! Isn't that marvelous?"

Greg's face fell. His expression looked scandalized. "Emily? Get back together with *Vinh*? What the fuck?"

"Language!" her mother yelped.

"Why are you having *anything* to do with that bastard?" Greg asked, his voice low but heated. "After what he did to you? He just fucking *abandoned* you when you needed him!"

"We talked it out," Emily said, not wanting to go into everything Vinh had told her. "Turns out, he had good reasons for not being able to drop everything and help me out back then. And . . . well, I figured out that it was wrong of me to expect quite so much of him. And to blame him for not meeting those expectations."

Greg's voice turned into a growl. "That sounds like gaslighting, Em."

Her mother waved her hands, fluttering like a distraught bird. "That was all in the past. They've worked it out."

"Oh, *God*. Please tell me you're not thinking about that!" Greg now looked sick.

"He paid the property tax bill and gave us money to fix the water heater and refill the house-repair fund," their mother added. "He's certainly acting sorry!"

"Did you take it?" Greg said.

Emily could feel the conversation jumping the tracks and rubbed her temples. "All right, wait a second . . ."

"Of course," their mother said, sounding defensive but also somehow cheerful. "If a man gives me money, no strings attached . . . well, I'd be an idiot to say no, wouldn't I?"

"Mom . . . ," Greg warned.

"Yes, well, you don't know how much it's taken to keep this house afloat!" Mom's voice trembled with indignation and sadness.

"And there's my opening," Emily leaped in. "This is why I wanted us all on this call together. Because *we can't keep the house.*"

Her mother reeled back like she'd slapped her. *"What?"*

Greg looked similarly stunned. "What do you mean, we can't keep the house?"

Emily sighed. "We haven't been able to keep it together for years," she said quietly. "We're barely staying ahead of the bills, and that's with me living at home and contributing to utilities and the mortgage. The repairs are going to start outweighing what we owe; the taxes are going up. And . . ."

She took a deep breath. This was going to be the hard part.

"I love you both so much," Emily said. "But this *isn't what I want.*"

Her mother pressed her hand to her mouth.

"I don't want to live at home, work any crappy job I can get, and put all my money towards a house I don't even enjoy living in. One that's slowly crushing me," Emily said in a quiet voice. "I want to take time and go back to college, maybe. Finish my degree, or at least get a certification for ethical hacking. I want to get a better job so I can stop being exhausted all the time. And I'm *lucky* that I have a shot at that. I'm privileged. But . . . I can't do it if I'm stuck on the treadmill here. If we don't make changes, we're all going to get sunk by this."

Her mother's eyes started to well with tears. She moved her hand away from her mouth to say, "But your father loved this house. This was his dream house."

"It was," Emily said. "I loved Dad so much—you know that. I miss him every day. He was just so fun and happy. He dreamed bigger than anybody I've ever known and was more optimistic than anyone too."

Her mother smiled, even though the tears had already started to run. Greg made a noise of assent as well.

"But he mortgaged the house to the hilt," Emily said. "He left us in debt. And as much as he dreamed about us having this lavish lifestyle, and me getting married and having a dozen kids, and Greg going off to college and then law or med school . . . what Dad wanted isn't necessarily what happened. And maybe it shouldn't be."

Her mother's lips quivered. "What are you saying?"

Emily looked over at Greg on the screen. "You keep going to college, taking a few courses, and dropping out," she said. "Do you even *like* school?"

He opened his mouth, then shut it with a quiet snap, frowning. Then, slowly, he shook his head.

"I like being a mechanic," he admitted. "And spending time with my pets."

"You could study to be a vet," their mother jumped in, looking a little frantic . . . as if all their father's dreams were vanishing into thin air.

"I don't want to be a vet, though," Greg protested. "I just like my plants and my pets. That's enough for me. I don't want it to be my job."

Their mother was gritting her teeth.

"It's funny you should mention this, Em. I've been doing a lot of thinking down here," Greg continued, "and I think I've figured it out, although I wasn't quite brave enough to bring it up yet. When I get back, I think I'll get my ASE mechanic's certification. I might get into a house share with somebody, so I have more room for the animals. Maybe a garden. But you're right—I'm not happy, and I'm not going back to college," he finished. "Sorry, Ma. I wasn't going to tell you until I got home, but I guess now's as good a time as any."

Her mother looked at her, pleading. "But . . . but, Emily, you're getting back together with Vinh," she said with conviction. "It sounds like he has tons of money! He could take care of all of this like it was nothing!"

"*Mom!*" Greg sounded pained.

"What? He'd be family!" Now her mother sounded near hysteria.

Emily put her hand on her mother's, calming the fluttering motion. She waited until her mother had calmed down enough to look in her eyes. "Even if I somehow managed to get back together with Vinh," she said, "I'm not doing it just so you can keep this house. And I don't think you should expect me to or want me to. Because this is *too much house*, and you don't even like it. Not really. It's too much to clean, too much to maintain. Too much to pay for."

Her mother bit the corner of her lip. "It's all I have left of your father," she breathed.

Emily suddenly felt eighty years old and heartsick on top of it.

"I understand," Emily said.

"No, you don't," her mother spat out, surprising Emily by yanking her hand away. "If you did, you wouldn't be saying all this. Jack loved me more than anything. He would've moved the *moon* if he thought it would make me happy. And the same with you kids. He paid for your colleges . . ."

"By *mortgaging the house*," Emily pointed out. "The same way he paid for the vacations we couldn't afford and cars we couldn't afford.

And he didn't tell you about it because he wanted to protect you. But then he died, and . . . well, all of a sudden, we had to deal with the fallout."

Her mother put her face in her hands, crying quietly.

"Mom," Greg said. "Remember that time that Dad took you to that fancy place down in San Diego? Donovan's or something? For your anniversary?"

She looked up, nodding. "He always got rib eye," she said. "And a baked potato."

"And then he took you for a walk to look at the art galleries?" he prompted. "And he got you that bronze sculpture of the ballerina you love?"

She looked puzzled. "Yes."

"Still have that?"

"You know I do," she said. "It's still on the table, in the study."

"What about all Dad's photos? The yachts?"

She nodded. "Sometimes I pull them out to look at."

"I've got Dad's cuff links and his class ring," Greg said. "And his Hugo Boss tux. And that baseball card he got signed by Tony Gwynn. Emily, what do you have?"

Emily thought she could see where her brother was going with it. "I've got photos with him too," she said. "That gold locket he gave me and the diamond tennis bracelet. And his collection of DVDs, the sci-fi movies we loved."

"We've still got memories, Ma," her brother said with more nuance and gentleness than Emily would've given him credit for. "The kind you can touch and the kind you just remember. You're not going to lose Dad if you lose the house. I don't think I'm going to disappoint him if I never go to college. And Emily's stepped up too much, for too long, to try and keep us on this track. She deserves her own life and to be happy. Do you think Dad would want Emily to give up all her dreams for the future for a house?"

Her mother let out a hiccup-y little sigh. She looked at Emily . . . and it felt like, for the first time, she was actually *seeing* Emily: what Emily had given up and how broken she now felt.

"I didn't . . . I thought you understood. I thought you felt the same way." Her mother sounded lost. "But your father wouldn't want you to be unhappy. He wouldn't want *me* to make you unhappy just to keep his memory alive." She shuddered, sounding suddenly appalled. "Oh my God. What have I been doing to you?"

"It's all right, Mom," Emily said. "We'll figure it out."

"I'll be home in March," Greg said. "And we can tackle things then."

Her mother straightened in her chair, and for the first time in her whole life, Emily saw something like determination in her eyes.

"No," she said. "I'm . . . going to start figuring this out. Myself. I'll let you know, and we'll talk about it—we are family, after all. But I've been leaning too hard on you kids. I need to do something on my own about all this now."

After that, Greg signed off, and Emily drew her mother into a hug. "Are you all right?"

"Not quite, darling," she said, then gave her a kiss on the cheek. "But . . . I think I will be."

Emily felt drained but also heartened. And for the first time in a long time, since her father had died, she felt like a weight had been lifted. Like she had a path toward freedom, if she just was brave enough to take it.

CHAPTER 40

Vinh was sitting at an elegantly appointed table in one of the most exclusive steak houses in Manhattan, one where you normally couldn't get a reservation for months, but his assistant had somehow miraculously finagled it. His mother's husband, Scott, let out a low whistle as he took in the waiting area, and the hostess quickly brought them to a small private room.

"I'm glad that you're visiting," he said after they had all sat down and given their drink orders to the server. "Any special reason you're in New York? Medical conference? Playing tourist?" He threw that last one in as a joke—he couldn't remember the last time his mother had taken a vacation.

His mother looked beautiful, if somewhat stern. She was only forty-nine years old, and other than the worry lines that would furrow her forehead, her hair was still glossy and black, her skin clear. She was wearing a small amount of makeup, never really having had a fondness for the stuff. She said it got in the way and was the last thing she thought about during long hours in her medical practice, especially when she was in residency. Scott, on the other hand, was only forty-five, a reed-thin white guy with a receding hairline and a pair of wire-rimmed glasses. He laughed a lot, was a huge fantasy football fan, and was father to two children—a teen and a tween, Vinh was pretty sure.

"I came out to visit my only son," his mother said, and there was a smile in her voice that he hadn't heard before—as well as a hesitancy. "Is that all right?"

"Of course," Vinh said, unsure how to respond.

The server brought their drinks—wine for his mother and Scott, a gin and tonic for him—and then they put in their orders, including appetizers. "How are you?" his mother asked once they had privacy again. "Your sister mentioned that you were in town this past month."

She didn't say it with any hint of passive-aggressiveness; there had been plenty of times where he'd swung through Los Angeles or San Diego and hadn't stopped to visit, since his mother's medical practice was usually very busy. They weren't that sort of family, he'd always reasoned.

So why was he feeling a tiny shred of guilt *now*?

"I had some stuff I had to take care of in Ponto," he said, shrugging it off. "It was nice seeing Tam, though."

"It's nice that you two are still close." His mother took a long sip of wine. "God knows that you two needed each other. Growing up with your father and me was not easy."

Vinh stared at her like snakes had suddenly sprouted from her head. He literally had no idea what to say to that. Their family didn't *talk* about stuff. Well, other than Tam, who often joked that she felt like a changeling who had gotten sneaked into the house. But by and large, their major communication patterns were screaming (his parents) and protectively reacting (the kids). He took a gulp of his G&T, feeling unaccountably nervous.

"I just wanted to say I'm sorry," she said, shocking him further.

"You're not *dying*, are you?" he blurted out.

She stared at him, then started giggling. Scott started laughing outright. "Oh my God. I suppose that's appalling that it's your first response," she said, shaking her head. "No, Vinh. I am not dying. I've got a perfect bill of health."

"Then . . . ?" Vinh still couldn't wrap his head around the conversation. "Why are we talking about this at all?"

"Because I'm starting to see just how hard it was for you and your sister," she said, her voice serious now. "Because I now understand what it means to be a parent—and how very badly I feel that we put you kids through what we did."

Vinh very briefly considered slipping a waiter a fifty to yank the fire alarm to get away from this highly uncomfortable moment. "It is what it is," he croaked. "I mean, it's the past—it's over with now, anyway. Not a big deal."

"It *is* a big deal," she said. "You know Scott and I coparent Tiffany and Jeremy on weekends. We try to make it for their recitals and things. And I've been better about guarding my work hours to make sure that I'm there too."

Okay, Vinh felt a very *brief* prickle of resentment as he remembered how many times he'd had to bum a ride home from track practice in middle school—or when they'd made the state semifinals in Academic Bowl and his parents had forgotten to pick him up again, leaving Tam and him to cram in the back of Hayden's parents' car and endure their pitying glances.

But for God's sake, that was years ago. Vinh shrugged. "That's good," he said instead and meant it. "Kids need that."

"But don't *you* need that too?" she said.

Vinh smirked. "Ah, but I'm not a kid."

"You're *my* kid."

Her words floored him. He quickly drank some more gin and tonic.

She took a deep breath, looking at Scott, who took her hand and held it on top of the table, stroking her knuckles.

"I've . . . also been seeing a therapist," his mother said.

Now, Vinh felt like he'd been dumped out of his chair. His grandparents—his father's parents, more to the point—had hated the *idea* of therapy, saying that it was a scam and warning against airing the family's business to strangers. They had dismissed the idea of mental health. The fact that his mother was going to therapy was frickin' *huge*.

"Do you feel like it's helping?"

She nodded and smiled. "It really has been," she said. "I was only twenty when I got pregnant with you and your sister. My family kicked me out for ruining my chances at becoming a doctor, so your father and I moved in with his parents . . . and you know how they are."

Vinh grimaced, thinking of their ultimatum: give up Emily, or Tam would lose her college tuition. "Yeah, I know how they are," he said, realizing he'd said the same thing to his father—even if his father had missed the connotations.

"I resented so many things, for so many years," she continued, her tone a bit sad. "I was angry at your father because I blamed him for losing that opportunity. I hated your grandparents, your father's parents. But felt like I couldn't do anything because they were the only ones who would take me in when I was pregnant. And—and this is hard to admit—I resented you two because I'd always dreamed of being a doctor, and you two seemed like the end of my dreams."

"Um," Vinh said, his voice raspy, "ouch?"

"It doesn't mean I didn't love you! That I don't love you," she rushed to reassure him. "I just wanted to have some dreams of my own . . . and it seemed like I was turning myself inside out to make everyone else happy. My therapist says I was setting myself on fire to keep everyone warm."

Vinh nodded, thinking about it. *That's what Emily does.*

Did Emily resent it? How could she not?

"But I also realize I could've handled it better," she said, and he saw Scott squeeze her hand.

Vinh shook his head. "Don't worry," he said, feeling strangely lighter. "If you could've done better . . . you *would* have done better. I really believe that."

"You do?" Now it was his mother's turn to sound shocked.

"I know you love us, Mom," he said. "And I'm glad that you got to become a doctor, even if it meant a lot of hard work. I know what it means to you."

"It's hard to juggle," Scott said when his mother looked speechless, swallowing hard, then drinking some water. "I used to own a start-up, and it cost me my marriage with Brit—that's my ex. She knew that my business was important to me, but she didn't sign up for me being gone all the time, especially when the kids were small. I messed that up royally, and when we divorced, I sold the business and did some work on myself. Now, I make my kids my priority, and I've got a better work-life balance. I know not everyone can—especially when you're struggling financially. But if you've got the money and a good job, it's worth negotiating for." He grinned. "Just putting my two cents in there."

Vinh's eyes narrowed as he studied his mother and Scott. "Did Tam put you up to this, by any chance?"

"Tam said you were in a bit of a funk but didn't give details," his mother said. "Scott and I are going on a cruise to Saint Thomas before the holidays, starting here in New York, since the kids are spending Christmas with Brit and her new husband. I just wanted to see you before we went, as long as we had the chance." She paused a beat. "I feel like I've missed too many chances before. I don't want to do that again if I can help it."

He felt his chest warm. "Thanks, Mom."

"Where are you going to be for Christmas?"

"Here," he said. "Although if I can swing a flight . . . maybe I'll go back to Ponto. Spend Christmas with Tam and Josh and the rest of the Herd."

"I am so grateful that you found them," she said. "I know how much they meant to you. It's hard to find friends like that. Friends that are family."

He nodded. "Yeah, it is." He thought about being back in Ponto . . . about hanging out with Hayden and Tobin, playing board games at the holiday party, joking with Asad and Freddie at Herdsgiving. Even hanging out one on one with Tam.

But it would mean seeing Emily, and that pain was still really fresh.

Maybe there's a way. A better way, he thought.

"Was it worth it?" he found himself asking Scott.

"Was what worth it?"

"Selling your business. Leaving your job."

Scott grinned.

"I'd do it again in a heartbeat."

CHAPTER 41

I have no idea what I'm doing.

Emily took a deep breath. She'd taken an oh-God-early flight out of San Diego to get to JFK in the afternoon, using some of the money Vinh had paid her. There was snow coating everything, and she was glad she'd remembered to pack a warmer jacket, even though it really wasn't up to what was needed. She thought she'd freeze her butt entirely off while she was waiting for her Uber. At least the driver had the heat cranking as they crawled their way through the slush and the traffic before finally arriving at Vinh's apartment.

After having the tough talk with her mother and brother, she felt like they'd finally moved past the weird limbo that they'd been trapped in since her father's death. She'd never noticed, so intent on keeping things status quo as best she could that she'd never really *grieved*. They'd just sort of settled into this weird state of perpetual motion—as if, by putting out continual fires and (barely) keeping everything afloat, she'd never looked at what she was actually feeling. She'd loved her father, and at times since his death, she'd resented him for leaving them the way he had—not just the debt but the suddenness, which hadn't really been his fault. It wasn't like he'd brought the aneurysm on himself. Now, she knew that it would take time to untangle the emotions, but she felt like at least she had the breathing room for it.

Her mother was a work in progress about the whole thing, which wasn't surprising. Overall, though, she'd agreed to sell the house. The reason property taxes had gone up so exponentially was because the market was ridiculously high—she'd be able to pay off the debt completely and have some left over for herself—to buy a smaller place, perhaps, or rent. She hated maintenance, hated the mental overwhelm that seemed to descend whenever something needed fixing. She didn't even spend time in their yard, so it wasn't like she wanted a lawn or a pool. She was crying more, but Greg of all people had suggested that she might consider therapy . . . and to Emily's relief, her mother seemed actually open to it.

Without the albatross of the house, Emily suddenly found herself in the enviable position of having *choices*. She might have some money to put aside—might be able to get that certification and get a new job.

Which also meant she could, theoretically, leave Ponto Beach.

Not that she wanted to. She still loved her complicated family, and she adored the Herd, who had been her lifeline and her safety net combined over the years. She didn't want to leave them. But she had to be honest. She and Vinh had lost their chance because of her selfishness and shortsightedness and because of his high-handed determination to do the right thing all those years ago. She didn't know if trying to stay together long distance would've worked. Probably, it wouldn't have. But now that they'd grown, and changed, and matured, it felt like they had a real chance.

This time, she wasn't going to let it slip away.

It was a Friday, the day before Christmas Eve. She'd been hesitant to leave so close to the holiday, but her mother had also bought a ticket to see her family in Connecticut. They'd actually taken the same flight, with her mother then taking a connecting train out of Grand Central to New Haven. Her cousin was going to be picking her up on the other end. When Emily had tentatively suggested accompanying her on the train, adding that she'd catch up with Vinh afterward or something, her mother had been firm.

"I'm going to be fine," she said. "After all, you've worked through Christmases and Thanksgivings before, and I gave you a hard time then—but it was that whole perfect-memory thing. Your father did love holidays. But that doesn't mean I can't enjoy it with my family."

"You sure?" Emily had asked.

Her mother's smile was sad but also hopeful. "If I were your age and I had Jack," she said, "I would grab him with both hands and never let go."

Which appeared to be her mother's stamp of approval: Vinh was her true love, her soul mate. The man of her dreams.

Emily was shivering in Vinh's lobby, her scuffed old roller bag trailing behind her. She hoped she wasn't tracking too much slush into the place, carefully dragging her feet over the thick mat in front of the door. The doorman smiled at her genially.

"Ms. MacDonald," he said. "So nice to see you again. Here to visit Mr. Doan, I presume?"

She nodded, suddenly getting a sick feeling in the pit of her stomach. "Is it all right if I, erm, go up? I have his door code," she said, feeling nervous. What if he'd taken her off the accepted-visitors list?

"Of course," the doorman said with a grin. "Go on up."

She did, riding the elevator, feeling the slight sway of the building, which did nothing to calm the shuddering feelings of nervousness in her stomach. God, at this rate, she'd have to pop some Pepto tablets that she'd packed in case of travel sickness.

She remembered the code, thankfully, and let herself inside. As usual, the place was immaculate. Since it was an afternoon on a weekday, she figured he was still toiling away at Aimsley. She still wasn't sure how they were going to negotiate that. She knew that he spent months overseas and barely stayed in the city at any one time. But that didn't mean that they couldn't be together. Maybe she could stay in Ponto

Beach, and they could do long distance from there. Maybe she could stay here, watch over his place, and go back to school while he worked.

However it worked, they would hopefully be together. If she hadn't ruined everything irrevocably.

Suddenly, she heard the door unlocking, and she stood, bouncing lightly from one foot to the other. This was it. The moment of truth.

She heard him laugh as the door opened. "So as you can see," he said, looking behind him as he opened the door for someone, "this is my condo."

Then a beautiful brown-haired woman walked in with a wide, warm smile.

CHAPTER 42

Vinh had had a busy day.

The holiday party and then dinner with his mother and stepfather—which still felt weird to refer to Scott as—had shifted things in him. He realized it had been slowly changing over time. He'd been disassociating, turning into a vengeful ghost in his own life. Something to fear, but something that ultimately had no connection to his own world.

In the short time he'd been back in Ponto Beach, he'd not only reconnected with love, but he'd also found things that he hadn't realized he'd given up. A new relationship to family, hanging with Tam, and now opening up dialogue with his mother. He'd probably always have a complicated relationship with his father's side of the family and his father himself, but that was all right. He didn't need to make himself miserable for the approval of people who made achieving the impossible not only expected but somehow not good enough. He'd spent his life trying to please them, trying to spitefully best them.

He needed to let that go.

He also had found the Herd again and couldn't believe he'd let himself lose them for so long. And despite feeling guilty as hell about that, he'd been welcomed back like not a day had passed. He'd had *fun* with them. He'd felt accepted and supported. He'd felt like he wasn't alone anymore.

Above all, he'd finally come clean with Emily, healing those old wounds. He had a *chance* with her. She might not be ready to move to New York, might not ever want to move there, and he understood. Ponto Beach was special. She had her own issues with her family, but he could hardly throw stones in that regard.

So he'd finally made some big decisions . . . and now he was putting them into action.

He guided the woman at his side—Camila—into his condo. "So as you can see," he said, gesturing to the interior, "this is my condo."

"It's beautiful," Camila cooed, then stopped abruptly. "Oh! Hello."

He looked over and then stared, stunned, at Emily in his living room. She looked stricken. "Emily?"

She grabbed her roller bag and started to head for the door, shaking. "This . . . was a bad idea," she muttered, tears in her voice. "I should have warned you, I guess. But I guess it's better I learned this now, huh?"

"Whoa! Whoa, whoa, whoa," he said, standing in front of her. "Baby, what are you doing here? What's wrong?"

She swiped at her eyes with one hand. "I didn't mean to interrupt anything," she said, her voice sharp, and she cut a quick glance at Camila, whose eyes had widened.

"Oh, God, no," Camila almost shouted. "No! Really. I'm not . . . we're not . . . I'm just here for the apartment!"

"Em, this is Camila Gutierrez," he said, holding Emily's hand and tugging her to him. "My *real estate agent.* Who is here to help me sell the condo."

Camila beamed. "So nice to meet you! You must be Emily."

Emily looked gobsmacked. "Um . . . yes," she said.

Vinh rubbed her shoulders, then pulled her tight against him, relishing the feel of her slight figure against his chest. He pressed a long kiss on the top of her head, then pulled back to look into her eyes. "When did you get here? And why didn't you tell me? I would've sent a car or picked you up," he said. When she didn't answer, just stared at him, he tilted her chin up so he could look in her eyes. "Are you all right?"

He watched her throat work as she swallowed; then tears welled up in her eyes. "I thought . . ." She shot another quick look at Camila. "I thought I'd ruined it. I thought I'd made a mistake."

Camila cleared her throat. "I'm going to take a look around, take some measurements," she said. "Let you two talk, okay?"

"Sure, look at whatever you like," Vinh said, not even looking away from Emily. "Em, what did you think you ruined?"

"Us."

He felt a thrill rush through him. "Us," he echoed, loving the way that sounded coming from her lips.

"I came here because I didn't want to be without you anymore," she said. "And I don't know what that looks like, but if you're serious . . . I want to try."

He held her tighter, kissing her softly. "I want to try too."

"So a Realtor? You're moving?" She took a deep breath. "Vinh. I'm not going to make you do that, give up everything for me. I want to be with you. If that means moving to New York, then I'll do it," she said. "I have some loose ends to tie up, things with family that still need to be worked out. But I'm tired of not taking risks. I'll just be miserable, and I'll lose anyway. I want to be with you." She grinned ruefully. "Even called in sick to come here. Although I don't think I'm going to have that job for much longer anyway."

He tucked her hair behind her ear and stroked her cheek. It was a simple movement, but he loved the silken feel of her hair, the downy softness of her cheek, the way she curled into his touch. He'd denied himself it for too long, and he was going to do it every day from now on if he had any say in it. He pressed kisses around her face. "You don't have to move to New York."

She frowned, a cute little line forming between her eyebrows. "Well, if you want to do long distance," she said, "I guess that would work. You are probably going to still be traveling a lot . . ."

"Emily . . ."

"But it's a digital world now, right?" she mused, and he could see her brain working. "Besides, we can totally sext. I mean, I haven't done it before, but I'm smart, and it can't be that difficult."

Vinh heard a laugh-covering cough coming from the bedroom. Camila had apparently heard that bit. He stifled a grin. "Emily . . ."

"And we'll figure out when we can see each other in person." Emily was on a roll now, in full problem-solving mode. She would've made a good consultant, he realized, if she wanted to. A determined Emily was an unstoppable Emily, or at least, she had been when they were young. It was good to see that coming back. "Because I'm not going for years without seeing you, got it?"

He couldn't help it. He kissed her again, silencing her with his lips. After a minute, he felt her go warm and pliant in his arms, sagging against him, molding herself to him. "Em, you don't have to move to New York because I'm moving back to Ponto Beach."

She gaped. "Wait, what?"

"I'm moving," he said. "And you won't have to worry about figuring out how to sext me because I also quit my job."

"*What?*" she yelped.

"After all the bullshit that happened, I realized that this isn't a place I want to work for," he said. "I talked with Tobin a little, too, about burnout. And I talked with Tam about figuring out what you really want." He grinned. "I know some smart people."

Emily was crying a little again, but her smile was bright. "Yeah, you do."

"I don't know what I'm going to do next," he said, "but I know I want to do it *with you.* And I want to go home."

"That sounds good," she whispered. "Going home. Making a home with you."

He smiled, smoothing away her tears. "As soon as humanly possible," he said and kissed the tip of her nose. "Because I love you beyond reason."

"I love you too."

Camila cleared her throat, and the two of them looked at her, their arms still wrapped around each other. "Well, thankfully," Camila said, her glossy billboard-worthy smile bright and just a *touch* avaricious, "I can say, if you'll excuse the pun, that I can sell this condo in a New York minute. This is fantastic. I can already think of several buyers." Vinh could almost see the dollar signs in her eyes, flashing like a cartoon.

"Good. I'm going to be moving as soon as possible," Vinh said. He felt Emily hug him tighter.

"You two are adorable," Camila said. "All right! I'm going to get stuff together, make some calls, but don't worry. I am going to sell this quickly, and you are going to make a bundle, okay?"

Vinh nodded. "I trust you. Thanks, Camila." Thank goodness the firm had a favorite agency.

Camila gave a little wave and saw herself out. Vinh looked at the roller bag. "C'mon. Let's move this, huh?"

Emily nodded. "I feel a little foolish," she said. "I was just so worried I'd fuck this up and you'd change your mind."

"Hey, none of that," he said. "I have been in love with you for, what, fifteen years? Longer?"

She grinned. "The whole time?"

"Even when we weren't together, I never stopped," he admitted. If he was in, he was going to be all in. "I know that's probably weird. But you were always it for me."

She sighed. "I didn't want you to be, for a while there," she said. "But yeah. No one ever measured up to you. Nobody ever loved me like you."

He felt that warmth radiating from his chest. "I'm going to spend the rest of my life making sure you don't doubt me again. Making you happy."

"If you want to make me happy," she replied, kissing him, "all you have to do is be there."

CHAPTER 43

Emily woke up in Vinh's arms on Christmas morning, and it was quite possibly the best Christmas she'd ever had, eclipsing the years she'd gotten the Barbie Dreamhouse when she was six and her first Alienware rig when she was fifteen. And she hadn't even gotten out of bed yet.

She had hoped for this outcome, wished with all her heart for it, but in a lot of ways, it still felt unreal. She'd spent time holed up with Vinh, ignoring the world around them. She was glad that the office shut down for a bit over the holidays and that she'd put in PTO for the days around Christmas. They'd stayed in and looked at the lacy snow piling up outside the windows. They'd eaten at the fancy restaurant Vinh liked—and a few hidden gems: hole-in-the-wall dim sum places, the best chopped-cheese sandwiches in the city, real thin-crust New York pizza. They'd watched silly movies, laughing at the antics.

Most of all, they'd talked. It was more than reconnecting. It was laying a groundwork, a foundation for their future.

He was still asleep. She knew there were a ton of books that described men as more innocent or harmless looking when they slept, but of course, Vinh wasn't one of them. His face was frowning, his forehead furrowed. He looked like he was wreaking vengeance on someone in his dreams.

He doesn't have nightmares, she imagined in a "Heisenberg from *Breaking Bad*" voice. *He is the nightmare.*

She snickered.

"Hmm?" he murmured in response, still half-asleep, eyes closed. Now, he had a slumberous smile on his face.

She spun, kissing his chest, stroking the taut muscles, moving her hands down his happy trail—and further. She scooted down under the covers, giggling. Then she took him into her mouth.

She glanced up to see that his eyes had flown open. "Merry Christmas to *me*," he croaked, his body going taut.

She laughed—or at least, as close to laughing as she could manage, considering her current activity.

She lost track of how much time it took to work him over. She luxuriated in the taste of him, the smell, the way his hands fisted in the sheets, and how he tried so hard not to move, to let her set the pace and make all the moves and choices. To be comfortable. And when he finally, inevitably, lost control, he warned her. She didn't care. She swallowed every drop, licking at him as he shook and shuddered.

"Wow," he muttered. "As soon as I regain feeling in my other limbs, I'm going to return the favor."

"No rush," she said, stretching and feeling pretty damned proud of herself. "I've got you for the rest of the day. We've got plenty of time."

He tugged her up, kissing her throat in the way that made her shiver. "More time than that," he said. "Lots more time."

She smiled, holding him tight. Loving him so hard she could barely breathe.

They finally got up, then showered and got dressed. Emily called her mother, who seemed to be happy at her aunt's house.

"Gram giving you trouble?" Emily asked when her mother was in her own guest room. "Or Gramps?"

"A little," her mother admitted. "Gramps has been happy to see me, in his way—but then again, as long as there isn't any fuss, he's pretty content. But your grandmother is so different than I remember, sweetheart. She'd always been so formidable."

"A battle-ax in Chanel," Emily joked, and her mother laughed.

"I wouldn't have said it that way, but yes. Now, she's still sharp, and she'll put you in your place in a blink, but . . ." Her mother seemed to struggle for words. "She's so frail, Em. I was shocked when I saw her."

Emily felt sad. She'd never been close to her mother's family because of the estrangement, and her father's family lived in Michigan somewhere. He'd lost his parents in his teens, bouncing around aunts' and uncles' houses until he'd struck out for California to escape the horrible winters and make his fortune. Other than the occasional Christmas card, she hadn't been close to that family either.

"It made me feel awful for how I've been acting since your father's death," her mother said slowly. "I'm not eighty, for God's sake. And I see your Aunt Lydia and the way she just relies on her husband and fusses over her kids and is a busybody in their lives and how they hate it. How in the world did you put up with me?"

"It wasn't that bad," Emily said.

"It's not going to be like that again," her mother said firmly. "I'm going to call a real estate agent as soon as I get home. And there are going to be some changes."

Emily took that as an encouraging sign.

Vinh called his mother and her husband, where they were vacationing in Saint Thomas. Then he grinned. "Wanna have some fun?"

She smiled, and he video called Tam, motioning Emily to stay out of the camera frame. "Vinh!" she greeted. "Merry Christmas!"

"Merry Christmas." His smile was small and sly.

"Please, please tell me you're not working today."

"I'm not working today."

There was a pause. "You know, I think I believe you," Tam said, sounding surprised. "What the heck are you doing?"

He finally revealed his grin . . . then reached out, tugged Emily into his lap, and kissed her soundly.

"Holy shit!" Tam's shout of surprise was loud, and Vinh and Emily both burst into laughter. "Josh! Josh! You gotta come see this!"

Josh tilted his head into the frame, taking in the sight, then started laughing too. "'Bout time you two got your shit together," he said.

"Considering how long it took you and Tam to figure it out," Emily shot back, "that's kind of the pot calling the kettle black, isn't it?"

Josh grinned back. "Fair."

"How did this happen? *When* did this happen?" Tam said, still processing. "And are you moving, Emily? I feel like I just got back. I'm going to miss you!"

"No, you're not," Vinh said. "Because I'm moving back to Ponto."

The squee of joy that Tam unleashed sounded almost inhuman. "I. Am. So. *Happy!*" she shouted, then kissed Josh, who grinned against her mouth.

"I'll tell you all about it when I get back there—which should be soon. I'll let you get on with your Christmas."

After they hung up, Vinh smiled at her. "So. You ready to celebrate *our* Christmas?"

She smiled. Before she could say anything, he tugged her to the bedroom, closing the door between them. "Don't peek!" he said, his voice muffled by the barrier.

She snickered, then went to her luggage to grab the present she'd gotten in the hopes that they worked out. It had been such a long shot, but now she was glad that she'd taken the time.

After a few minutes, he opened the door. "Okay. Merry Christmas, Emily."

She looked out at the living room . . . then burst out laughing.

He had a tiny little Christmas tree in a pot on the dining room table, decorated with some ornaments and tinsel. Something suddenly clicked.

"Wait, is that from the lobby?"

"The doorman likes me," Vinh said, sounding abashed. "If I'd known you were coming, I would've done something more . . ."

"It's fantastic," she said. Then she saw that he had a small box under the tree on the table. "What did you do?"

He smiled. "Open it and see."

She did, feeling nervous. He was ridiculously rich, and let's face it, she was broke. She didn't want it to feel like a competition, but she still worried she'd come up short.

Now that she looked at it, it was kind of a small box, she realized. And she freaked out even more. *There's no way this damned thing is what I think it is.*

Taking a deep breath, she undid the beautiful store-wrapped packaging. Then she gasped.

It *was* a ring. She didn't know much about jewelry, but it was what she would've picked out: what looked like a titanium band, simple and strong, with a square-cut emerald. He remembered that she hated diamonds.

She looked up at him, stunned.

"It doesn't have to mean engagement," he said quietly. "I know we're just getting back together, and we have a ton to work out. But I feel like I've waited my whole life to be with you, and I wanted you to know: I'm all in. When you're ready, I'm ready."

"When did you get this?" she breathed.

"As soon as I quit my job."

She felt like she was melting. "I got you a present too," she said, instead of acknowledging his statement. She handed him the shoebox she'd wrapped in garish red-and-green paper that she'd had at the house.

He smiled, even though she felt like he might be disappointed at her lack of response to his unspoken question. He tore through the paper, then opened the box. Then went very, very still.

"What do you get the guy who can buy himself anything, amirite?" she said, laughing nervously as he sifted through the contents.

They were memories.

Movie tickets from the first official "date" they'd gone on—the Spike and Mike's Animation Festival. Photos of them on camping trips with the Herd. Them outside *Rocky Horror Picture Show*, grinning and goofing around. Her diary from middle school, where she waxed rhapsodic about the boy she'd met and was fascinated by, his somber demeanor and quiet smile, his raw intelligence and puckish, if rarely shown, sense of humor. There was a program from the Academic Bowl where they'd finally kissed, on a dark campus, waiting for their rides. A small toy dinosaur he'd won from a claw game.

"I almost burned this," she admitted. "I was so hurt. Instead, I wrote a list of why I should never get back together with you. Why I hated you."

He put the box down, holding her to him.

"I burned the list instead," she said. "We can't change what happened in the past, and even if I didn't like what happened, I'm not sorry that it happened. I think we wouldn't have made it if we'd kept going the way we were. I didn't understand your life, and you needed to work out your stuff without me. Now we can just move forward."

"I'd change a lot of things about my past," he said, his voice clogged with emotion. "But I would never change being in love with you. And I'm glad I'm getting a second chance."

"We both are."

"And now we're going to work on our future."

She steeled herself. Then she put out her hand.

"You're it for me," she said. "One way or another. So why don't you put that on me, and we'll get started."

His smile was like the sun. Then he got on one knee, taking the ring from the box.

"Marry me?" he asked, holding the band in his hand. "Stay with me, love me?"

She felt her breath catch in her throat. Then she smiled and turned the page.

"Forever," she said as he slipped it on her finger.

Then, in true Vinh-and-Emily fashion—she pounced on him.

EPILOGUE

Three years later—Herdsgiving

"What the hell is *that*?" Vinh asked, staring as Hayden put a platter down on Tam and Josh's dining room table, which was already laden with food.

"It's my own creation," Hayden said, rubbing his hands and sounding frighteningly like Frankenstein unveiling his monster. "It's meatloaf wrapped around a pie full of spaghetti Bolognese, covered with mashed potatoes. I call it: Cottage PieLoafen."

"You said you were bringing salad," Tam muttered. "I hate you right now."

"Salad! Ha!" Hayden proclaimed. "Salad is for the weak!"

Josh burst into laughter. "It's the spaghetti that makes no sense to me."

"That's the only part?" Asad chimed in. "Really, Josh? *Really?*"

Josh and Tam burst into laughter. Vinh did too, shaking his head.

"No work today, Vinh?" Tam teased him, nudging him and handing him a tumbler of whiskey.

He grinned back. "My boss is a bastard, but he isn't that bad."

She laughed. He worked for himself now. He'd taken some time off to decompress, on Tobin's suggestion, when he'd first gotten back to Ponto Beach, and it had been one of the best decisions he'd ever made in his life. He and Emily had painstakingly talked out what they wanted and how they were going to get there. He'd gotten a small house near downtown Ponto Beach, not beachfront or anything but a place with a nice fenced backyard. He'd even tried some container gardening, although his tomatoes had all gotten eaten by worms.

Slowly, he'd built up a select clientele, working as a freelance consultant. He didn't take any jobs that would require him to be away from Emily for longer than a few weeks.

"Hey, you," she said, sidling up and kissing him.

"Hey back," he said, kissing her more soundly, loving the way she sighed into it.

"You two! Get a room!" Tobin called from the kitchen.

Vinh didn't stop what he was doing, simply flipping Tobin off without even looking over, setting off another round of laughter. "You okay?" he asked Emily when he finally pulled away.

"Yeah. Just checking in with Greg, seeing how Mom and the family are."

Her mother had sold the house and then made the surprise decision to move back to Connecticut. Her grandparents seemed pleased, even if they drove her mother up the wall, and her mother was happy enough helping out with taking care of them—running errands, taking their grandmother for haircuts and manicures, things like that. Emily's aunt seemed happy to get the break too. Greg and Emily switched off going back East to visit.

"Still liking the new job, Em?" Tobin asked.

"So very much," she said, and the simple satisfaction in her voice made Vinh unspeakably happy. It had taken two years to go through the training, and then she'd had to get accepted to simply take the exam— which, unsurprisingly, she'd passed with flying colors.

"Yeah, well, we miss you at the café," Juanita said. "Cyril says nobody made a vanilla latte like you did."

Emily grinned. She'd worked at the café so she had a more flexible schedule while she was in training. Now she'd been at her new job for about eight months, a boutique cybersecurity firm in La Jolla that was starting to make waves, and she loved every minute of it. Vinh only ever wanted her to be happy, so to see her so relaxed and thrilled was a dream come true.

"So is it everything you thought it would be?" Emily whispered at him. "Kind of bananas, kind of chaotic . . . but good?"

He kissed her.

"Couldn't ask for more." He smiled. "Well, maybe one thing."

She smiled. They were finally going to get married. It wasn't right for everyone—Tobin and Lily were just fine living together, no ring or ceremony required. But seeing Josh and Tam in their marriage bliss had only convinced him that he wanted that. They'd held off while Emily was getting her certification and he was getting his business together, but this had always been the endgame.

She smiled back. "This summer, then?"

He nodded. Then he kissed her again, soft and slow, like a promise.

Because it was.

Acknowledgments

First and foremost, I want to thank the team at Montlake Romance, especially Alison Dasho, Krista Stroever, and Jillian Cline. You've taken such good care of me, encouraged my voice, and made sure that I was supported. I couldn't be happier to write for you if I were twins.

Tricia Skinner, my phenomenal agent and dear friend. I couldn't do what I do if I didn't know you had my back. Thank you for your constant vision, guidance, and strength.

My husband and son, who are getting really good at answering questions like "If you were going to destroy someone in a business setting, what would that look like? What would hurt the most?" and "What do you think about these text messages? Are they cringe?" Thank you for listening to my weird conjectures and encouraging my cheese habit. I love you guys so much.

Most of all, to all my readers . . . thank you, thank you, thank you for loving my work as much as I do and sharing it with others. All I write is for you.

About the Author

Cathy Yardley is an award-winning author of romance, chick lit, and urban fantasy. She has sold more than 1.2 million books with publishers like St. Martin's Press, Avon, and Harlequin Books. She writes fun, geeky, and diverse characters who believe that underdogs can make good and that sometimes being a little wrong is just right. She likes writing about quirky, crazy adventures because she's had plenty of her own: she had her own army in the Society for Creative Anachronism, she's spent New Year's on a three-day solitary vision quest in the Mojave Desert, and she had VIP access to the Viper Room in Los Angeles. Now, she spends her time writing in the wilds of East Seattle, trying to prevent her son from learning the truth about any of said adventures, and riding herd on her two dogs (and one husband).